AN INTERNATIONAL SPORTS ROMANCE

JOHANA GAVEZ

ISBN: 978-958-49-3239-6 (Paperback)
ISBN: 978-958-49-3240-2 (E-book)

Edited by Crystal Shelley of Rabbit with a Red Pen Editorial Services
Cover Design by Johana Gavez



For any inquiries regarding this book, please email:
contact@johanagavez.com

To my fiancée who believed in me even when I didn't, cheered me on for months and months and supported me every step of the way. Our love is my biggest inspiration.

In loving memory of Danna, the sweetest dog anyone could have asked for and my companion during the writing process.

# Chapter One

**Tumblr chat, six months before**
**Firegirl94:** I'm sorry, but I just have to slide into your chat to tell you that your fanfic of The Bold Type is the one thing sustaining me during this hiatus. Can't wait for season two. It's been 100 years :(
**Chickentender09:** That's so nice of you to say. I love praise and encouragement, so keep it coming :P I will try to not take 100 years to update, even if real life sometimes gets in the way.
**Firegirl94:** Real life—that pesky little thing always getting in the way. What's more important than pleasing your fans? And yes, by fans I mean me.
**Chickentender09:** Law school. Believe me, scrolling through Tumblr and writing fan fiction is way more entertaining, but sometimes guilt over the amount of debt I'm amassing wins and forces me to focus on my studies.
**Firegirl94:** Ouch . . . I guess I should encourage you to study, then.
**Chickentender09:** You should. But not gonna lie, talking to you beats studying.
**Firegirl94:** I'm happy to be your distraction. Message me anytime you need to avoid your responsibilities ;)

◈

The fuzzy yellow ball hovered in the air, suspended against the blue sky as if time couldn't affect it. Dani's gaze followed its path, her brown eyes not missing a beat, and she moved to attack it with practiced ease.

The dry sound of the strings hitting the ball was music to her ears, the racket in her hand an anchor to reality. It kept her body grounded while her brain flew away to another realm—a world where the only things that mattered were the quick movements of her feet over the hot concrete and the precision of her shots.

Anger, happiness, frustration, loneliness. Tennis had brought to her life those emotions and more. But in that warm, humid afternoon under Melbourne's sun, every stroke, every smack of the tennis ball gave Dani peace. Each one allowed her to ignore the world around her and embrace her instincts instead.

Dani's body moved over and over, in an infinite loop. Run, jump, hit, turn, run, hit. The motions allowed her to forget . . . what, she wasn't sure. Her loneliness? Her longing for more—for someone? It didn't matter. With her mind blank, focusing only on the next step, the next shot, she felt free.

A sonorous *thwack* left her racket when she hit the ball with her forehand and used the entire weight of her body to send a lightning-fast stroke toward the corner of the court.

"Harder!"

Igor's deep, thunderous voice resonated against the stadium's empty seats. He stood on the other side of the court, feeding Dani a new ball as soon as she finished hitting a shot. Though it didn't look like a demanding job, a drop of sweat still slid from the crown of his round, bald head down his thick, furrowed eyebrows.

*Easy for him to say*, Dani thought, suppressing an eyeroll.

*Thwack*. The ball flew off her racket as she hit it with even more force and speed, a manifestation of her annoyance with how people were always demanding things from her. She had been playing tennis since she was four years old, and for almost twenty years, people had been telling her what to do and how to do it. Run faster, hit harder, keep going. They didn't care if every single muscle hurt, if she was sad or upset. Winning was the only option. The worst part was that her body never failed to respond to the demands.

Igor was no different. Some would say he was too strict a coach, but Dani disagreed. His thin lips were always pursed, making him look tougher than he was, and true, he demanded full commitment and effort every single time. But she expected the same from herself, so their relationship worked.

The memory of their first exchange was still clear in Dani's mind.

"I don't care if it's training. You run every ball like your life depends on it. If you get your body and mind used to not always giving one hundred percent, they won't."

There'd been no "hello," no "nice to meet you." He didn't have time for pleasantries.

"Why would your body give one hundred percent when ninety percent is enough?" he'd continued. "It could be match point in the most important match of your life, but your body won't know it. If you get used to giving your all every single time, your body will never fail you when you need it."

"I always give my best," she'd answered, part amused by his intensity, part insulted by his insinuation.

"You think you do, I'm sure. But you can give so much more, and I'm going to show you how."

She had hired him on the spot. Three years later, the results spoke for themselves. She won her first Grand Slam the year before in Australia and was inching closer to overtaking Olga Podoroska for the top ranking. She was happy to admit that Igor's belief in her abilities—the possibility of achieving more—inspired her to push her own limits.

Her tennis career couldn't be better, but there was something missing in her life. Having the same routine for years could bore even the most dedicated. Wake up, eat a healthy breakfast, practice for two or three hours, then rest. One hour of specific training at the gym. Two hours of playing in the afternoon, either a match or more practice. Repeat everything the next day.

"Let's take a break." Igor's words were a welcome interruption.

She walked with no hurry, dragging out the chance to rest as much as possible. As she flopped down on the chair and rehydrated, the muffled sound of her phone made her look down at the bag on the floor. Would it be who she hoped it was? Not her parents or her manager adding things to her schedule, but the girl she had been messaging with on Tumblr for months.

Tumblr was Dani's favorite social media platform. She'd created an account as a teenager, and even if the website was less popular every day, she kept her account out of nostalgia. All her other social media accounts were about work, about her public profile. But on Tumblr she could be a faceless icon following her favorite TV shows and books. There, Dani could forget about who she was to the world and be herself, not only a tennis player. By far her favorite part of using the platform was the conversations she had with Ari, or Chickentender09.

As much as she craved answering the message right away, Dani fought the urge. Looking at her phone would mean irritating Igor and violating his strict no-phone rule, which would cause him to extend the training session. "You can go two hours without Instagram," he would say. "I'm sure your fans will survive, even if you don't post another picture of your sweaty abs."

A tennis ball bounced against her forehead, yanking her away from her thoughts. Igor's laughter let her know it wasn't an accident.

"Why are you so happy?" he teased. "I'm sure it's not because of me."

Dani grabbed the tennis ball at her feet and threw it back at him with as much force as she could muster. He caught it without effort.

"I'm thinking about what I'm going to say in my acceptance speech when I win the Australian Open again next week," she replied. "It seems like the perfect time to announce that I fired you."

"Oh, is that so? I should let you go back to the hotel, then. Sleep all day, no training," he said as he walked toward the middle of the court, racket in hand.

Dani stood from her seat, took one last sip of her drink, and did a quick sprint toward the baseline. "Maybe you should."

◈

During the next hour of training, Dani didn't think about the message waiting for her. While she was on the court, her focus was only on playing. But as soon as Igor told her to pack up, her mind instantly flitted back to it.

She jogged all the way to the chair and let the racket slide out of her hand so she could reach into her bag. By the time the racket hit the ground, she was holding the phone and opening the message. A photo of an empty suburban street adorned with rows of snow-covered trees greeted her in the app.

**Chickentender09**: Slipped on the ice taking this picture after class because I know you love snow. You're welcome.

Dani couldn't stop the rush of happiness she felt anytime she read a message from Ari—nor did she want to. She hoped Igor wasn't looking at her because it was impossible to keep a smile from taking over her face.

She loved snow, or at least the idea of it. The first time she had seen any in person was when her family had moved from Colombia to Spain. She was twelve when they'd arrived in Madrid in the middle of winter, on a brief stop to sort paperwork before settling in Mallorca. A tennis academy awaited her there, and her dad had a job lined up tending the grounds.

The day after arriving, Dani woke up to speckles of white covering the windows. She jumped out of bed and ran screaming toward the street before her mom had time to react.

She loved the beach and Mallorca as much as she loved the green mountains of Medellín, the city she had left behind. Both felt like home, while snow felt magical and distant. She'd told that same story to Ari months before.

Dani aimed her phone up to take a picture, making sure it showed only the clear sky.

**Firegirl94:** Here, have a little sun.

She walked toward the locker room, one finger tapping incessantly against her thigh, the urge to add something more to her message refusing to go away. She managed only a few steps before retrieving the phone and sending a follow-up to the photo.

**Firegirl94:** Sending you a hug too. I hope it helps warm you up, even if the sun doesn't.

# Chapter Two

**Tumblr chat, five months before**

**Chickentender09:** I can't believe we've been talking for a month, and I still don't know your name. I'm Ari btw.

**Firegirl94:** Ari. That's pretty. A pretty name for a pretty woman, I bet.

**Chickentender09:** Don't think your charm will stop me from noticing you avoided my question. What are you, a spy?

**Firegirl94:** You got me . . . I was really hoping you would let me get away with it. I'm sorry, I'm a little weird about what I share online because of my job, but I guess it's not like you'll be able to track me down just by my name . . . unless you're the spy.

**Chickentender09:** I understand being in the closet. I wouldn't want my parents to find this account either or read my F/F fan fiction. I don't think I'm ready for that conversation yet.

**Firegirl94:** It's not that exactly. In my case it's more about work. I don't know how accepting my job would be. You can call me Dani. That's what my friends call me.

◈

The walk to the one-bedroom apartment Ari rented outside of campus was only two blocks, but she already felt exhausted by the time she got there. The cold pierced her legs through the two pairs of leggings she had on under her jeans, and the weight of her blue coat was too much for her small frame. Was walking extra blocks to get takeout truly worth it? She didn't feel like cooking, but she couldn't bear the thought of stepping out into the cold again either. *Nothing wrong with eating instant ramen again.*

As soon as she entered her apartment, the layers came off. First, the scarf soared through the air and landed on top of the desk she used as a dining table and workspace. The coat followed. That one Ari at least tried to hang on the hook by the door, but when it fell to the floor, she stared at it and shrugged while walking to her bed. Shoes went flying next, one landing near her bed to the left, one settling by the kitchen entrance to the right. Sweater and shirt came off together in one movement. Jeans and leggings were the last to go. She took them off while standing in front of her closet as she looked for an old T-shirt to wear for the rest of the day.

She would have stayed in only her panties, but her best friend would be showing up later and she'd rather not retraumatize him with her nakedness. The way he'd screamed the last time it happened was enough to make her sacrifice a little comfort for his sake.

Her stomach rumbled, making her regret the choice of not getting takeout, but she ignored it. She walked to the kitchen, not for food but for the tea she could never go without for long. While the water boiled, Ari retrieved the jar next to the stove that housed her beloved tea, opened it, and buried her nose inside. The familiar black tea and cardamom aroma filled her nose.

With a warm mug in her hands, she was ready to settle in bed for the rest of the night. She plopped on top of her covers, and as soon as her body hit the soft mattress, her laptop was open. She alternated between drinking her tea and scrolling, and without thinking, she opened Dani's Tumblr profile. It'd been almost two months since Dani had posted anything new. Thankfully, they stayed in touch via messages.

Sometimes Ari wondered if the air of mystery Dani insisted on was part of why she was fascinated with her. Ari couldn't deny she had a small crush on her internet friend, even if it made her feel a little silly. There was no harm in it, besides making her spend way too much time staring at old posts and rereading their messages. She knew nothing would ever come of it, and maybe that was what made it better. It felt safe.

The sound of the door opening made Ari look up from the computer. Tom was the only other person with a key to her apartment and the only one who would come in without knocking as if he owned the place. Whenever Tom entered a room, it was impossible to ignore him. His tall and muscular frame moved through the world with a heaviness that contrasted with the lightness of his character. His steps were strong and loud, his voice strident, his arms bulky, but his eyes were always soft and warm, his words encouraging, his hugs safe.

"Oh my God. You're not going to believe what I found out today," he said while dropping a takeout bag on the kitchen counter.

She raised her eyebrows to let him know she was listening, but as soon as he started talking, she focused on the computer again.

"Mark. You remember Mark, right?"

"Uh-huh," she mumbled, even though she had no idea who he was talking about.

"Of course you don't. He's the cute bartender I met the last time I was in New York."

"Oh, I remember him. He was nice."

"He was a dream! And he texted me. He's coming this weekend to our isolated corner of America because his sister studies here. Can you believe my luck?"

She glanced up and grinned. "And he wants to see you? That's amazing."

Tom was a sensitive soul, in love with love. Ever since Ari had met him, he'd never stopped trying to find his one true love, as he liked to call it. It didn't matter how many failed dates he had or how many heartbreaks. He always bounced back.

Meanwhile, Ari had barely dated since her first year of college, back when she was getting her philosophy degree and law school wasn't even on her mind. Maybe there was someone out there for her, but she didn't want to put herself through the work of meaningless dates that led nowhere. She refused to risk getting hurt when the odds of someone liking her back were close to none.

"Yes!" he exclaimed, making the bed bounce with his frantic movements and excited stomps. "I think a date is in my near future. And you know what? I think he may be the one." He walked over and lay next to her.

Ari laughed, leaning into him. "You say that about every guy you meet, Tom."

"That means I will eventually be right," he shot back.

She was about to answer him when a message notification pinged on her laptop. She considered clicking to another page before Tom could comment on it, but she was dying to see what the message said. His squeal told her it was too late to hide it anyway.

"She is so flirting with you!" he said.

Ari fought the urge to roll her eyes. She hadn't wanted to tell Tom about her friendship with Dani at first, but it was hard to keep it a secret when she checked her phone all the time.

Not that there was anything to hide. But she knew Tom, who believed love made everything better. Ari found it too hard to listen to his daydreams about the future relationship he imagined she and Dani would have, when she knew there was zero chance of it happening. She would rather avoid hearing about it.

"I hope it helps warm you," he read while leaning on her to see the screen better. "That's so sweet. I bet she would be the kind of girlfriend to take off her jacket and give it to you if you were cold."

"I have no way to know," Ari said. She didn't want to give Tom more ammunition for his fantasies, but she thought that yes, Dani would be the kind of girlfriend to do that.

Tom bounced on the bed while looking at her with puppy eyes. "What are you going to answer back with?"

"Nothing. I'll answer later—when I don't have someone looking over my shoulder," Ari retorted, closing her laptop. She looked pointedly at Tom, exaggerating every movement so he knew she was joking, but also making it clear she didn't want him meddling.

He sighed as loud as possible. "Fiiiine. I'll watch TV, then."

Ari got up from the bed, smiling at her friend's antics on her way to the kitchen. It was only fair that she be the one to serve the takeout Tom had brought. As she opened the bag, the smell of hot food hit her, reminding her of how thankful she was to have him in her life. If not for him, she would eat even more instant ramen and cereal than she already did.

While Tom was distracted with the TV, she reached for her phone and opened Dani's message. She didn't reply, only wanted to read the words again and take her time to savor each one without him looking over her shoulder. If she'd learned one thing about Dani by now, it was that she was a natural flirt. Ari's brain told her to not read much into the message, but her heart didn't listen.

◈

Ari settled again on the bed, handing Tom a plate. "You're still watching that show? I'm tired of their queerbaiting."

"Oh, come on. You know I love it, and all the actors are so hot."

"I love how your motivation to watch something is how hot the actors are."

He shrugged. "I also like the plot. Besides, I know you're going to be on your laptop all the time and won't pay attention to whatever I put on. Let me have this."

"Okay, I guess you're right. I need to work on my essay anyway."

"Mm-hmm . . . work on your essay. Not send a message to anyone, I bet."

Ari didn't even pretend to be bothered by his callout. They both knew he was right. She would sit with the Word document of her essay open and untouched for hours as she switched to scroll social media every few minutes. She'd give up for the night with only a couple of new sentences added to her work. Despite knowing this, she still opened her laptop and typed carelessly on it for a few seconds, staring right back at Tom just to rile him up.

He laughed his loud, resounding laugh before taking a bite of his food. He had barely finished chewing when he spoke again. "Well, if you get tired of all that hard academic work, you can always watch with me. The women are hot too."

Ari didn't bother to glance at the TV screen. "I'm good."

"You can look. I won't tell your internet girlfriend you've been admiring other women."

"She's just a friend."

"Right, and that's why you're constantly daydreaming about her. And why you've had the message app open this whole time and keep looking at it like someone stole your puppy."

Ari glared at Tom with all the anger she could muster in that moment. She loved her best friend, but she hated how right he was.

Yes, she had a big, embarrassing crush on someone she barely knew. She wasn't in denial, but admitting it to someone else made it more real, and it also opened her up for disappointment. She was fine with keeping her feelings to herself and not thinking much about them. She knew that Tom—annoying but well-meaning, romantic Tom—would make it a bigger deal than it was.

She considered going with her usual go-to reaction: deny, deny, deny. Tom wouldn't buy it, but he would drop the topic, at least for a couple of days. But a part of her didn't want to keep denying it. She thought about the message Dani had sent her and the way butterflies fluttered in her stomach when she read it.

"Fine. I may have a small crush on her."

Tom's squeal left her ears ringing. "Yes! I'm so excited! You're finally letting yourself fall in love." He knocked the wind out of her with an enthusiastic hug.

"I should have waited until after we finished eating," she said when he let her go, pointing at the bits of taco filling that had flown from her hand and were now spread all over the bed. "I said I had a *crush*. I'm not going to fall in love with some random woman I haven't even met. Don't be silly."

"Yeah, yeah, whatever. Ari is in love, Ari is in love," he sang.

She grumbled under her breath, regretting all her life choices up to this point, and she was one second away from hitting him with a pillow to shut him up. He seemed to pick up on her increasing annoyance because he soon stopped his teasing. A full grin remained plastered on his face, but Ari gave an inward sigh of relief that he at least calmed down.

He settled next to her, looking at the laptop resting open on top of her legs. This time, she didn't hide the window—her Tumblr dashboard, with a message pop-up clear on the screen. Her fingers lingered over the keyboard as she itched to write something but wasn't sure what.

Tom's watchful gaze unnerved Ari, even though he wasn't doing anything but looking at her. She felt pressured to write something, anything. She kept telling herself that it was a simple message, like the hundreds she had already sent Dani. But Tom's presence, and having admitted out loud she had a crush, added extra weight to this one.

She started typing. Stopped. Deleted the message. Glared at Tom for good measure.

He was quiet the whole time and didn't even flinch at her glare. He rolled his eyes and made a dramatic motion of zipping his mouth shut. Ari focused on the laptop screen again and typed a new message. *The weather looks nice where you are.* She heard Tom's groan in her mind, even though he was silent in reality. He sat patiently, letting her take her time, but she imagined how it would sound. She deleted the message and closed the laptop, then let out an exasperated sigh.

The entire process had taken ten minutes—probably the longest time Tom had ever gone without speaking since Ari had met him. She could tell he was trying to be supportive and give her space.

She also knew it wouldn't last long.

Almost immediately after the thought crossed her mind, Tom let out a loud "Oh my *God!*" as the only warning before he reached over and grabbed the laptop. He jumped from the bed and held the computer high above his head. By the time Ari reacted and tried to stop him from doing whatever it was he wanted to do, it was too late. He handed the laptop back to her with a smile.

"Here. You're welcome, girl."

Ari stared at him, mouth open. Petrified by what he had done, she couldn't even gather the energy to yell at him. Meanwhile, he settled on the bed again and munched on his food while watching TV, as if nothing had happened.

Ari stood immobile for what felt like an eternity, glaring at the back of his head, even though he couldn't care less. When she finally gathered the courage to open her laptop, the words of the message she—well, Tom—had sent glowed back, taunting her.

**Chickentender09:** I wish you were here to warm me up.

Ari had assumed that Tom sent an embarrassing message, not such a flirty one. She'd never said anything like that to Dani before.

She should be yelling at Tom or hitting him over the head, but her body had gone numb. She stood there, eyes fixed on the screen, mouth still hanging open. After a while, her legs started to give out, forcing her to sit on the bed again. All the while, her eyes never left the words. Trying to delete the message would be useless, and she considered sending something else to defuse the situation to make it look like a joke, but nothing came to mind.

"Girl, breathe. It's just a freaking message."

Tom's voice broke Ari out of her trance. She turned back at him, willing her eyes to show him how infuriated she was.

"Just a message?" she said between gritted teeth. "You may as well have sent her a nude with how explicit that was."

"Now you're overreacting. It was *barely* flirting, and it's not like I said 'Come fuck me now' or something."

Ari groaned at the thought of Tom sending a message like that. She wouldn't put it past him. But to be honest, the one he sent sounded just as bad to her.

A part of Ari's brain tried to remind her that Dani had always been flirty and loved to tease and joke around, so she probably wouldn't bat an eye at the message. But another part of her was in overdrive. What if Dani freaked out and blocked her? If that happened, Ari would lose her forever. She didn't know enough about Dani to find her on any other platform. No email or phone. Nothing.

For Tom, it was easy. If someone said no, he would have a new Grindr date lined up for the next day. For Ari, it wasn't. She would lose the only person who had made her heart race in years.

Maybe it was a sad statement that their relationship was so fragile it could end with the push of a button. But Ari wasn't the one asking for it to be that way. It had happened without her expecting it.

Something about Ari's face or demeanor tipped Tom off about the state he'd put her in. He moved to wrap an arm around her and looked at her with worry in his eyes. "Hey, are you okay? I'm sorry. I didn't think it was such a big deal."

Ari didn't answer at first, her worry sounding ridiculous in her own mind. She knew Tom was messing with her and trying to help. He had no way of knowing how much the messages she exchanged with Dani meant to her.

She almost couldn't get herself to voice her concerns, so when she finally did, her voice came out almost in a whisper. "I don't know what I would do if she got mad and stopped talking to me."

Tom gripped her tighter. "That's not going to happen. From what you've told me, she seems to care about you too. She won't let a silly comment stop that."

He was right. Ari knew he was. But she still couldn't get herself to stop worrying.

"Look," he said, "if she gets mad, you can tell her your stupid best friend was dicking around."

Finally, Ari managed a small smile. "Maybe I'll do that. Tell her all about how much you suck."

She looked at her laptop again, debating what to do. Dani usually took a long time to answer her messages, which would allow Ari to do damage control before Dani even saw it. But she was tired of worrying so much. She was going to listen to Tom. It was just a silly comment; it didn't have to mean anything. Maybe she was panicking for no reason.

# Chapter Three

**Tumblr chat, four months before**

**Chickentender09:** Do you ever feel like you're not enough?

**Firegirl94:** I don't think I have, sorry. You probably chose the wrong person to ask this question. I've been told I have a healthy ego.

**Chickentender09:** I can see that . . . Forget about it. It's just one of those days, you know.

**Firegirl94:** Hey, no. Don't dismiss it, I'm here for you. Let it out. Tell me what's up.

**Chickentender09:** My mom called. One of my older brothers got engaged and she is beyond happy. It made me wonder if she would be that happy for me if I ever got engaged to a woman, which is so not fair to her 'cause she doesn't even know I'm gay. But being the youngest kid and the only daughter makes me wonder sometimes. All my other brothers are married, with kids on the way and good jobs. I know they all expect the same from me. I don't think my mom will reject me or anything, but I know at least a part of her will be disappointed.

**Firegirl94:** I don't know your family, but I know you. I can't imagine anyone not finding you amazing. From what you've told me, I'm sure your parents will be proud of you no matter what. It feels overwhelming now, but when you are ready, you'll see that it will go better than you expect.

**Chickentender09:** I hope so. I really want to tell them but always chicken out. Soon, though. And then there's school. I've been looking at summer associate positions at big law firms where I would be defending awful corporations but would get paid . . . or I could apply to do amazing work with small NGOs but not getting paid, and I can't afford that. I haven't even graduated yet and I'm already compromising my values for money. Attending law school because I thought being a lawyer was the only way for me to change the world was the stupidest decision of my life.

**Firegirl94:** There's nothing stupid about caring. About wanting to make the world a better place. I can't tell you the path to follow, but don't feel guilty about having to choose what's best for you. Maybe you have to take that big law money now, but as long as your heart stays in the right place, I know that one day you will make up for it and be able to follow your dream.

**Chickentender09:** How do you always know what to say to make me feel better?

**Firegirl94:** It's one of my many talents ;)

◈

It was turning out to be one of those frantic, running-around-from-place-to-place days for Dani. Arantxa, her manager, showed up after practice to talk for hours about her upcoming interviews and promotional obligations, only letting Dani go because she had a match. A routine first-round match, which she won in less than an hour. After recovery and the mandatory press conference, she found Arantxa waiting for her again, ready to walk Dani from one commitment to the next. Arantxa was relentless about her work. She never let Dani slack off, even when Dani would rather do anything else than pose for pictures or give interviews.

She could only admire Arantxa's passion, because it wasn't easy to be a manager. They followed their players around the globe, sacrificing time with their own families, unable to settle down. It took a particular personality to want to do that kind of job.

Looking around at the luxurious hotel, Dani realized she was projecting. She dreamed about settling down, waking up every day in the same bed, the same city. Arantxa always seemed more than happy to spend her days in fancy accommodations.

As they walked, Arantxa's heels clicked against the hard marble floor, the echo announcing their presence. Dani was walking fast—faster than she usually did—but she was still struggling to match Arantxa's pace. Even in her three-inch heels, Arantxa kept a steady two-foot lead. She always moved with purpose, with the determination of someone who couldn't afford to waste a minute of her time.

They were making their way toward a private room at the hotel's restaurant to have dinner with a journalist. Arantxa would never allow her to be late, but Dani wasn't worried. They would wait for her no matter when she arrived, and if they didn't, she would have one less interview to do. Answering unrelenting questions wasn't her idea of fun.

"Are you ready for this?" Arantxa said, glancing over her shoulder at Dani.

“As ready as always. Unless there’s something I need to worry about.”

“Not worried, just ready. I know you’ve done a thousand interviews in your career, but this is not your usual sports media. This is for one of the biggest lifestyle magazines in the world, and Mary Felton is their most determined journalist. She won’t be happy with canned answers.”

Dani shrugged. For her, it was just another interview. “This is like the third time you’ve warned me. I’m sure I will be fine.”

Arantxa came to an abrupt halt, turned around, and took a step toward her. “She won’t care about tennis. She will ask about political stuff. Your personal life. Love.”

Dani stared ahead, tension radiating from every muscle in her body. “You know I don’t talk about my love life.”

“I know.” Arantxa’s eyes softened, her laser focus on business forgotten for a second. “That won’t stop them from asking, so you have to be ready.”

Dani furrowed her brow. More than ever, she was dreading sitting in front of a journalist with no way to escape. “I’ll handle it.”

Arantxa nodded, turning away and resuming her walk at a pace even faster than before.

Soon they were sitting at a table with two glasses of wine and a sparkling water in front of them. They made small talk for a few minutes, and Dani let Arantxa handle the usual pleasantries. Once the formalities were out of the way, Mary opened a recording app on her phone and placed it in the middle of the table—a reminder that no matter how much they wanted to pretend this was an informal conversation during dinner, it was anything but.

Mary turned to Dani. "After your victory at the US Open last year, the American public wants to know more about you. I'd like to start this conversation going back to your childhood. What was it like to leave your country so young to pursue a dream?"

Dani wished she could communicate telepathically with Arantxa to tell her, *See, you were exaggerating*. The interview was only starting, though, and she wasn't going to lower her defenses just yet.

After an hour of nonstop conversation, things seemed to be going well. The questions were more personal than professional, but nothing crossed the line. And Mary hadn't asked about Dani's love life. At least not yet.

Dani could always hope the issue didn't come up, but she knew it was almost impossible. The fact that she'd never had a public relationship made it even more appealing for the media to try to find out about it. It had been easy so far to keep her sexuality hidden because she'd been single for so long.

Dani had confirmed she was a lesbian after kissing one of her training mates at the tennis academy when she was fifteen years old, but her single-minded focus on tennis stopped her from having lasting relationships. She still hadn't met someone willing to deal with the forty weeks a year she spent traveling. Not that she tried hard to find them. Focusing on training, on winning, gave her an excuse to stay single.

Mary left for the restroom as they were about to order dessert. During the dinner, Dani's phone had gone off a couple of times, and as usual, she was dying to look at it. She looked up to check if the journalist was anywhere in sight, and when she saw no sign of her, she took her phone out and hit the blinking message notification.

**Chickentender09:** Tom spilled pico de gallo all over my bed last night. I can't even be mad at him because I would starve if he didn't bring me dinner.

Dani smiled. She loved messages like that from Ari. It made her feel like she was right there sharing Ari's daily life. She could imagine her laughing at Tom and making fun of him for being so clumsy.

"I don't think I've seen you smile that big this whole interview."

Dani bit her tongue to stop a curse. Of course Mary would come back right then. Dani tried to not panic—the first rule of keeping control of a situation was to mask your reaction. That's what she always did on the tennis court. No broken rackets, no emotional outbursts, nothing a rival could use to their advantage. That's what she did with Mary too. No reason to show she was uneasy.

She swiped up to hide the message and then placed the phone screen facedown on the table with measured movements. Fast enough to prevent the woman in front of her from seeing more than she already had, but slow enough to not appear in a rush, even if she was. Out of the corner of her eye she could see Arantxa's disapproving look.

"Maybe you're not as funny as you think you are," Dani said with a smile. She tried not to be rude, but she wanted to make it clear that it wasn't a topic she wanted to discuss.

"That smile didn't look like it was because of a joke. It seemed more like one that's reserved for someone special," Mary observed, clearly taking advantage of the opening Dani had given her.

"That's quite the leap."

They stared at each other for a long minute, neither of them backing down.

Mary broke the silence first. "You're saying there's nobody special in your life?"

"There are a lot of special people in my life. My parents are always by my side supporting my career. My coach and my entire team are there for me. My fans give me so much love everywhere I go. I'm really fortunate."

It was a nonanswer, an obvious attempt at diverting attention from the topic. Dani knew it was going to fail, but she had to at least try. This woman could keep asking—that was her job and her right—but Dani would not make it easy. She never did.

Mary smiled. Not a warm, happy smile, but more of a sardonic smirk that let Dani know she wasn't buying her words. "It's hard to believe that a young, attractive woman like you doesn't have a line of admirers bidding for her attention."

"All of my energy goes to tennis. I don't have time or desire to focus on anything else."

Mary broke their staring contest to write something down in her notebook. Dani observed with attention every movement of the pen over the paper, unnerved to feel like a subject being studied.

Mary set down the pen. "That sounds lonely."

Dani wavered. She should be angry at the assumption, but she did feel lonely, even if she hated to admit it. This time her voice was lower, not as forceful. "Maybe. But it's my choice. It's the same choice I've made since I was four years old and started playing tennis. To be successful, I can't allow any distractions."

Mary nodded and seemed to let the topic go as she asked about Dani's opinion on Colombia's recent peace agreement. Dani didn't love that topic either, but it was better than being hammered with questions about her romantic life.

◈

Arantxa and Dani stayed at the restaurant long after Mary had left. The expensive bottle of rosé still had more than half left in it, and because Dani wasn't drinking, Arantxa had to finish it—a task she was always glad to undertake as long as Dani kept her company.

"Well, that was almost a disaster." Arantxa wasn't one to beat around the bush. She said what was on her mind, and she clearly wasn't pleased with the interview.

Dani hid her guilt. She knew how hard Arantxa had worked to get her exposure in mainstream magazines, which would broaden her appeal to sponsors. And instead of playing along and trying to be charming to make the best of the opportunity, Dani had been so focused on not giving away too much about her personal life that she'd almost blown it by being rude.

It was one thing to be standoffish during the mandatory press conference after her matches, or the interviews with tennis-specialized media, but she could have been friendlier to Mary. Not that she was going to admit that to Arantxa.

Dani shrugged instead. "I don't think it went that bad."

Arantxa poured more wine into her almost-empty glass and took a long sip. "Then you are more naive than I thought. She let you off the hook today, but she knows something is up."

"There's nothing to figure out. I meant what I said."

"I'm sure you did. But don't think I didn't notice how excited you got when you read that message."

Dani glanced at her phone, still placed facedown on the table. It had vibrated a couple more times since the interview ended, but she opted to not look at it until she was alone. After being called out less than an hour ago, she wanted privacy before checking it again. That desire was probably more telling than anything else.

"It's just a friend."

"That's how many relationships start."

Dani felt no judgment in Arantxa's voice, which sounded almost encouraging. As passionate as Arantxa was about Dani's career, she also cared about Dani as a person. The link they shared went beyond their professional relationship. It was impossible to work closely for years and not care for each other.

"When am I going to have time for a relationship when you have me giving interviews until midnight on a match day?" Dani was trying to divert attention from the topic, and for a moment she thought she succeeded.

"Don't go putting this on me now," Arantxa said with a smirk. "If you want to date, you know I will be the first in line keeping reporters away."

"I know. I've never doubted it."

"Good. Money is important, but your happiness is more important." She took one last sip from her glass before standing up.

They walked in silence back to the lobby elevator. Arantxa stepped off first onto her floor, and as the elevator doors began to close, she stopped them with her hand.

Arantxa looked at Dani with soft eyes. "I also want to be the first in line to meet whoever it is you are talking to. I have to approve."

Dani couldn't help but smile, even if she still believed there would be no dating for her in the immediate future. "I promise you will be."

As soon as the doors closed, she took her phone out. There were several new messages, but there was one she read over and over, the flirty tone throwing her off. What would happen if she answered it with more intention?

Before then, it had never crossed her mind. But since reading the message, it was the only thing Dani could think about. She'd never talked with someone as freely as she did with Ari. She also couldn't deny that their interactions made her happy—in a way she'd never felt with anybody else.

She thought about what she would do if she was in a place where she felt more confident: the tennis court. The answer was obvious. She never shied away from attacking, from taking initiative in any of her matches. She'd rather lose knowing she'd tried everything she could than win by waiting around for her opponent to make a mistake. Taking a risk with Ari shouldn't be different.

As Dani walked to her room, she started typing, suddenly wishing she'd drunk some of that rosé. Or at least had Arantxa there to give her advice. She deleted her attempts at a message a couple of times until she was confident it sounded flirty enough. Reading it one last time, she hit Send as fast as she could before she regretted it.

**Firegirl94:** Do you invite any stranger on the internet to warm you up or am I special?

Dani moved to close the app and go to sleep, the clock telling her it was one in the morning. But she saw that her message had been read, and soon enough the three small dots in the corner of the screen told her that Ari was online and getting ready to answer her.

Dani held her breath as she waited for a new message to appear. Unable to sit still, she took the opportunity to change into her sleeping clothes, brush her teeth, and wash her face. She was settling under the covers when finally, something showed up.

**Chickentender09:** You are special.

Short, but more than enough to confirm that she and Ari were on the same page. Ari could have made a joke or changed the topic, but she chose to be vulnerable, to open up. The least Dani could do was reciprocate that vulnerability with her own.

**Firegirl94:** It's very bold of you to say that to an internet stranger ;)

Dani added the winky face at the end to make sure Ari knew she was playing. But she also rushed to send the next message before there was any chance for a misunderstanding.

**Firegirl94:** We can fix that if you want. We could FaceTime one of these days. I promise to behave.

Dani's heart beat harder inside her chest. Her message may not have looked like much, but for her it was a big step. She was opening the door to her life, telling Ari that she wanted her to be part of it.

# Chapter Four

**Tumblr chat, three months before**

**Chickentender09:** All my friends have dates tonight so it's you and me on this Friday night . . .

**Chickentender09:** Please answer. Don't tell me you are also on a date. That would absolutely destroy my morale.

**Firegirl94:** It's morning where I am, but no, no dates for me. Don't worry.

**Chickentender09:** That surprises me. You seem like you would be popular with the girls.

**Firegirl94:** I am when I try ;) It's been a while since I had a relationship. My job makes it hard. My career will always come first and not everyone is willing to accept that.

**Chickentender09:** I see. In my case I don't see the point when things will most likely end in heartbreak. Anyone I've ever dated always gets bored with me and ends up leaving. I'd rather not have my self-esteem destroyed again.

**Firegirl94:** I understand being cautious with your heart, but sometimes the risk is worth it. You will never know unless you allow yourself to be vulnerable, as hard as that is.

**Chickentender09:** Well, it's not like there are any prospects right now, so I guess I will cross that bridge if I ever come to it.

◈

Ari woke up with the blankets tangled around her legs, and the first sound she heard was Tom's snoring. His apartment was close by, but with the snow still falling steadily deep into the night, they'd decided it would be better if he stayed. He was curled on the small sofa Ari had across from her bed, one of the few pieces of furniture she owned. She had no clue how he fit on it, but he slept soundly with his knees bent up to his chin.

Out of habit, Ari reached for her phone as she did first thing every morning to check social media and text her mom. She rushed to open the Tumblr app, only to find no answer from Dani.

Not one minute later, a string of words appeared on her phone screen. She thought her mind was playing tricks on her or that the haziness of sleep made her read things that weren't there. She shook her head, rubbed her eyes, and read the message again. And then for a third time. Dani was flirting back. There was no other explanation, but Ari refused to believe it. She jumped from the bed and rushed to Tom's side, shaking him with all her strength until he woke up.

"What the hell?" he grumbled.

It wasn't the gentlest way of waking him up, but this was an emergency. She hadn't dated in years, she had absolutely no game, and most importantly, she wouldn't need to have any if Tom hadn't played cupid. The whole situation was his fault, so the least he could do was help her out. Besides, once he learned what it was about, he would be furious if he missed the chance to help.

"Whatever," she said. "I need you to read this."

Tom looked at Ari like she was losing it, then fell back on the couch and turned away from her. "I'm sure it can wait. Let me sleep."

Ari grabbed him by the shoulder, forcing him to look at her again with a strength she didn't know she possessed, and pushed the phone screen in front of his wide eyes. "She's flirting back and I'm panicking. I don't know what to do."

In one movement, Tom bolted upright and took the phone from Ari's hand. As he read, his brow furrowed in concentration in what Ari felt was more for show than anything else. It was a one-line message that he shouldn't need more than ten seconds to read, but he kept looking at the phone, narrowing his eyes, and nodding as if he was trying to decipher a secret code.

"I detect a heavy case of flirtation with a side of *I told you so*." Tom kept his face straight for a full second before bursting out laughing.

Ari huffed, not finding it as amusing as he did. Her mind was still churning at a thousand revolutions per minute, thinking about what the message could mean. She let him laugh for a few more seconds before punching him in the arm. "Are you going to help me or just mock me?"

He rubbed his arm as if the blow had hurt, when Ari knew that even if she tried to hit him with all her strength, it wouldn't register.

Finally, he stopped laughing enough to speak again. "Okay, calm down. You want to flirt back, right?"

She almost punched him again but limited herself to an incredulous look. As if her freak-out wasn't a clear sign that she cared so much because she wanted this—whatever it was—to continue.

Tom threw up his arms. "Just making sure!" He started typing at a frantic pace, and Ari panicked, but for a different reason this time.

"What are you writing?" She tried to peek over his shoulder.

He stood up, moving away from her. "Just telling her you think she is super hot and that you want to kiss her and have her babies."

Ari grabbed the phone out of his hands in a frenzy, desperate to stop him from sending another embarrassing message. When she glanced at the screen, she found the chat box empty, and her panic turned into confusion.

Tom shook his head. "I was just messing with you. Look, I can write something for you, but it's clear you like this girl. Just be honest."

"I don't know how to flirt!"

"You don't need to!" he exclaimed. "You've been talking to her for months and she clearly likes you enough just as you are. Let your guard down, stop overthinking things, and be yourself."

She let out a sigh while falling dramatically on top of the bed, phone now in her hand. "I hate when people tell me to be myself. I'm not that interesting," she grumbled.

Tom lay next to her and stared at her as she typed a message, then spent several minutes with her finger hovering over the Send button.

"Let me see what you wrote," he said. As soon as Ari loosened her hold on the phone and let him have it, he hit Send.

"Noooooo!" she cried. "It wasn't ready."

"It was perfect. Really, relax."

A new message notification pinged almost immediately, causing another wave of nerves to flood Ari's body. Tom held the screen out to her and let her read Dani's response.

"Internet stranger," she scoffed, reading aloud. "She is so much more than that."

"Yeah, I can tell." Tom offered the phone back to Ari. "Are you going to act like a rational person now? Is it safe to return this?"

"Yes, give it to me. I'm good now," she insisted, and he raised an eyebrow at her. "Well, I'm panicking because it seems like she may be into me too? But I'm ready to embrace it. I'm going to talk like I've talked to girls before in my life."

"I'm going to trust you," he said, handing the phone over slowly. "Don't blow this for us. I want a sister-in-law!"

She rolled her eyes but smiled despite herself. Tom being his usual silly self helped her relax. She took a deep breath to calm the butterflies dancing in her stomach and typed a new message.

When Dani suggested they FaceTime, a battle between elation and fear started raging inside Ari. She pushed both feelings down as deep as she could and answered before her insecurities took over.

**Chickentender09:** FaceTiming sounds great.

◈

There was a bounce in Dani's step that wasn't there the day before, and she wasn't the only one to notice it. Granted, the fact that she hated working out in the gym and had never been shy about declaring it every morning didn't help her case.

"For someone about to do squats with over two hundred pounds on their shoulders, you seem awfully cheerful," Igor commented soon enough.

"What can I say, maybe the gym is growing on me."

He looked at her with narrowed eyes. Usually, that gesture would be enough to make Dani confess everything to him, but not this time. To avoid Igor's inquisitive look, Dani closed her eyes and focused all her strength on lifting and squatting.

"Only last week, you told me that gyms were modern torture chambers. It's quite the change, that's all."

Dani stopped lifting and opened her eyes to find him staring at her. She knew there was no way to avoid giving him an answer, but she delayed it for as long as possible. First, she waited for her physical trainer to help get the weight off her shoulders, then she stalled by taking a sip of water and drying her sweaty hands with a towel.

"Can't I be happy?" she asked innocently.

"Oh, I love that you are happy. It's just unexpected."

"Well, sometimes unexpected things are the best ones."

As soon as the words left her mouth, Dani realized she meant them more than she thought. If she had to pick a word to define her life, it would be "predictability." Despite how professional tennis demanded constant travel and living out of a suitcase, she always knew what her life was going to bring day after day. Train, play, win, lose. Even her never-ending travel was predictable, dictated by the tennis schedule.

Meeting Ari had been the one unpredictable thing in her life. And now, the mere thought of

FaceTiming with her sent ripples of electricity through Dani's entire body.

Igor frowned but didn't comment. Dani could tell that he was curious and had noticed something shift for her, which were both natural after sharing so many years together. But he never meddled in her personal life, and it didn't seem like he would start now.

"Well, since you are so motivated, let's get some burpees and high-jump circuits done."

"Ugh, no. I hate those."

Dani could swear she saw him smile before he turned around to help set up the area for the jumps. "Glad to see you are still you," he said.

Dani shook her head, amused. Even her current state of happiness was not enough to make her enjoy working out in the gym. She loved the tennis court, could run and play for hours without getting bored, so it was no surprise that during her routine, the one thing on her mind was Ari. She was eager to share more of herself with Ari, but her biggest worry was how to open up about her life without attracting unwanted public attention.

She wasn't ashamed of being a lesbian; she wasn't even worried about losing sponsors. Society wasn't perfect, but it was no longer the time of Billie Jean King. Her sponsors would be more worried about negative backlash if they dropped her over being gay. And even if some did cancel contracts, she trusted Arantxa to find new ones that were better and more inclusive.

No, that wasn't it. What worried her was that she'd signed up for a life of being watched. It was not something she enjoyed, but it came with the profession she chose. Ari hadn't made that choice, which meant that protecting Ari was Dani's priority.

The first thing Dani would have to do to accomplish that goal was to be honest with Ari. Tell her who she was. It was not fair to think about the possibility of a relationship when Ari didn't have all the relevant information. At the same time, it would be odd to drop it all on her out of the blue, so Dani decided to not do a big declaration. Thinking about saying something like *Oh, by the way, I'm kind of famous* felt pretentious. She would let things progress naturally, like any two people getting to know each other would.

**Firegirl94:** Good morning from Melbourne, Australia.

Her morning greeting wasn't a big deal, but she thought of it as a small way to share more of her life with Ari. For the first time, she was also in the picture she sent. Kind of. The photo showed just her back; she was ready to share more with Ari, but she was also a tease. Dani knew the picture made her look good. It had been taken right after training, so she was only wearing shorts and a sports bra, with her tanned back on full display and drops of sweat making her skin glisten in the sun.

**Chickentender09:** Melbourne? No wonder you're always replying at random hours. I just finished dinner, and now I'm having some tea.

Dani stared at the message from Ari, which also had a picture attached. Hers showed a woman sitting in a kitchen, a beautiful red-and-gold ornate teacup in front of her. Ari was facing the camera but was looking down in the teacup's direction as it approached her lips. Wavy hair covered the side of her face—an obvious attempt to get back at Dani.

Dani smiled. Soon there would be no hiding behind carefully crafted messages or elaborately set up pictures. She couldn't wait for that video call they'd promised each other. She couldn't wait for the chance to look into Ari's eyes and hear her voice for the first time. Her motto had always been "There's no time like the present," so she crafted another message as soon as her work in the gym was over.

**Firegirl94:** Are you free tomorrow for our video date? I can't wait to talk to you.

# Chapter Five

**Tumblr chat, two months before**

**Firegirl94:** I'm bored and my flight is delayed. Care to entertain me?

**Chickentender09:** Suddenly I'm panicking and have no idea what to say. I don't handle pressure well.

**Firegirl94:** Sorry, didn't mean to sound demanding. Just tell me whatever. What have you been doing at school?

**Chickentender09:** School is the same. I should be writing an essay right now, but I don't want to, so I'm reading to distract myself.

**Firegirl94:** What are you reading? Maybe I can buy the book and we can read it together.

**Chickentender09:** *No Exit* by Jean Paul-Sartre

**Firegirl94:** . . . That's what you read for fun?

**Chickentender09:** Lol, I was in the mood for it, I guess.

**Firegirl94:** OK, no judgment here if you don't judge my collection of thrillers. Tell me about the book.

**Chickentender09:** I'll bore you.

**Firegirl94:** Never. I love learning stuff from you.

**Chickentender09:** I was just thinking about how I'm always worrying about the expectations others have for me, or what I think they expect, and it made me want to read the book again.

*I have a date today* was the first thing on Ari's mind when she woke up. "I have a date," she said out loud while standing in the kitchen eating breakfast. *I have a date*, she texted Tom while walking to class.

It had been a while since the last time Ari went on a date. She tried to downplay it by remembering it was only a video call, but it didn't work. The entire day she was unable to focus on anything—her classes or her work at the library—because she kept thinking about Dani. The mix of excitement and dread fought to return to the surface.

She hadn't had many relationships. She'd met her only official girlfriend, Lara, in her first year of college, and sometimes she wasn't even sure if what they had counted as a relationship. One day at a party, Lara had come up to her, told her she was pretty, and kissed her. From then on, they saw each other only when Lara wanted. When she called, Ari rushed to meet her at her dorm. Sometimes they hooked up, and sometimes they spent time together doing nothing, lying in bed, watching TV, reading.

Lara always told Ari how much she loved her, how happy she was to have her as a girlfriend, until something happened one day and Lara had a 180-degree turnaround. From then on, their time together always ended with Lara's cutting words or screams to just leave her alone while she closed the door in Ari's face.

After a week or two, the cycle would start again because Ari always went back. She basked in the moments when Lara made her feel like she was the most special woman in the world, while a nagging voice in the back of her mind told her that relationships shouldn't be this way. One day, she didn't go back. No matter how much Lara begged, how much she called, Ari ignored her.

Since then, Ari had barely dated. The fear of losing herself again, like she had with Lara was stronger than her desire for love. With Dani, she felt safe enough to at least give it a chance after months of chatting, and she couldn't contain the excitement of going on a date with someone she liked. She'd forgotten how thrilling it could be.

Two hours before the scheduled time for their video call, Ari decided to shower. The long, hot shower helped relax her tense muscles and distracted her anxious mind. Between that and standing in front of the closet trying to decide what to wear for what seemed like hours, time flew by. In the end, Ari opted to put on her usual home clothes—sweatpants and a T-shirt.

She jumped on the bed, placed a couple of pillows behind her back to get comfortable, and opened the laptop on her legs. She typed a message to send to Dani, but a knock on the door interrupted her. Tom's timing was just perfect.

She fought the urge to roll her eyes. "Go away!"

"You're aware I have a key, right? I'm just being polite . . . and cautious in case you've already gotten to the virtual sex part of the night."

"Goddammit," Ari mumbled, more annoyed at the images Tom had put in her mind right before she talked to Dani than at the disruption. "What do you want?"

That was all the invitation Tom needed to come in. "I wanted to check how things are go—" He examined Ari from head to toe. "Thank God I did. That's what you're wearing?"

"Yes? This is me. No point in pretending to be something I'm not."

Tom groaned but dropped the subject. He started moving around the apartment instead, reaching behind Ari to pick up some dirty clothes hanging on the edge of the bed that she hadn't noticed.

"You realize that most people try to make a good impression on their first date. It's not lying, it's called caring."

"I care," she said. At Tom's skeptical face, Ari spoke again with more force. "I do!"

"I'm all for showing your true self, but you could at least pick up your dirty underwear." He reached next to her pillow to pick up some shorts she had forgotten too. He used only the tips of his fingers to grab them, dangling them in front of her with a grossed-out expression.

"Those are shorts, not underwear. And the camera won't show all that."

"What if she asks you to see the apartment? Or you have to move the camera to another place? She's going to see this mess."

He was still walking around picking up stuff when a message from Dani appeared on her screen.

**Firegirl94**: Hey, beautiful. Ready for tonight?

She answered back to let Dani know she was ready while grabbing her phone and waving desperately toward the door. "Get out, dude!"

Tom stood at the door, ready to close it, when her phone started to ring. She hit the Answer button as fast as possible.

"Hey," Dani said with a bright smile.

"H-Hey," Ari whispered, momentarily stunned by Dani's beauty. She cleared her throat and tried again, louder and with more confidence. "Hey."

She had no clue when Tom had closed the door and left. She was too lost in the woman in front of her, in the soft brown eyes staring back at her through the screen and the flawless smile that grew with every second Ari remained speechless.

Dani tilted her head, watching her with what looked like appreciation and a hint of amusement. Ari was aware that the longer she stayed silent, the more awkward it would be, but she couldn't bring herself to speak.

She didn't believe in love at first sight. How could you love someone when you knew nothing about them, only because fate or some outside force decided it? She refused to imagine she didn't have a choice. The moment she saw Dani, though, she almost had to change her mind. Even with miles of distance between them, Ari's heart skipped a beat when their eyes met.

But she knew Dani, Ari realized. It wasn't love at first sight—only the confirmation of the feelings she'd harbored inside for months now.

Technically, they'd already met. But her body was reacting in ways she'd never experienced before. Ari saw her own reflection on the phone screen. Saw her lips move without her authorization, her tongue licking dry lips while her eyes roamed over Dani's face. She swallowed hard and forced herself to speak, even if Dani seemed happy to let Ari bask in her beauty.

Ari cleared her throat. "How's Melbourne?"

The question was basic, but Ari congratulated herself on being able to articulate something. Anything. She could only imagine the field day Tom would have at her expense if he could see her too affected by a woman to hold a conversation.

"It's hot. So hot. Summer in Australia is brutal. Well, it's brutal everywhere, what with climate change and everything. I hate the heat, but it's part of the job and I've gotten used to it. This is like the eighth summer I've spent here."

Ari was relieved that Dani was more talkative than she was and not overwhelmed by their first interaction. That made one of them.

"Why do you travel so much again?" Ari managed to ask. "I'm not sure I caught that last time."

*Okay, that was better*, she told herself.

"I like your hair," Dani said out of nowhere. "The way it curls around your face makes you look so cute."

A blush rose to Ari's cheeks. Here she was trying to string words together in a coherent sentence, and Dani had no problem flirting after less than five minutes.

"I, umm . . . Thank you?" Ari tucked a strand of her shoulder-length hair behind her ear. Probably the same one Dani had called cute.

"Sorry, that was too forward. I couldn't help myself," Dani said with an expression that made Ari doubt she regretted her words at all. "As for your question, I'm a professional tennis player.

We have some big tournaments in Australia during this time of the year. There are tennis tournaments all over the world, so I travel to play in them."

"Oh, that sounds exciting. Are you like a sailor? With a girl in every city?"

"None for me right now. But I'm hoping that may change soon." It was hard to miss the way Dani said the last few words, without breaking eye contact and closing them with a wink.

Ari was proud of herself for her comeback—playful and flirty but also a callout. Perfect balance between everything. A part of her wanted to make sure Dani was serious about whatever it was they were starting. She seemed to be, but it didn't hurt to get more information with a little banter.

Of course, Dani had turned it around into an opportunity to flirt even more. Ari didn't mind, though. She'd gotten an answer to her question, and she couldn't deny that it felt good to have someone showing interest so openly. Dani's approach also helped her relax. There was no chance to second-guess things when the other person was so direct.

"Has anyone ever told you that you're a huge flirt?" Ari retorted with a grin.

"Most people say I'm super cold and emotionless, actually."

"I find that hard to believe."

"Well, I don't show this side of me to everyone."

The mood changed with that confession. Dani was still smiling and looked relaxed, but it was easy to tell there was weight behind her words, a vulnerability that hadn't been present before.

"I'm honored," Ari answered with a bow. It was partly a joke, an attempt at lightening up the conversation again, but it was also sincere. She sensed that the easy banter they had so far was growing into something beyond friendship, and she was eager to find out more about Dani. "So, are you any good?"

"At what? Flirting?"

"No. Tennis. I already know you're good at flirting," Ari said. The chuckle that Dani let out warmed her heart. It felt great to be the one making her laugh.

"At least my efforts have not been wasted. For a second there I wasn't sure if you were catching on."

Ari rolled her eyes and looked down, trying to hide another blush.

"You don't follow sports much, do you?" Dani asked.

"Not at all. My dad loves soccer, so that's the only sport we watched growing up, and I can't say I fully understand it. It was more a way to spend time with him. Why?"

"No reason. It's refreshing. People around me are obsessed with sports, and one sport in particular. It's their bread and butter, and they talk about it all the time. It's nice to have a break."

"Well, you'll be happy to know, then, that I get tired going up and down the stairs of my building. Exercise is not my thing."

Dani laughed again, which was quickly becoming one of Ari's favorite sounds in the world.

"Ahh . . . Now I think I should worry about you. I don't need you to be at a professional-athlete level, but maybe you should walk around the block once in a while. We don't want you collapsing at thirty."

"I walk half a mile to campus every day so I should be fine, but I will leave the serious exercise to you. I'm more the intellectual type."

"Oh, are you saying I'm the dumb jock in this relationship?"

"I didn't say 'dumb' . . ."

Ari enjoyed their banter, and it flowed in a way that made her forget all the worries and nerves she had before the call. With every exchange, she grew more confident at how things were turning out.

"Well, I can't complain," Dani said. "It gave me this body, after all." She accompanied her retort by standing up, moving away from the camera, and twirling to show off her physique.

Until that moment, the frame of the camera had only allowed Ari to see Dani's face, neck, and shoulders. Ari could tell that she was wearing a sports top, the bright orange stripes over her shoulders giving it away. But she was not ready to have a full view of Dani's body. Just her smile, eyes, and face had left her speechless minutes before; the complete view almost made her choke.

The outfit wasn't extraordinary—a sports top, yoga pants, and tennis shoes. Ari gave an inward sigh of relief that both of them were wearing their regular clothes. But the fact was that Dani didn't have to try to look good.

The first thing that caught Ari's attention was the uncovered spot between the top and the yoga pants, where defined abs hypnotized her. When her eyes moved up, they found big, muscular arms, and she could only imagine the back muscles she would see if Dani turned around—Ari had a thing for backs. When Dani spun with slow, calculated movements that gave Ari a perfect view of what she'd been imagining seconds before, she thought she was going to pass out.

Dani was dragging out the moment to torture her; Ari was sure of it. Should she try to hide the obvious impact Dani was having on her? Retreating was her first instinct. Being exposed was scary. The way Dani brought out things in her that nobody else had in a long time nagged at the back of her mind. But in that instant, she couldn't help but give in and show her feelings as clear as day in the way she looked Dani up and down.

"I can't complain about the results, that's for sure," Ari finally said.

Dani sat down again. "It's good to know that all my hard work is paying off."

"As if you didn't know before."

"I knew, but it never mattered to me until now. If I can get you to look at me like that again, it will be worth it to go to the gym tomorrow."

"You are so full of it. If you're a professional athlete, you have to go anyway."

"You got me. But believe me, this is way better motivation than anything my trainer can yell at me while I'm doing weights or whatever torture he designs for the day."

"Well, I would return the favor, but I can't compete with the results of a personal trainer."

"Tease."

"I need to keep the mystery. Can't give away everything on the first night."

"Fair. Besides, I thought we agreed you were the brains. Show me some of those smarts you were bragging about."

"I started reading *The House of the Spirits* a few weeks ago, but I'm trying to read the original version in Spanish and my grasp of the language is worse than I thought it would be."

"I've read that book. It's been a while, but I loved it. We can read it together. Your dumb jock enjoys reading."

"I'd love that. I really want to improve my Spanish. My dad spoke it to us a little when we were kids but back then I really didn't care to learn the language. I didn't see the point but now I regret it."

"When I first moved to Spain, I faked a Spanish accent because kids would make fun of my Colombian accent, so I get it. It's never too late to learn. Besides, you have me now. I can be your personal Spanish tutor."

Ari smiled softly. The care and support Dani offered without even thinking might be the one thing that made Ari truly fall for her.

They talked for hours. Ari blushed without fail at Dani's flirting, and her heart fluttered in her chest every time she managed to make Dani laugh or stare in concentration while she spoke. She could have stayed like that all night if it weren't for her eyelids betraying her. They closed without her consent for seconds at a time until she forced herself to snap them open again.

One of those times, when she managed to open them again, Dani's warm eyes and smile were the first things she saw.

"Hey, sleepyhead, I'm sorry for making you stay up so late. I will be in the US in a few weeks, and we won't have this annoying time difference then. Go to sleep."

"Yeah, I guess I should. I loved talking to you."

"So did I."

Ari had only enough energy to put her phone on the nightstand before losing the battle to sleep. As her eyes drifted shut and her mind lost consciousness, a smile never left her lips.

◈

When Dani glanced at the clock, it surprised her to see it was almost five in the evening. No wonder Ari had struggled to stay awake by the end of their call; it was close to three in the morning for her when they had hung up.

The image of Ari looking sleepy was still fresh on Dani's mind. She found it adorable how her eyelids closed on their own every few minutes, but Ari had insisted on shaking the sleep away again and again. Dani understood. She also hadn't wanted their conversation to end.

Now that her video chat with Ari was finished, all she had was time on her hands and her own thoughts to keep her company. She could call Igor to schedule a last-minute training, but after going through the work of telling him she would only do one that day, she didn't want to change plans again.

She'd also asked Arantxa to clear her schedule from sponsor obligations and media interviews. Her manager was less discreet, so it wasn't a surprise when she received more scrutiny from her. Dani smiled at the memory of their conversation.

"You need me to make sure there's no press or sponsor obligations tomorrow?" Arantxa had asked.

"Yes, I need to be undisturbed for a couple of hours."

"Igor told me you weren't doing your afternoon training session either. I think he thought it was me stealing you away. Seemed quite shocked it wasn't."

Dani shrugged. "He could have asked me."

"You know how he is, never one for conversation. I want all the details."

"Details of what?"

"Come on, don't play coy. The last time you canceled a training session, you were awfully ill, so don't pretend this is just a coincidence. I haven't forgotten that text-message-big-smile situation from the other night."

"It's enough that I have to protect my private life from journalists and fans. I just want a day for myself."

"Well, I'm not some random fan or a journalist, I'm your friend. Granted, your options are limited because of the constant travel, but I'm what you got, take it or leave it."

"I'm gonna go with leave it," Dani answered.

"Funny. Come on, you can tell me."

"There's nothing to tell."

Even through the phone, Dani could tell Arantxa wasn't buying her words. The prolonged silence on the other end of the line was too much for her to take.

"Yet. Nothing to tell yet," Dani confessed. "I promise you will be the first one to know if something worth mentioning happens, which it won't if you keep pestering me. When I said I wanted the day for something personal, I wasn't planning on spending the one before it bickering with you."

"Fine, fine. Keep your secrets, but I'm onto you."

Now Dani wondered if she would be breaking her promise to Arantxa if she didn't share what had occupied the last hours of her life. Dani was interested in Ari, but she wasn't sure what, if anything, would come of it. Should she involve other people already, when everything was still in such early stages?

On one hand, Dani considered Arantxa a friend, and it would be exciting to share with someone else what was happening. But Arantxa was also her manager. As much as she cared for Dani as a person, there was still a business side to their relationship.

If things progressed further between her and Ari, then Arantxa would need to know about it. She would oversee where and how things became public, if they ever did. Dani always tried to keep her private life as far away as possible from the public light, and in that case, it would also be Arantxa's job to help keep it that way. Telling Arantxa made it real. It added too many complications, too many things Dani didn't want to think about.

Right then and there, the only thing Dani wanted was to remember the way she'd made Ari blush every time she flirted with her. The shy smile that adorned Ari's lips when Dani complimented her, or how Ari didn't realize she tucked a strand of her hair behind her ear when something made her nervous. Dani let out a loud sigh. Dating was complicated enough on its own—the last thing she wanted was to have to worry about the implications for her career.

◈

Dani decided to look Ari up on Instagram to pass the time. Ari had shown no reservations about sharing details about her life, like her name or her school. She'd even given Dani her personal email address so they wouldn't have to limit themselves to chatting on Tumblr like they'd been doing, which made it even easier to find her.

Ari didn't seem too active on social media. She had several pictures up, but most of them were landscapes or random objects. Pictures of her were few and far between, but that didn't stop Dani from staring at them for longer than was appropriate. There were a couple of pictures of Ari with a tall, muscular guy who she assumed was Tom. Ari talked about him so much that Dani almost saw him as a friend already too.

Acting on impulse, Dani hit the Follow button on Ari's profile, knowing that it would be impossible for Ari to miss the five million followers Dani had. They would have a conversation about it, eventually. For now, she was content revealing herself like this, in stages, and letting Ari reach out if she wanted to find out more.

Dani texted Arantxa. **Let's get dinner together. I have a promise to fulfill.**

She took a shower and changed before meeting Arantxa in the lobby. Arantxa insisted on going to the same restaurant again; apparently, the wine was that good. Dani couldn't drink it in the middle of a tournament, but maybe when she won the championship, she would try it.

For the first few minutes, Arantxa led the conversation. She asked generic questions, told Dani about her day, dished about celebrity gossip and what had happened in the reality shows she loved to follow. Nothing heavy or important, nothing work related. But after they finished eating, Arantxa switched to inquisitor mode.

"So, you're going to tell me about your secret affair?"

Dani gave her an annoyed look. "You're worse than any journalist out there."

"Well, the definition of 'affair' is a secret relationship, so the word fits."

"It's not a relationship. Not yet at least. And it's not a secret if I'm telling you, is it?"

Arantxa shrugged, reluctantly admitting Dani was right. "Who is it? Another player?"

"What? I barely have any friends on tour and you think I bagged a girlfriend?"

"Well, you barely have any friends in general. If it's not someone who's around, like a player or coach, then I'm lost."

Dani took a sip of water and braced herself for the reaction to come. "I met her online," she finally said.

She would have laughed at the way Arantxa almost knocked the glass of wine down in her surprise if not for the fact that it had attracted the attention of people around them. The last thing they needed was for the wrong person to overhear them.

"What?" Arantxa whispered. "A groupie?"

"She's not a groupie. Drink your wine and let me talk."

Dani explained to Arantxa the details of how she'd met Ari anonymously at first, protected by their usernames and with no idea who the other was. How they had been talking for months, just as friends, but recently things had changed. She told Arantxa all about how she wanted to pursue something with Ari but wasn't sure what was going to happen.

Arantxa sat back in her chair. "And you're sure she is not a stalker."

"I'm sure. There was no way for her to know who I was when we started talking, and honestly, she doesn't seem to know a thing about tennis. Either she's a great actor, or she really has no clue."

"Okay," Arantxa said, taking another sip of her wine, "what do you want me to do?"

"Nothing. Nobody knows about it, and we haven't even met in person. I guess I just wanted to share it with someone, make it more real."

"It sounds plenty real to me."

"Do you think it's silly?"

Arantxa shrugged. "I'm not one to call anybody silly for falling in love." Dani opened her mouth to protest that "love" was a strong word, but Arantxa waved her away before she could say anything. "Crush, liking someone, whatever you want to call it. There's nothing wrong with wanting to find a connection with someone else, and God knows you need one."

Dani sighed in relief. Her manager's words made her feel better about the whole thing.

"Love is always a risk," Arantxa continued. "But you've never been afraid of taking risks before. I don't see why you would be now."

# Chapter Six

**Tumblr chat, one month before**

**Firegirl94:** Happy New Year. One of the highlights of my year was talking to you, I hope you know that.

**Chickentender09:** It's still early afternoon here, but Happy New Year! It was one of my highlights too.

**Firegirl94:** Any plans for tonight? Hit the city, party all night?

**Chickentender09:** I think you know by now I'm not a party girl . . . the number of Friday nights we spent chatting is evidence of that. I'm home, and all my brothers are here for the holidays, so it will be a family affair.

**Firegirl94:** I guess I better not tell you to find someone to kiss at midnight, that would be awkward. Here :-* You can kiss me.

**Chickentender09:** Thank you. Best New Year's kiss I've ever had. I'm sure you have no problem finding someone to kiss, so I will refrain from sending one back.

**Firegirl94:** It's hard to kiss someone when your mouth is stuffed with twelve grapes. That's our tradition, one grape = one wish. I used one to wish that our friendship only becomes stronger this upcoming year.

◈

Ari glanced at her watch again, as though time would magically stop and prevent her from being late to work if she stared hard enough at the numbers. She tried to walk faster, her legs burning from the effort. In the end, though, it didn't help. She loved working at the library, but being half an hour late because she'd overslept was unacceptable. She tried to sneak in without being noticed, but her luck had her running into her boss the minute she stepped inside.

"Hi, I'm so sorry. It won't happen again," she blurted before her boss could even register who she had run into.

To her relief, the other woman shook her head and waved her away. "Get to work. No point in wasting more time."

Ari was happy to run away to her desk and focus for the next few hours. It was hard to ignore the constant vibration of her phone, but she knew it was only Tom desperate to hear all the details about her date the night before. She was eager to share everything with him too, but the last thing she needed was to get caught on her phone instead of working.

She was able to ignore his messages, but not her rumbling stomach after missing breakfast. Deciding to kill two birds with one stone, she shot him a quick message asking him to bring her coffee and something to eat.

Twenty minutes later, Tom waved at her from the door, then entered the library and walked between the shelves as if looking for something. They had established a system when she started working here: when they wanted to talk, she took a cart full of books that needed reshelving, and Tom walked beside her while she did it. That way she didn't neglect work, and the rows of shelves offered a protective cover for their conversations.

"Morning, sleepyhead. I assume that means things went well," he said, offering her a Starbucks cup.

Ari took her time enjoying the first sip of coffee. "It went great," she answered as a smile took over her face.

Tom surprised her by not making any comments. Instead, he leaned on the stack of books between them and smiled back. There was a glint in his eyes, but he said nothing— unnerving in a different way. She assumed he was already picturing a wedding and kids, even though she was only just adjusting to the idea of liking someone.

"When's the next date?" he asked.

Ari shrugged. She hoped it was soon. The few hours since she and Dani had last spoke already felt like an eternity, but she wasn't worried. She had no reason to believe they wouldn't be talking again. "We didn't have a chance to set up anything. I'll message her later."

Tom picked a book from the pile and flipped through it absentmindedly. "You haven't talked at all since last night?"

"I kind of passed out and had to run to get to work on time. I haven't had a chance to message her," Ari said without looking at him. She grabbed a book from the cart, put it in the correct spot, then moved on to the next.

"What are you waiting for?"

Ari was about to berate him for being on her case, until she realized she wanted to text Dani right then and there. Really, there was no reason she couldn't do it. "I guess I can message her right now."

Tom's enthusiastic nod made his opinion clear. Ari needed little encouragement to take her phone out and open their conversation history. A few unread messages awaited her from the night before.

"She said she can't wait to talk again."

Tom let out a high-pitched squeal that forced Ari to shush him.

"Sorry. Come on, show me," he shot back in a more appropriate tone of voice, pulling their faces together to stare at the screen. "She is so into you. This is amazing."

Ari blushed at his words but didn't contradict him. She was starting to believe he was right.

"Did you post something on Instagram?" he asked.

She frowned as Tom's random question brought her back from her thoughts. She barely used social media, so why was he mentioning that out of nowhere? "Huh?"

"There's an Instagram notification on your phone."

Strange. She furrowed her brow, trying to remember the last time she had used the app. "No, I haven't posted anything," she said, opening it out of curiosity but expecting it to be a bot or some creepy guy.

"Someone new is following me. Daniela Martínez." Ari didn't know Dani's full name, but it had to be her. Who else could it be?

Tom gasped. "Oh! She is checking you out on social media. Things are getting serious."

"Shut up," said Ari, equal parts embarrassed and excited about the fact that Dani was looking her up outside of Tumblr. "Should I check her profile out?"

"Hmm . . . duh? Of course! She opened the door by looking at all of your, what, ten pictures? Now we get to have fun. And it's perfect because I get to see how she looks, and my investigative abilities are way better than yours."

"She's super hot, I can tell you that." Ari couldn't stop herself from sharing that piece of information with Tom. He eyed her with curiosity —she didn't usually talk about people like that. "Let's wait until tonight to check it. I have to work, and I'm sure we'll spend hours on it."

"Ugh, I hate you because you're right. We need an appropriate setting and time for this, so even though it kills me to not do it now, I will be strong." He punctuated his words with over-the-top hand gestures, clutching at his chest and sighing. If anyone saw him, they would believe he was in actual pain about having to wait.

"You are so dramatic. Meet me at my apartment tonight. I got some Italian leftovers from last night, so no need to bring anything."

"The minute you finish work, I'll be at your door waiting."

Ari knew it was not an empty promise—he would be there. But this time, she didn't mind. She was dying to find out more about Dani too.

◈

As soon as her shift ended, Ari's focus switched to getting home as quickly as possible. The day had dragged on painfully slow, her brain unable to focus on anything but Dani. The memories of their date, the anticipation over their next conversation, the possibility of finding out more about her from social media.

Ari felt uneasy at first. Diving into someone's life without them knowing felt like an intrusion, but she rationalized it. Everything posted on social media was a curated view into a person's life, after all. She would see nothing that Dani hadn't chosen to share with the world. It was no accident that Dani had followed her. It was almost an invitation, and Ari couldn't find the strength to decline.

Of course, the day she was in a rush to get home, she ran into one of her professors at the library door. And not just any of them, but Samantha Edison, the person who had advised her during her whole academic career and had helped her with recommendation letters.

Professor Edison smiled in greeting. "Ari, great to see you. How's that summer associate hunt going?"

"It's going well. I already have a couple of interviews set up. Thank you again for putting in a good word for me."

Ari was thankful for all her help, that much was true. She doubted Professor Edison would want to hear about how much she hated the idea of landing a summer associate job and spending the summer surrounded by people who looked down on her and would never understand what it meant to be raised from nothing. Telling Professor Edison—who had put her good name and reputation on the line for her—about how conflicted she was about sacrificing her dreams for money was not the best idea.

"Be sure to let me know if you need anything from me. I'm sure my friends at Collins and Schuster would love to have you."

Ari nodded, happy when Professor Edison cut their conversation short. The reminder of her dilemma brought her mood down from the high it had been at since talking to Dani, but she tried to push it aside and rushed home as planned. Tom was sitting on the floor outside her apartment.

She rolled her eyes at him. "You have a key."

He stood up slowly, leaning against the door while he waited for Ari to find her key. "I was so excited I forgot it, and I didn't want to risk going back to my apartment for it and have you start the fun without me."

"I would never dare," she answered with fake solemnity.

Inside the apartment, Tom took charge of heating the leftover Italian food and setting the table with practiced ease while Ari changed clothes. "I got myself some wine and bought you some of those coconut water drinks you like."

"Wine?" Ari answered back from the restroom.

"Yes, wine. This is like *my* virtual date with your future girlfriend. I need to make it special."

His explanation made total sense, in a Tom sort of way. At the world "girlfriend," Ari's stomach twisted into knots, not out of excitement but out of dread. As much as she tried to manage expectations, they were already sky high. She could only repeat again and again that it wasn't a big deal if things didn't progress further with

Dani, even if deep down she knew she would be devastated if things didn't work out.

"We've had one call," she fired back. "Don't jinx it."

"Fine, fine, but I have a sixth sense." He said it with so much conviction that Ari almost believed him. Almost.

"Just like you had a sixth sense about each of the ten different guys you dated last year?" Ari couldn't stop herself from throwing a dig at him. Tom had said similar things so many times over the years about his own relationships. She thought his intentions were pure, but she preferred to remain realistic.

"Not going to comment on that. Sit down and eat your food. And give me your phone!"

Ari sat and dove into the food right away, starving after missing breakfast and lunch. She handed Tom her phone so they could start their mission.

Not five seconds later, Tom mumbled, "Holy fuck."

She raised an eyebrow, curiosity eating at her, but he remained silent as he scrolled.

A minute later, he spoke again. "Are you sure this is the person who followed you?" he said, turning the phone toward her.

A picture of Dani at the gym filled the screen. Ari could recognize that back without a problem, every inch of Dani's face and body fresh in her memory from the night before. "Yeah, that's her. She's actually wearing the same clothes that she had on last night."

"Holy fuck," Tom said again, eyes wide.

Ari's breath hitched at the change in his demeanor. By that point he should be making jokes and teasing her, but he seemed fixated on the picture. "What's up? You're scaring me."

He furrowed his brow, jokes and teasing forgotten as he swiped from one picture to the next on Dani's profile. "Did she tell you where she works or anything about her life?"

Again, the question struck Ari as odd. What was Tom so worried about? "Um . . . Yeah, she told me she's a professional tennis player," she answered, hoping he would stop playing twenty questions and explain himself soon.

Tom let out a loud scoff. "A professional tennis player? That's like the understatement of the century."

He didn't stop scrolling, going at light speed over Dani's feed. Finally, Ari had enough. She forced him to stop by placing a hand over his, and he looked at her again. It was as if he woke up from a trance the moment their hands touched.

"She won the Australian and the US Open last year. I knew that name sounded familiar, but I didn't connect it at the time. She is like an *international superstar tennis player*!" he exclaimed.

Ari shrugged. Dani was a tennis player, as she'd said. She still didn't understand why Tom was freaking out. "So . . . she didn't lie?"

Tom's shock changed into exasperation at her lack of reaction. He opened a new picture and shoved the phone in Ari's face to show her a photo of Dani on the cover of some magazine called *Hola*.

"No, she didn't lie," he said. "And okay, it's not like she is Beyoncé-level of famous, but she is rich and famous. I watched one of her matches on TV the other day!"

Ari looked at the picture again, noticing also for the first time the amount of likes and comments it had. Thousands of them. Realization dawned on her. "Oh," she whispered.

"Yeah, oh. You are dating a freaking celebrity."

Ari remained in place while Tom moved around her apartment, walking from one end to the other and back again, still scrolling on her phone. At first, the newfound information didn't seem important to her. But slowly it started to dawn on her that despite their months of conversations and the connection she thought they had, she was unaware of this significant, fundamental fact about Dani.

The doubts started to flood her at full force. Why would a successful, famous tennis player want anything to do with her? In her confusion, there was only one thing that was clear: there was no way Dani wanted to date her. Ari had misunderstood her intentions for sure, and the only thing Dani wanted from her had to be a friendship at most.

"We are not dating," she blurted.

Tom stopped his pacing, looked at her, and waved her off. "Oh my God, I need time to process this." He reached for his forgotten glass of wine on the table and took a sip, then another, and then another, until the glass was empty.

She wanted to laugh at his reaction, but her words came out annoyed instead. "*You* need time to process? I'm the one who's been talking to her."

As usual, Tom didn't register her reaction or her tone, or else he ignored it altogether. "I'm the one who understands how famous she is. I'm more affected than you."

Ari then listened to him explain just how popular a tennis player Dani was. Not only was she one of the current players always in contention to win the big tournaments, but she was a favorite of sponsors and advertisers. Ari's mind was a whirlwind of questions, and a lot of conversations she'd had with Dani suddenly made more sense: the way Dani was always careful about revealing too much about her personal life, the offhand comments she made about feeling watched.

On the outside, Ari appeared as calm as usual. But inside, her mind was going a thousand miles a minute over all their conversations, looking at them with fresh eyes. How many times had Dani stopped herself from revealing more, out of fear of being exposed? Were some of the things they shared lies? As she tried to process those thoughts, another one crossed her mind.

"What if this is some weird catfish situation?" she whispered.

Tom stopped mid-rant. He looked back at Ari, snapping out of his own feelings to focus on her. "It would have to be a very elaborate one. This is Daniela Martínez's account. I checked. It has like five million followers, and it's verified. It's not some weird knockoff. And you saw her last night, right?"

Ari nodded, unable to form words, worried that her voice would break. Tom's eyes softened; his lips moved to form a sheepish grin. She fought with the insecurity growing inside her enough to keep it from taking over, but not so much to stop from asking, "Why would a famous tennis player want to talk to me?"

Tom moved closer, squatting in the limited space in front of the dining table and taking her hand. "You tell me, girl."

They fell silent after that, both lost in their own thoughts. Tom kept scrolling on Ari's phone, looking at all the pictures Dani had posted over the years. On the tennis court, vacationing on beaches next to turquoise water and in beautiful mountain towns, gracing the covers of magazines, and modeling for professional photo shoots.

Ari stared at the pictures over his shoulder, realizing what he meant by "super famous." It was obvious that Dani's lifestyle was light-years away from her own, as a student with only debt to look forward to when she graduated. Ari rarely shared her worries and problems, not even with her best friend, so it was a shock even to her when the one thing that kept screaming the loudest in her mind came out of her mouth before she could stop it. "Do you think this is some kind of game to her?"

Tom's jaw dropped slightly at her words. He put the phone down and turned around to look at her with nothing but love in his eyes. As much as he liked to tease her, he was also a sensitive soul who knew when to drop the jokes.

"What do you mean? Like she goes around befriending people online and seducing them?"

"It sounds silly when you say it like that, but I don't get it." Ari winced at the way her voice sounded sad and defeated. She wanted to push the feelings away, but the more she dwelled on it, the more her insecurities came out.

"What don't you get?"

"Why would she be interested in me?"

"Because you are a beautiful, smart, funny, and sensitive woman that anyone would be lucky to have in their life."

Ari smiled at him, unconvinced. "I'm sure there are a million women around her who are hotter or smarter. Why me?"

"I can't speak for her, but maybe you should ask her yourself. But don't doubt for one second that anyone would be lucky to have your attention. Even tennis star Daniela Martínez." Ari blushed at his words. She was ready to refute him, but he beat her to it. "Don't sell yourself short. I won't allow it."

"I'm not going to. It's just a lot to take in."

"Tell me about it. I know how to Instagram-flirt with a regular person, but this celebrity thing is unfamiliar territory."

The ridiculousness of that statement made Ari laugh. The day before, flirting for the first time in years was her main worry, and now she had to think about what it might be like to date a celebrity. She could only marvel at the weirdness of it all.

Tom went back to scrolling on his own phone once he'd made sure she was no longer spiraling. Ari distracted herself by drinking tea, and after pausing to sit with her thoughts, she opted for taking things at face value and talking to Dani about it instead of letting her imagination run wild. After all, during the time they had been in contact, Dani had always been genuine with her.

The first thing she needed to do was ask Dani about it. Ari grabbed her phone, still open on Dani's Instagram account, and a small message under her username caught Ari's attention: *Followed by Tom.Samuelson.*

"Did you follow her?"

He shrugged. "Yeah."

"That's so embarrassing! She's going to realize I've been talking to you about her. She knows my best friend's name is Tom."

"So what? She gets a ton of notifications a day. I doubt she will even notice. But if she does and follows me back because I'm your friend, that will give me so much clout. I may even slide into some hot tennis player's DMs."

Ari couldn't get mad, even if she wanted to. It was impossible to be anything but amused. "You are incorrigible."

"Hey, dare to dream."

She laughed and decided to not dwell on it. Instead, she focused on what was on her mind, taking a screenshot of Dani's profile and sending it in a text to her.

**Got a shock when I checked my phone today. Sounds like I'm being pranked or something.**

Dani replied in less than a minute.

**I'm glad to see you've recovered from last night ;) It's not a prank. Surprise?**

Ari let out a small laugh as she typed back.

**Yeah, quite a surprise. I'm a little shaken by it, to**

**be honest.**

**I'm sorry. I should have been more careful about how to let you know. I didn't want to make a big deal out of it.**

Ari read Dani's text multiple times, struggling to find the words to express the way the discovery had affected her. After she tried and failed for several minutes to send an adequate reply, Dani messaged her again.

**Can I call you? This seems like something we should discuss in person. Well, you know what I mean. Not by text.**

Ari's response was a short *Sure*. She still didn't know how to convey what she felt, but maybe seeing Dani would make it easier. When her phone started ringing, Ari turned around to keep Tom out of frame and signaled at him to stay put. She took a deep breath and swiped up to answer.

"Hey," Dani said.

That simple greeting was almost all she needed to silence her doubts. The way Dani looked at her, her face full of warmth, was enough to make Ari relax. As she had the night before, Ari stayed silent, drinking in Dani's presence, losing herself in the sight in front of her.

Again, Dani took the lead by speaking first. "I don't have much time, but I had to call you." She looked distraught, her eyebrows tight and her forehead full of tension. Ari assumed Dani thought she was upset. Many people would be, given the situation, but Ari wasn't. The only problem she had with finding out about Dani's life was that she felt more inadequate than ever.

"I appreciate you calling. It also gives me a chance to make sure I'm not being pranked or catfished," Ari said, half joking, half not.

"No catfish, I promise. I'm sorry I caught you so off guard; I didn't think things through. I thought telling you myself in conversation would be more awkward, but I guess I was thinking of my own comfort and not yours. I'm sorry."

"It was quite the shock, but I'm processing it."

Dani's posture relaxed at the words. "I will be here for anything you need processing with," she said in a soft voice.

Ari's heart started beating harder when Dani leaned closer to the camera, tilting her face sideways in the most adorable way. "Thank you."

As fast as it happened, the moment ended. Dani shifted again, sitting straighter, as if someone she didn't want around had come into the room. Ari noticed the area behind Dani for the first time. It didn't look like a hotel room, with rows of what appeared to be lockers lining the walls.

"I have a match," Dani said. "But I will call you later if that's okay?"

Ari nodded, then realized Dani was about to end the call. "Wait!" she yelled without thinking.

Dani stopped, her hand hovering in the air to end the call. Long seconds ticked by in silence. Ari knew what she wanted to ask, but it sounded silly in her own mind. She considered telling Dani it was nothing, but she knew the issue would bother her for days if she didn't bring it up.

"What?" Dani cocked her head but said nothing more.

"Why talk to me?" Ari asked. "I'm a nobody. I don't get it."

"Because I enjoy talking to you. As simple as that."

Ari nodded, allowing herself to believe Dani's words. She realized she was holding her back from an important match. "Oh, right. Break a leg."

"What?" Dani's face was a mix between amusement and confusion.

"Oh, I mean good luck in your match. Don't you guys use that expression, like in theater?"

Dani laughed, and Ari's heart fluttered just as it had the night before. She liked Dani, no way around it.

"No, we don't use that. It would be bad if a tennis player broke a leg, I guess. But thank you."

Ari stayed rooted in her seat, staring at the screen of her phone long after Dani had hung up.

Tom's strident voice brought her out of her daydream. "You two are the cutest!"

# Chapter Seven

Dani sat in the locker room staring at the wall, lost in the memory of her conversation with Ari until the tournament supervisor called for her. With her match minutes away, it was time to walk through the tunnel that led to the main stadium.

Under normal circumstances, her focus would be on her upcoming match and nothing else. She valued concentration above everything. She didn't even listen to music while waiting for her match to start, like a lot of players did. Instead, she always found the most secluded corner of the locker room, closed her eyes, and spent whatever time she had doing breathing exercises and clearing her mind.

She usually put her phone on silent, or even on airplane mode, at least an hour before play was due to start. She wanted nothing from the outside world bothering her. This time, she had broken her own rule, too anxious and curious to wait. It had been a long day, with Ari not talking to her since their call. Dani knew that the time difference affected them, and she'd tried to occupy her mind with other things, but as much as she'd wanted to resist, she kept checking her phone every other minute.

It was just her luck that Ari contacted her right as she was getting ready to walk out to the court. Even if the timing was unfortunate, Dani had to read the message. Her initial excitement over hearing from Ari turned into worry with the change in tone. She started fearing that the way she'd let Ari find out more about her hadn't gone as she'd hoped. The ways her actions could be misinterpreted started dancing in her mind, and the urge to clear the air became impossible to stop. If she didn't call right then, she would have to wait two or three hours, at a minimum, to address the topic. The only option was to call Ari since waiting would affect her concentration more than breaking routine.

Dani didn't regret her choice, but now it was time to focus on tennis again, and it was proving harder than expected. She had no time to find her usual mental zone. She stepped out onto the court, hoping she would find her rhythm after a few minutes of playing.

The walk through the tunnel to enter Rod Laver Arena always made her feel like a rock star, especially when she passed the place where her picture adorned the wall with all the other former champions. Being next to so many legends of the sport was sobering and reminded her of her primary goal: winning. Not only today but every day.

As she got closer to the court, she took a minute to bask in the public's roar. She closed her eyes and visualized the sea of faces that would greet her once she stepped out into the stadium, the way they would clap, cheer, and will her to another victory.

The bright Australian sun shone as intense as ever, making drops of sweat fall down her face even before she hit the first ball. The cameraperson who followed each of her steps served as a reminder of how this wasn't the time or place to dwell on personal thoughts. A furrowed brow, a smile, a frown; anything and everything was broadcasted to the world in HD and subject to scrutiny. Experience had taught her that people created narratives from the most minuscule muscle movements, so she tried to not give them a thing.

Was Ari watching? That possibility was an added motivation for Dani to win. It would be embarrassing if Ari watched one of her matches for the first time, only for her to lose.

Despite her determination to impress Ari, Dani found herself down in the score. A constant stream of balls went long or into the net, making her unforced error count climb. But it was not an unsurmountable deficit, at least not for her. She always fought for every point, and no matter how bad things looked, she trusted herself and her game enough to at least try to turn things around. The fact that she found herself down 5–0 and one game away from losing the set was not enough to deter her confidence. In tennis, like in life, nothing was guaranteed. Nothing was certain until you played the last point. That sentiment was something Igor had drilled into Dani's mind, something she believed as much as she believed in God.

No, being down 5–0 wasn't the end of the world. It was unexpected, but remediable. A look at Igor in the stands told her he didn't understand why she was playing poorly either. He never gave much away, but Dani read his expressions better than anyone. The way he kept taking off his cap and scratching his head told her he was uneasy, and she didn't blame him.

Her rival—a young, promising player in her first year as a professional—had come out swinging, attacking every short ball and going for the lines as often as possible. Her strategy was paying off. For now. That kind of tennis was high risk, high reward, and Dani knew it firsthand because she played that way when she was younger. With time and experience, a player learned that, on a bad day, all those balls landing an inch inside the line could start landing an inch outside. That playing just a little bit safer could be more effective than going for everything in each shot.

But Dani understood why her opponent didn't care about margins. It wasn't long ago that she herself was in the same position, eager to prove herself by beating one of the best players in the world. Her competitor wouldn't go away without a fight, but if Dani came back and took the set from her, it may be enough to break her. Easier said than done, though. Dani needed to focus on winning one game—the rest would come later.

The change of ends couldn't come fast enough. Dani knew the match was on her racket. Her own mistakes were giving her rival an advantage, but she was the defending champion and was determined to not lose in the third round.

Dani tried to use the ninety seconds of rest allotted to try to clear her mind, to no avail. Something that was second nature to her had become impossible, because Ari appeared in Dani's mind without fail every time she closed her eyes. Her baffled expression at the fact that Dani wanted her in her life, the small quaver in her voice when she'd asked why, the cute way she'd wished her good luck.

*This is why I don't allow distractions.* She regretted that thought one second later. It wasn't Ari's fault that she wasn't able to focus. Dani was a professional tennis player who had competed in over a hundred matches. It was Dani's fault alone if she didn't turn things around.

Her anger at herself for allowing something so simple to throw her off her game fueled the next few points. It wasn't her usual game—she was taking more risks than usual and adding power to shots she preferred to control—but it worked. Her rival struggled to handle the alternative approach and the additional pace on the ball. Soon the score was even at 5, and fifteen minutes later, Dani won the first set 7–5.

Her opponent's eyes revealed that something had broken in her after her lead was taken away. Dani knew the feeling. After playing on edge for so long and feeling victory within her grasp, having things turn around was an emotional hit. The errors returned in the second set, but not on Dani's side of the court this time. The balls her opponent had been hitting just inside the lines now were landing outside, and the more mistakes she made, the more frustrated she became.

The rest of the match flew by in a blur. Once Dani found her rhythm, nothing shook her out of it. Her mind finally focused only on tennis. She won the second set 6–1, devoid of all the drama from the start of the match. For her, it was a bigger win than the score suggested. She'd climbed out of a hole, one she hadn't been sure she would get out of an hour before.

Back in the locker room, Dani fought the urge to check her messages again. Focusing on Ari instead of tennis had affected her too much during the match, and exercising some self-control, forcing herself to wait, was a way to implement the self-discipline she would need to have to prevent something like that from happening again.

She did her post-match routine and the mandatory press conference. The only thing left to do before she could rest in her hotel room was to talk to Igor. It was a tradition they'd established from the start; after every match, they would sit and talk about what went well and what she could have done better. It didn't matter the score or the tournament, he always made sure they did it.

She walked to the players' lounge, where most of her team was waiting. If she had to deal with Igor, at least she would eat at the same time. To his credit, he held off on saying anything until she'd gotten her food, and he even sat in silence while Dani made small talk with Arantxa. His silence unnerved Dani more than his criticism, but it didn't last long. The minute Arantxa wandered away to pick up dessert, the unspoken truce ended.

"That was quite the hole you dug for yourself today."

Dani's jaw clenched. "Got out of it, didn't I." Igor's direct approach was part of the success of their relationship, but it hit hard. She took a bite of her food instead of looking at him. Her obvious tension didn't deter him—it never did.

"You pulled it off, which surprised me. You were all over the place. This should have been a routine win but instead you were anxious, distracted. Focus and calm are your biggest strengths."

He was right, but Dani wanted to antagonize him. To disagree with him for the sake of it. This time, she dropped her chopsticks and stared at him. "I would say that getting back from a 5-0 deficit requires a lot of focus and calm."

"I'd rather you not get yourself in those situations in the first place. It happens, and you can't win every match 6-1, 6-1, but I saw nothing to make me think this was the other player's doing."

She'd been berating herself for the same reason for hours now, but admitting it to Igor was a different thing. If she did, he would have additional questions she didn't want to answer. Not this time, at least. Not to him. "We all have our off days."

"That's all it was, an off day? Because I can deal with that. You're right, it happens. The important thing is to fight and to win so we can do better the next day. But if there's more going on, tell me. You've been distracted lately."

She looked down and started eating her food as a way of stalling. Not meeting his eyes made brushing off his judgment easier. "It was just an off day," she repeated. "Nothing to worry about."

Silence spread between them, his inquisitive eyes locked on her and fixated on her every movement. Hers remained down, staring at the food she moved around her plate.

He pushed back his chair and stood. "I set up two practice sessions for tomorrow. The first one is at eight in the morning. See you then." The sound of heavy footsteps walking away accentuated the words.

Dani didn't enjoy lying to Igor, but what had happened in the match wouldn't happen again, she would make sure of it. There was no point in making it a bigger deal than it was, and talking to Igor about her love life was not on her agenda. It wasn't on her agenda to talk to anyone about it, to be fair.

But Arantxa never cared about what Dani wanted. She'd returned to the table as Igor left and didn't waste a second. "So . . . rough day, huh?"

Dani glanced up from her plate and met Arantxa's inquisitive stare. "It wasn't the best."

"I, for one, don't see what the big deal is. You won and made things more exciting."

The joke was an attempt at breaking the gloomy aura surrounding her, and Dani tried to force herself to take the offer of levity, but the weight of her near failure lay heavy on her shoulders, mind, and heart. "So happy to hear my pain entertains you." What was intended as a joke came out as an accusation.

Arantxa, to her credit, didn't bat an eye at Dani's sour mood. Instead, she reached across the table to steal a piece of sushi from her plate. "Oh, come on. Don't be dramatic," she said, still chewing. "You won the second set 6–1. It's not like you were two points away from defeat."

"I'm not upset about the result, just mad because I blew the first few games. My mind was somewhere else."

"Now that's surprising. Focus is like your thing."

Dani sighed but didn't reply. Everybody reminding her how out of character she'd been today was not helping.

"Relationship drama?"

Dani answered with a glare.

"What? You're going to tell me it's not about that? It can't be a coincidence."

Dani stared at Arantxa with ice in her eyes, refusing to give away anything for a full minute. Arantxa met her challenge, unfazed by the intense, angry look. In the end, Dani relented. "Ari found out who I am, the whole rich person thing. She freaked out a little. We are fine, but it kind of disrupted my match preparation."

"So cute to see you act like a regular human being. Shaken by your emotions."

Dani huffed out a breath. The one person she decided to open up to was only interested in mocking her. Her glare came back stronger. "I'm not shaken," she said with more force than before. "I'm a creature of habit. Changes to my routine throw me off, that's all."

"If you say so." The smug smirk spreading on Arantxa's face fired Dani up.

"I do." The bite of Dani's tone left no room for discussion.

Arantxa raised her hands in fake surrender before moving her chair over next to Dani's. She leaned closer, speaking in a warmer, softer voice. "This seems serious. Not a random, anonymous internet friend anymore."

Dani stopped to think before answering. It was obvious her interest in Ari was evolving beyond a friendship—she would have never taken that first step of setting up a call otherwise. The fact that things were changing too fast stressed her out, but it also felt right. She didn't think she could slow down even if she wanted to. Talking to Ari was the one thing that made her happier than anything else in her life at the moment, and she didn't want to fight it.

"Yeah, I guess it is serious," Dani said. "I wouldn't be exposing myself like this if it wasn't."

The relief it brought to share her feelings with someone was great, but seeing Arantxa's eyes widen with surprise was better. The reaction was understandable, as Dani hadn't dated in years. She had in fact rejected several offers by Arantxa to set her up with women she knew. Most of them were Arantxa's own exes, which was an additional reason to decline. If there was one person who Dani knew wouldn't judge her, it was her manager.

The only downside was that Arantxa's support, though unconditional, always came with a generous dose of teasing. This time was no exception. "No sending nudes, though. I don't need to deal with that."

Dani rolled her eyes, while trying to control the thoughts invading her mind because of the implications of Arantxa's advice.

◆

Dani breathed a sigh of relief as she entered her hotel room. She craved the time alone, away from prying conversations, no matter how well-intentioned. She didn't want anyone around her, but the emptiness of the room suddenly unnerved her. She turned the TV on to at least have some noise to keep her company while she lowered her body into a makeshift ice bath. She hated them, but they were a necessary evil that soothed her aching muscles.

She was already chest-deep in the water when the TV commentary caught her attention. In her rush to put on something—anything—she'd landed on a network covering the Australian Open. The last thing she needed was to hear more opinions about her.

*"The biggest news of the day is the scare that defending champion Daniela Martínez had earlier today. What do you make of it, Chris?"*

*"The pressure of coming back to the place where you won your first Grand Slam and trying to replicate that success is never easy for a player."*

*"True. Most players have struggled after winning big, and she comes from a great season, even getting close to the number one position in the ranking. Do you think we should expect a sophomore slump?"*

Dani tried to ignore their words and refused to get out of the bathtub. She closed her eyes and took a deep breath, trying to fill her senses with anything else and block out the voices.

*"I wouldn't go that far. I've always said that you write off a champion at your own peril. They have that extra mental gear that allows them to come back, even when things look bad. Just like she did today. Soon we will know if this was an off day in her road to the title or evidence of a bigger problem. Right now, I wouldn't read much into it. She won the second set 6–1, and she is going to come out in two days looking to dominate and put to rest any doubts about her performance."*

She groaned as she stepped out of the bathtub and reached for her robe. The trail of water she left behind was the last of her worries while she focused on finding the remote and muting the TV.

She looked at the clock on her phone; it was past three in the morning for Ari. Despite the long shot, she decided to text her.

**Did you watch the match? I promise I'm better than that.**

Dani stared at her phone for fifteen minutes before accepting that she wouldn't be receiving an answer anytime soon. She contemplated reading a book or catching up on one of her online language courses, but her mind wasn't in it, and it would be a waste of time to pretend like she could focus on anything but Ari.

She went back to her Instagram scrolling. Maybe it wasn't the best idea—after all, it had been her brilliant plan to reveal herself using social media that had caused all her problems—but in that moment, this was the only way she could feel closer to Ari.

A notification caught her eye. Because she received so many on a regular basis, she ignored most of them, but the name stood out this time: Tom. Since he had followed her first, it was fair game to look at his profile. As she hoped, he was an avid poster. Where Ari had twenty pictures total, he posted twenty a day. Some Dani didn't care about, but others had Ari in them. Most of them were around their school campus. In most of Ari's own pictures, she never smiled, but she was often mid-laugh in Tom's pictures, looking happy and carefree.

While scrolling through Tom's photos, Dani contemplated if texting Ari again would appear needy. Her finger hovered over the Message app icon on her phone, anxiety rising inside her. She scoffed at how unlike her it was to doubt herself, and she opened the app—there was no time to second-guess. She wanted Ari, no reason to pretend she didn't. The message included a link to a picture she'd been staring at for more time than she would admit.

**I love your laugh in this picture. I hope you are not still mad at me so I can see it for myself soon.**

That text was more vulnerable than Dani was usually comfortable with, but since their last call, she couldn't shake the edginess Ari's words had caused. It pained her to see how insecure Ari looked. How she didn't believe that Dani wanted her in her life as even a friend, let alone as more than that.

As difficult as it was for Dani to expose herself and her feelings, she also understood that people couldn't know what they were never told. If she wanted to pursue Ari, and if she wanted to help their relationship start on firm foundations and eventually evolve into more, they needed honesty and vulnerability. These had never come easy to Dani, and it was one reason her past relationships had failed. But she was ready, and she hoped Ari was ready too.

Dani would open the door, but both needed to pass through it.

◈

Ari was starting to hate the time difference. She had woken up to a message from Dani, and it was obvious that she had wanted to talk. Ari cursed the fact that she wasn't there for Dani when she needed her.

Ari answered the message on the spot just in case Dani was still around, and a minute later her phone was ringing. "I promise I won't tell you to break a leg ever again," she said, hoping her attempt at a joke would make the worried expression on Dani's face disappear.

"I assume you watched me get my ass kicked yesterday?" Dani answered, the hints of a smile tugging at the corners of her mouth. "I hope my rivals don't find out about you; they'll want to use your jinxing powers to beat me."

Ari's heart soared at being able to make her laugh, but that happiness didn't last long. As quick as their jokes started, they ended, and Dani's expression turned serious again. Ari mentally prepared herself for the worst-case scenario: Dani realizing that talking to her had been a mistake and ending their friendship once and for all. She held her breath as Dani spoke again.

"Are you sure we're good? About the whole me-hiding-important-information-from-you thing?"

Ari averted her gaze, embarrassed by the way she had reacted and the way she was letting her insecurities get the best of her again. "We're fine. It shocked me, but I've had time to process it now and I think I was overreacting because of the surprise."

"I'm happy to hear that. Still, I could have handled things better. I could've told you in another way so I didn't catch you off guard."

Ari couldn't help but feel even more charmed by Dani's worry and apology. In her past relationships, she was always to blame for anything that happened, and she didn't think she'd ever heard an apology from Lara. She already knew Dani was different—there was no comparison—but details like this confirmed it even more.

"That would have been nice." The corner of Ari's lips raised in a teasing grin. "Not sure how you can prepare someone for such a big revelation. I'm still wrapping my head around it."

"Yeah . . . my bad," Dani replied, flashing a charming smile of her own. "I know you don't like tennis; I wasn't sure you would care."

"I guess this is a perfect time to tell you I didn't even realize you were losing yesterday until way too late. If Tom wasn't a tennis fan, I would have thought you were an influencer."

Dani's eyes widened. "Influencer? Oh my God, no!"

Ari let out a chuckle. "That's where you draw the line?"

"You promise we're good?" Dani asked again.

"We are. I'm still processing, but we're okay." This time Ari didn't avoid Dani's eyes. She hoped the sincerity in her own put Dani at ease.

"There's only one reason I'm talking to you and why I told you who I am beyond my online profile: I like you. I enjoy talking to you, being your friend. It's not a game to me or a joke. You are amazing, and that's all there is to it."

Heat rushed to Ari's cheeks, but she was grateful for the reassurance. She hated to appear needy, but Dani's words meant the world.

"I don't get why you think that, but I want to embrace it," Ari said. Despite how hard it was for her to understand what Dani saw in her, she wanted to believe it. Every time Dani repeated how much she liked her, Ari accepted it a little more.

"I wish you could see what I see, the amazing woman you are. I'm the lucky one for having you share part of you with me. I can't force you to believe me, but I hope you give me the chance to show you."

Ari smiled back, her heart melting, ready to give Dani anything she asked for. "I would like that."

They hung up shortly after that, with Ari firmly on cloud nine. Part of her wanted to lie back in bed and stare wistfully at the ceiling while she daydreamed about Dani, but she had class and work, so she reluctantly started to get ready for the day. She drank her morning tea while checking all the unread messages from her mom. The first thing she saw was a picture of her parents with a cake and her brother standing next to it.

**Your brother got a promotion to chief surgeon! We're so proud of him. Please call to congratulate him. I'm sure he would love to hear from his baby sister.**

Ari sighed. She loved her three brothers, but all of them being so much older and having their lives sorted out didn't make it easy for her. She felt like nothing she did would measure up to them. Even becoming a successful lawyer would only be meeting expectations, not surpassing them. But that wasn't her mom's fault, or her brother's. She made a mental note to text him later.

She scrolled through the rest of her mom's messages and stopped on another picture, this time a huge pot full of steaming tamales.

**Your grandma made a huge batch of tamales this week. You know how she is, never listens when we tell her she doesn't need to. I'm sending you some by mail tomorrow.**

**I would never say no to Grandma's tamales. Can't wait for them to get here!**

It had been less than an hour since she hung up with Dani, and a text from her appeared on Ari's phone as she finished replying to her mom. She opened it eagerly, surprised that Dani had sent her something because she'd said she would be busy with training for the next several hours. It took Ari a few seconds to realize that the attached photo showed a bunch of tennis balls arranged on the floor to form a word: her name with a heart next to it.

**Tennis used to be the only thing on my mind, but now it's you.**

# Chapter Eight

**From: ari3nunezar@virginia.edu**

**To: dani@danielamartinez.com**

Dani,

I should be paying attention in class, but as usual, I'd rather talk to you. Besides, now I have your e-mail and your phone number and don't have to limit our chats to Tumblr, I can't help but want to talk to you all the time.

I'm so happy our lives crossed paths. It still blows my mind for so many reasons that in such a big world, with billions of people scattered around the globe, we ended up talking to each other.

I don't believe in fate. It makes me sad to think our paths in life are pre-established. I'd rather believe that I'm the only architect of my future, that the choices I make have a meaning and a purpose, but I can't find any explanation besides fate as to why we crossed paths. Whatever the reason, whether chance or fortuity, I'm grateful we did.

I watched your match the other day, and I'm sure you won't be surprised to know that I barely understood what was happening. But something that stuck with me was when the commentator said you've been playing since you were four and a professional player since you were sixteen. Here I am, at twenty-four years old, struggling to figure out what to do with my life. Maybe having my path set as a kid would have made it easier.

**From: dani@danielamartinez.com**

**To: ari3nunezar@virginia.edu**

Hey Ari,

I'm grateful for the fact I found something I'm good at and I'm able to make a living from it. But I'm not going to lie, sometimes I wonder what I would be doing if I hadn't decided to become a tennis player as a kid. I wonder what I've missed. I'll never go to college, for example.

I have no idea what I would do if I weren't a tennis player. In a sense, it's nice to have a set path, but it's also restrictive. By the time I was able to turn pro, I'd been working toward that goal for so long, had sacrificed so much already, that any other choice was impossible. Your life, instead, is full of possibilities. Or maybe this is another case of the grass being greener.

I can't really give much advice; I can't pretend to ever be able to understand the situation you are in. I understand expectations, though. I understand that weight. I can only confidently say that you will always feel pressure from people surrounding you, even when they don't mean to, but you are the only one who can choose what to do with it. You can suffer it, embrace it, or shake it. It's your call, even if right now it feels like there's no option. Expectations can crush you, if you let them, but they can also empower you.

◈

If someone had told Ari a week before that she would be spending her Friday night watching a tennis match—a tennis match where the woman she was kind of dating would try to win one of the most important tournaments in the world—she wouldn't have believed it. Not because Friday nights were exciting affairs for her. She usually spent them online and eating takeout, so in that sense, it wouldn't be too different.

It was more about the surreal fact that she'd found someone she connected with after years of claiming she didn't care about love. "You can't get your heart broken if you don't date" had been her philosophy since her first relationship had ended badly. But here she was, not only interested in someone, but interested in someone who turned out to be some rich, low-key celebrity. Someone who, against all odds, liked her back.

It still baffled her when she thought about it. To be less weirded out, she attempted to focus on Dani the person, the one she talked to without reservations, and tried to forget about Dani the millionaire. It was easy when Dani used her husky voice to flirt and looked at her with mischief in her eyes—because that made Ari forget even her own name.

All week she'd stayed up late to watch Dani play. She was still not an expert on the topic, but at least she understood the rules of the sport a little better now. The first match she watched, when she'd jinxed Dani somehow, she only realized how bad things were because Dani looked miserable every time the camera focused on her and because Tom was panicking about it.

Now Ari sat on her bed, virgin margarita in hand courtesy of Tom, staring at the TV and waiting for the finals to start. The commentators talked on and on about the importance of the match and how Dani would become the number one player in the world if she won.

As they waited for the two competitors to walk out on the court, the camera focused on a bald man who looked like he had never smiled in his life. His eyes stared with laser focus in front of him as yellow letters appeared on-screen under his face: *Igor Belaskayi, Coach.*

The TV network shared his name for viewers like her who didn't differentiate who was who in the tennis world. Ari had seen him several times already during the week, and she had to admit that he looked intimidating, with an angry scowl always on his face no matter if Dani was winning or losing.

Next to him, a woman with short, slicked-back hair also watched, and *Arantxa Navarro, Manager* appeared under her face soon enough. The contrast between the two members of Dani's team couldn't be more evident. While Igor wore a simple T-shirt and cap, Arantxa looked like she'd stepped right out of a magazine into the tennis stadium. She wore minimal but perfect makeup, sunglasses that looked as expensive as Ari's entire wardrobe, long gold earrings that framed her face, and a tailored suit. Despite the expensive outfit, her warm smile made her look more approachable than the man next to her.

A minute later Dani appeared on screen, walking with purpose onto the court. Ari had seen a similar image several times in the past week, but it still took her breath away. Dani walked with her head held high, her body straight. Every step, every inch of her body screamed confidence. A definite turn-on.

Of course, Tom noticed. "Do you need some privacy? I can feel the heat radiating from you."

"Shut up," Ari mumbled, but she didn't deny it. They both knew that saying she didn't want Dani would be a lie. Instead, she allowed herself to stare without remorse.

At least, she did at first. Soon, the tension of the match was too much, and all she cared about was Dani winning. Ari knew how much this match meant, so she had to remind herself to unclench her jaw when she saw the first set go to Dani's opponent.

From what she'd seen, Dani wasn't playing badly. She was attacking and moving her rival from one side of the court to the other, but no matter how precise or how fast her shots were, the other player always got to them.

"She can still turn this around, right?" Ari said, staring intently at the TV.

"Yeah, of course. Olga Podoroska is playing great, and she's a difficult opponent, but if Dani keeps her level of play up and the score stays close, she's in position to regain control of the match."

Ari trusted Tom. He understood the sport, and he wouldn't lie to her. She leaned forward, eyes fixed on the screen. She only relaxed when Dani took the lead in the second set, with a string of great serves and a couple of mistakes from her rival in crucial points.

Ari sat back, trying to relax now that things didn't seem as dire. The corner of the screen showed that the score was 6–5 in Dani's favor. That meant she needed only one more game and then each player would have a set.

Dani's serves started landing low into the net, and soon the commentators were going on and on about her apparent nervousness. Tom cursed, and Dani wore a deep scowl.

"What happened?" Ari asked.

"She was serving for the set and screwed it up," Tom said with a sigh. "She only needed to win this game to take the set and level the match. She had the advantage of using her serve, but she started double-faulting and making mistakes. She just lost her lead."

"Well, that sucks, but it's not the end, right?"

"They're going to a tiebreak now. Whoever wins this game takes the set. She can still win it, but it's going to be harder. To be honest, most players crumble after losing a chance like that."

"Well, she is not like most players. She's stronger than that."

Tom said nothing. Ari wasn't sure if he believed her or thought she was being naive and didn't want to burst her bubble. She admitted it was ridiculous that after following the sport for such a short time, she now was talking as if she were an expert. But it wasn't about tennis, or how players usually reacted. If there was one thing Ari knew about Dani, it was that when she wanted something, she went for it.

Ari sat straighter, all her focus back on the TV screen. Tom remained unusually silent too, but he probably sensed the stress irradiating from her every pore. She had no idea how Dani did it—Ari wasn't even the one playing and she could feel the tension in her entire body. Every point made her hold her breath and clench her muscles.

Ari let out a relieved sigh once Dani won the second set. For a moment, she wasn't sure if she should be glad or sad that she didn't understand the sport. The commentators mentioned something about Dani being one point away from defeat and saving several match points. Though Ari didn't understand tennis, she understood human emotions, and when they showed Dani, she was bouncing in place next to her seat in the brief break that players were given between sets. Her scowl was long gone.

The crowd was easier to read than the players were. There were screams as the *oohs* and *aahs* became more and more frequent. The clapping grew louder, and people even jumped out of their seats as they shouted Dani's name. When they panned the camera over Dani's team on the bleachers, no sleuthing efforts were necessary to read their emotions. The usually poised and elegant Arantxa was on her feet, pumping her fists and screaming what sounded like "vamos," which even Ari could understand with her rudimentary knowledge of Spanish. Igor wasn't speaking at all, only his fist raised, eyes fixated on Dani.

"This is good, right?" Ari asked Tom for confirmation because she needed to hear out loud what was obvious.

"More than good. She is amazing."

Ari smiled. Yes, Dani was amazing in many ways.

The rest of the match wasn't easy. There was plenty of stress, but through it all Ari was sure Dani would win. She had no real reason to believe it besides her own selfish desire to see Dani happy. Her knowledge of the sport wasn't enough for her to be able to discern between the abilities of the two players, and the match itself was too close for comfort. But even when the third set went to a tiebreak again, she never doubted that Dani would end up on top.

The determination in Dani's eyes hadn't wavered since the match started. That was what gave Ari confidence, and Dani proved her right. A powerful crosscourt forehand landed just out of Podoroska's reach, which gave Dani the win. Ari jumped out of bed and screamed, the same way Arantxa and Igor did on the screen.

"Someone is invested," Tom said.

Ari's cheeks flushed, but she sat back down and shrugged at him nonchalantly.

"Can't wait for next year when we're cheering for her from the VIP section of the stadium," he said with a grin.

Ari bumped his shoulder. "If that happens, who says I'm going to take you."

"Please! Who else would you take? I haven't endured all these ramen dinners with you for you to ditch me the minute things get exciting."

"Hey! Are you calling me boring?" Ari suppressed a smile; it was rare that she had a chance to return some of his teasing.

"Hmm . . . no. Of course not. Never," he shot back with another grin. "Let's focus. She is about to give her victory speech."

Ari snickered at his obvious deflection but shut her mouth anyway. All her attention was now on the beautiful woman holding a trophy on her right arm, close to her body almost as if cuddling it, who was walking toward a microphone stand in the middle of the court.

Ari had heard Dani's voice that same morning, but that didn't stop her from getting butterflies in her stomach when Dani started speaking. The speech was generic—platitudes about being grateful to the sponsors and all the people who made the tournament possible, and acknowledgments to her coach and team. Ari still listened with unwavering attention, enjoying the sound of Dani's voice.

"I also want to thank someone special for the late-night calls that kept me sane during these stressful weeks. It made all the difference."

Ari's heart started racing at those words. Was Dani talking about her? Who else could she be referring to? But then again, maybe Dani had some friend back home she also talked with. Ari knew it was presumptuous to assume Dani was thanking her, but she couldn't help the feeling of hope that had worked its way into her.

Tom turned to her. "Wow. You already made it into a Grand Slam winning speech? That was fast."

"You think she was talking about me?"

"Well, she didn't say your name, so maybe she's talking to ten other women and this is a great way to charm all of them at once."

Tom kept a straight face, and even though Ari knew it was ridiculous and that he meant it as a joke, the rush of anger and jealousy that surged through her caught her by surprise. She must have shown it on her face, as Tom hurried to course-correct.

"I'm joking! Not even I have the time to juggle so many people at once. I'm sure she only has eyes for you."

Ari sighed. "I know, but I don't want to assume. She said we would talk after the match. I'll ask her then."

The downside of Dani winning was that she would have more commitments to attend to. The wait would be torture for Ari as she wondered if Dani had meant the words for her. She preferred to be cautious and never assume, but she was already failing. Her heart was bursting at the thought of occupying such an important spot in Dani's life that Dani needed to share it with the world.

◈

From the moment Dani stepped off the court with the trophy, chaos ensued. It wasn't until forty-eight hours later that she had time to call Ari. She meant to do it as soon as possible, but after a Grand Slam win, there were a hundred commitments to attend to: the post-match press conference, the individual interviews with different media outlets, the official photo shoot with the trophy, the celebratory dinner with her team. Arantxa salivated at the new sponsorship opportunities coming her way, and Igor still expected Dani to go over their training plans for the next few weeks.

Dani only had enough energy to crawl into bed and pass out by the time she reached her room. The next morning, when she woke up around eleven, her first instinct was to reach for her phone. She ignored the congratulatory messages from her parents, as well as Arantxa's text asking if she was awake and when could they meet to talk. She also dismissed Igor's text saying he booked a court for training in the afternoon. There was only one person she wanted to talk to.

When Ari's warm eyes greeted her through her screen, she felt like that was all the reward she needed after a long two weeks of focusing on winning.

"I had no idea watching tennis was so stressful, but it was worth it. Congratulations."

Dani had heard the word "congratulations" so many times in the last few hours, the word had lost impact—until Ari said it. The way Ari had supported her during the tournament, even when she didn't understand why it was important, made it more significant.

"You watched the whole thing?" Dani said, trying to hide how much it meant to her.

"Of course! I wouldn't have missed it for anything," Ari answered, and Dani couldn't help but believe her. "Tom and I had a watch party."

The sincerity in Ari's words made Dani's heart fill with love. The mental image of Ari and Tom sitting in their pajamas at the other end of the world, eating popcorn, and cheering along was the most adorable thing she could imagine.

"That's cute," Dani said with a smile.

There was a pause in the conversation as they stared at each other in silence, both happy to bask in each other's presence. There was no pressure to fill the space with superfluous talk, and no awkwardness in the quiet. Dani couldn't think of another person who had ever put her at as much ease as Ari did. Would it feel the same way without the distance between them?

"I have a question for you, but it's embarrassing," Ari said, interrupting Dani's thoughts.

Dani frowned, curious about the coming question. "You can ask me anything."

"I don't want to sound conceited . . ." Ari bit her lip. "I was wondering if what you said at the end of your speech was about me."

Dani had to suppress a laugh, not wanting Ari to think she was making fun of her. To Dani, that part of her speech couldn't have been more obvious that it was about the woman she was falling for. The fact that Ari still had doubts baffled Dani, but she didn't want to dismiss them. If Ari needed confirmation, she was happy to give it to her. "You mean the part about being thankful for our late-night calls? Of course it was about you. Who else would it be about?"

"I didn't want to assume."

"Well, I'm giving you permission to assume from now on." Dani paused to give Ari a chance to absorb her words. "I meant all of it. Our conversations helped me so much to stay relaxed and forget tennis for a while. It kept me sane through the stress of defending my title."

As she spoke, Ari's expression brightened. That simple reaction encouraged Dani to keep going. She longed to see Ari embrace what she had been telling her for days now, how much she meant to her. "I have to keep you around. You are my lucky charm now; I can't change my routine, or else I'll stop winning. Those are the rules."

"I'm always happy to talk—you don't have to make up excuses."

Dani smiled, a sweet smile at first that soon turned into a cheeky grin. "Now I have a question for you."

"Okay . . . Should I be scared?"

Dani couldn't miss the opening Ari had given her. She lowered her voice and looked at Ari while she enunciated every word. "That depends. Only if you are scared of me." As she expected, Ari became flustered under her gaze, and Dani enjoyed every second. "I'm messing with you; I have a serious question. When I'm done in this part of the world, I'm going to the United States. In around a month, I will be in California first, then Miami."

Dani paused, expecting Ari to say something. When it became obvious that Ari didn't get what she was trying to say, she switched to a direct approach. "I would love if you traveled to any of the cities I'll be in, or somewhere else if you prefer, so we can meet in person." She wanted to laugh at the deer-in-headlights look Ari was giving her. Eyes wide, mouth agape.

"You don't have to answer me now," she continued. "Just think about it. I won't mention it again, but if you decide it's something you want to do, let me know. I'm happy to pay for you and Tom to stay wherever you choose for a week. If it's not something you feel ready for right now, don't worry. I'm happy to be in your life only virtually if that's what you feel comfortable with."

The sincere words seemed to calm Ari down. Her body posture, tense a few seconds before, relaxed. "I do like the idea of meeting you, but I just don't know if I'm ready yet."

"Of course." Dani smiled back to show she was okay with Ari taking her time to decide. Even if Ari knew who she was and that there was no risk of being catfished, it was still a big step to move from the virtual to the physical world. She'd laid her cards out, and now Ari had to decide whether she would accept them.

◈

When Dani got to the hotel's restaurant to have brunch with Arantxa, her manager already had a Bellini in her hand and had gotten one for Dani too. Dani tried to wave away the server putting down a drink in front of her, but Arantxa stopped her and told the server to leave it.

"You won a freaking Grand Slam; you can have one weak-ass cocktail to celebrate."

"I had champagne last night at dinner," Dani retorted, pushing the drink in Arantxa's direction.

"One sip when we toasted. Come on, indulge me. We need to celebrate."

"Let me get some food first, I'm starving."

"Stayed up last night having another one of those inspiring conversations?" Arantxa said with a hint of teasing in her voice.

"I fell asleep five seconds after returning to my room, but I called her today. For the record, she was the one who had to suffer the late nights because of the time difference. Are you monitoring my sleeping habits now?"

"No, that's not my job. Mine is to take care of your image, and I thought we'd agreed you would let me know if I needed to get ahead of any potential news. You declaring your love to the world on live TV with no warning isn't helping me do my job." Her voice held more vehemence than usual.

"Are you talking about my speech?"

Arantxa nodded while taking a long sip of her drink.

"It was not a love declaration. I was only expressing gratitude for a friend."

"Well, I'm sure that great romantic move charmed her. But if you were planning to hide things, you blew it."

"I don't know why you're making a big deal out of like five words nobody paid attention to."

"You've been in this long enough to know there are people who pay attention to every word. And one of them did."

Arantxa showed Dani an image on her phone—a tweet from tennisgossip.com, a low-level but popular tennis blog.

**Daniela Martínez has fallen in love, and judging by her speech tonight, she is ready to share it with the world. Will the elusive tennis star finally come out with the big secret we all kind of already know?**

Dani rolled her eyes. Rumors and comments about her sexuality were nothing new. A small subset of tennis fans and journalists loved to speculate, nothing more than that. "This has you worried? Nobody takes this website seriously. They can try all they want to make up a juicy story for some clicks, but they have nothing substantial to back it up."

"Some people are really talented about making a lot out of nothing, and you didn't help by gushing over a mystery person yesterday. Just be careful is all I'm saying."

Dani tried to appear unaffected, but Arantxa was stressing her out. "I guess this is as good of a moment as any to tell you I invited Ari to Miami?"

"Yeah, that's excellent information to have," Arantxa said absentmindedly while looking down at her phone. Dani leaned forward to glance over and noticed she was still scrolling through tweets. This time Arantxa didn't show her whatever had captured her attention, opting to read it out loud instead: "It's obvious that the recently crowned Australian Open champion has someone special in her life. Why she insists on covering up her suitor in an air of secrecy is anybody's guess. Maybe the tennis darling has something to hide."

Dani's blood boiled. She had nothing to hide—she liked her privacy, that was all.

"Why it's so hard for people to mind their own business, I'll never know," Arantxa said, voicing the thoughts running through Dani's mind.

As much as she agreed with that statement, Dani tried to downplay how mad thc comment made her. This was exactly why she never checked her own social media mentions. "Ignore them. I won't give them the benefit of dignifying their tabloid talk with an answer."

Arantxa put her phone away and sighed. "Consider it ignored. But I want you to be careful. I know you've never paid attention to the rumors, but they exist, and I want things to be on your terms." She rested her hand on top of Dani's. "Time to stop with these downer topics and talk about the good stuff. I've gotten a hundred press and sponsorship requests since yesterday. I got some proposals from Colombian companies. They are not as lucrative, but I know you like doing those."

Dani smiled at Arantxa's enthusiasm for her job and let her talk about all the plans she had for the next few weeks without complaining. She felt like it was the least she owed her manager, and friend, for always looking out for her. Despite herself, her brain fixated on the tweets. It was easy to tell other people to ignore them. Harder to apply it.

# Chapter Nine

**From: dani@danielamartinez.com**

**To: ari3nunezar@virginia.edu**

I don't mean to make you jealous but I'm currently sunbathing in Dubai. (After three hours of training! It's not all fun and games.)

Here's a picture of the great view.

**From: ari3nunezar@virginia.edu**

**To: dani@danielamartinez.com**

It snowed again last night, and I slipped on the ice on the way to class and spilled tea all over myself. Getting your message was adding insult to injury.

I have to admit the view of the beach looks great . . . Too bad someone walked in the middle of the shot and covered half the picture with their body. I couldn't fully appreciate the scenery with them in the middle.

**From: dani@danielamartinez.com**

**To: ari3nunezar@virginia.edu**

My bad. I didn't realize I sent you one of the selfies I took for my Instagram instead of a picture only of the beautiful landscape. Let me make up for it.

**From: ari3nunezar@virginia.edu**

**To: dani@danielamartinez.com**

I'm starting to worry about you. Ten pictures and not one of them had a glimpse of the beach or the sunset, only blurry body parts and views of the floor. I just hope you only make these mistakes with me and won't end up posting the wrong thing to your social media.

Maybe I can give you a few tips. I took this picture of one of the cherry blossoms behind the business school building. I love to think of the contrast with how they will look in a couple of months. Now there are only dry branches and snow, but soon it will be full of color and life.

**From: dani@danielamartinez.com**

**To: ari3nunezar@virginia.edu**

That is a beautiful picture, but your words are what make it prettier. I love the way you always see beyond the evident—I would have only seen a bare tree and passed it by without a second thought. I love looking at the world through your eyes.

**From: ari3nunezar@virginia.edu**

**To: dani@danielamartinez.com**

We all have unique ways to view the world. For me, everything you share is brand new too, and I love expanding my world through what you teach me.

**From: dani@danielamartinez.com**

**To: ari3nunezar@virginia.edu**

I have a twenty-hour flight from Dubai to Mexico in front of me. Maybe I will finally get around to reading all those books you recommended. I'm not looking forward to the hours in the air. I always struggle to sleep on flights, but I can't wait to eat some tacos. It's been too long since I had some, and nothing beats eating tacos in Mexico. I'm sorry but American ones are just not the same.

**From: ari3nunezar@virginia.edu**

**To: dani@danielamartinez.com**

You know my dad is Mexican, right? And that I'm from California? Like, you really want to get into a debate with me about tacos?

**From: dani@danielamartinez.com**

**To: ari3nunezar@virginia.edu**

I do remember that . . . but have you eaten tacos in Mexico after a twenty-hour flight and months of not having one?

**From: ari3nunezar@virginia.edu**

**To: dani@danielamartinez.com**

It's been a long time since I visited. Last time we went I was only a kid, but nothing beats my grandma's cooking, I'm sure there are no tacos in the world better than hers.

**From: dani@danielamartinez.com**

**To: ari3nunezar@virginia.edu**

I concede. Nothing can compete with grandma's food.

◈

The sound of a tennis ball hitting a racket acted as background noise while Ari studied, a soothing melody she'd added to her routine in the last several months. Since watching the Australian Open, she'd developed a habit of following Dani's matches as much as possible because it made her feel like she was part of Dani's life, even with the distance between them. Right then, they were as close as they had ever been, with Dani playing at Indian Wells in California, close to where Ari was born and raised.

In less than two weeks, Dani would fly from California to Miami, and Ari still hadn't decided if she would join her there. True to her word, Dani hadn't mentioned the invitation again, giving Ari all the time in the world to decide. From the first moment Dani had brought up meeting in person, Ari had wanted to do it, but there was something holding her back from taking the plunge.

She wanted to meet Dani in person, dreamed of seeing her flirty smirk up close and losing herself in her arms, but she was also afraid. The possibility of everything they'd been building crashing down the minute they broke the virtual barrier terrified her. What if they didn't get along in person like they did online? Ari wasn't sure if she wanted to risk what they had for what could be.

She clicked away from the essay she was writing and opened her inbox to reread some of the emails she'd exchanged with Dani in the last month. She took her time to drink in every word, from the most mundane messages about what they were eating that night or watching on TV, to the deeper conversations about their lives, their hopes, their dreams.

She closed her eyes and pictured Dani smiling at her, winking when she blushed at her comments, or tucking a stray piece of hair behind her ear. Merely the fantasy of it made her heart flutter inside her chest. She sighed loudly, aware of the fact that she was the only one preventing those dreams from becoming a reality. Spring break aligned with the dates of the Miami Open, so she didn't even have to worry about school. Her own fear was the only thing standing between her and Dani.

Agreeing to meet went against everything Ari usually did—taking risks had never been her strength. But when it came to Dani, she couldn't live with the weight of a missed opportunity. No matter how scared she was, she wanted to at least give herself a chance to know how their connection felt in person.

With her decision made, she finished her essay and opened a new tab on her browser, searching for a flight for the next weekend. She found several options within her budget, despite waiting until the last minute to book. She reviewed the various itineraries on her screen while her fingers tapped rhythmically on the side of the touchpad for several minutes, until she grabbed the mouse and bought the tickets before she could talk herself out of it. She stared at the airline confirmation page and breathed out slowly.

Tom opened the door to her apartment and walked in. He glanced at the TV and back at her with a grin on his face. "I can't get over how cute it is that you follow all her matches." He put his hands on his waist and tried to look stern. "Not sure it's going to help your grades, though. School before love."

Ari could remember at least five times when Tom had ditched class because of a Grindr date, so the fact that he was advising her to put school first was ironic. But she was sure he would sing a different tune as soon as she told him about their upcoming trip. "I finished the essay we have due tomorrow. It's not half-bad."

"I'm also done. Mine is trash but whatever, I can't wait for spring break."

"Speaking of spring break, what would you say if I told you that I want you to go with me to Miami?" She dragged the words out with fake innocence.

As expected, she'd piqued his interest, and he raised his eyebrows. "I would tell you I was planning on going to New York, but I would be open to Miami if it has anything to do with a certain someone who will play there on those dates."

"Well, in that case . . . Dani asked me after the Australian Open to meet her in Miami." Ari braced herself for what she was sure was coming—the high-pitched scream he always let out when something surprised him.

It took Tom five seconds to process the information, but the moment he did, she lost him. Ari could barely get another word in before he started rambling about how amazing everything would be.

"I bet Dani is going to get us a big-ass suite for our stay. And will we have, like, official team credentials? I'm sure we will. It's going to be so awesome, access to everything, VIP booth at the stadium." He paced the apartment, naming all the things he was dreaming for their trip.

Ari didn't dare interrupt him, but she winced at his words.

"I'm not liking your expression right now," he said. He traced his finger in a circle at her face. "What did you do?"

Ari bit her lip. "I haven't told Dani yet that I am coming to the tournament." At the judgment flashing in Tom's eyes, she rushed to add, "Yet! I'm going to tell her, of course. But I want to do it after we have planned everything. Gotten our own hotel and stuff."

He took a deep breath, as if trying to calm himself, and grabbed his forehead. "You are a broke college student; you should take the help."

"She offered to cover all our expenses, yours included, but I don't know. I feel weird about it."

He mumbled incoherently to himself, but she was able to make out something that sounded a lot like "What's the point of a rich girlfriend if you're going to pay for stuff yourself." But he sighed exaggeratedly before addressing her again. "Look, I get where you're coming from. But do you have any idea how expensive hotels are in Miami? It seems like a big deal to us because we're broke, but to her, spending a couple of thousand dollars is like if we bought a coffee, while it will take you *months* to pay it off."

Ari hated his logic, because she knew she should accept Dani's help instead of putting herself in even more debt.

"Look," he added, "I'll follow your lead, but what if I paid for my flight and we can let Dani help with the hotel? That's technically a fifty-fifty split, right?"

Ari looked into Tom's expectant eyes and slowly nodded. It made sense to let Dani pay for the hotel, especially because Dani herself had offered to.

While Tom went over her wardrobe, complaining because she didn't have any appropriate clothes for Miami, Ari emailed Dani a copy of her ticket. Once she hit Send, there was no going back. She thought that doing so would fill her with dread, that she would spend every minute before their trip stressing out about it and all the ways things could go wrong between her and Dani, but to her surprise, the only thing she felt was excitement.

◈

Dani had almost lost all hope that Ari would join her in Miami. The trip was only a week away, and there had been no mentions or even hints at the possibility. Dani hadn't said anything after she'd brought the topic up initially, and at times she regretted her promise of not pressuring Ari, but she knew it was the right thing to do. She was already asking Ari to accommodate her with the time and the place, taking her out of her comfort zone. It was only fair that she at least give Ari time to think about it. That didn't mean she didn't agonize over the decision every minute that went without an answer, though.

Seeing the email with the subject "Miami" in her inbox sent a wave of nerves to her stomach for the first time in a long time. There was no reason to think it wouldn't be good news, but the chance that Ari was saying no to her invitation once and for all was always plausible. She tried to push down the anticipation building inside her, and she readied herself with a deep breath as she opened the email.

Dani scanned the contents and fist-pumped as if she'd just won a big point in a match. In less than a week, she would meet Ari in person. She forwarded the flight information to Arantxa, asking her manager to handle the rest—the hotel reservations, airport pickup, official accreditation to the tournament, and all the other details Dani was forgetting but Arantxa would take care of.

Then she started research of her own: there was one thing she had to do herself, and that was planning an amazing first date. Since Australia, her interest in Ari had only grown. She was sure that seeing each other in person would only confirm what she already felt in her heart. She hoped it would be the same for Ari, but even if it wasn't, she would make Ari's flight all the way to Miami worth it. Dani would make sure that, if nothing else, she showed Ari a great time.

# Chapter Ten

**From: ari3nunezar@virginia.edu**

**To: dani@danielamartinez.com**

I can hardly believe that in only a few hours, I will see you in person. I just finished packing and should be sleeping, but I can't.

The upside is that thinking about the trip almost made me forget about all the other stuff I've had on my mind lately. I've got an interview right after I get back. It's at one of my dream organizations, and if they hire me, I'll spend the summer working with some of the best human rights lawyers in the world. They've been assisting asylum seekers, and just the idea of being able to help them win a case makes me so excited. Of course, they don't pay much, so if I get the job, I will have my usual dilemma of choosing between the job I really want and the one that pays well.

But those are problems for after spring break. I plan to really enjoy my time there and relax . . . Easier said than done, but that's the plan.

I really need to go to bed now if I don't want to oversleep and miss my flight tomorrow. But I have one last thing to say. Well, it's more of a request. You have to promise me that no matter what happens after we meet, we'll always be friends.

**From: dani@danielamartinez.com**

**To: ari3nunezar@virginia.edu**

I can't promise we will *only* be friends, but I promise we will always be friends.

◈

The knot in Ari's stomach threatened to take over her body as the plane shook from side to side while taking off, but not because she was afraid of flying. There was only one reason for her nerves: in less than three hours, she would meet Dani in person.

As much as she tried to tell herself there was no reason to worry, Ari couldn't stop her mind from going into overload as she imagined all types of scenarios. The worst one—and the most unlikely—was Dani laughing in her face, declaring everything had been a joke while cameras emerged to record her reaction.

The second was that they hit it off as friends, like they had been doing for the past few months, but with no chemistry or attraction. That was a genuine possibility. No matter how much Ari tried to pretend she would be fine if that turned out to be the case, the truth was that she would be devastated.

She'd allowed herself to embrace the flirting Dani did whenever they talked. She'd let a seed of hope that they'd become more than friends plant itself in her heart, and it had only continued to grow. Meeting Dani would be the test, the make-it-or-break-it moment.

A hand on her leg shook Ari out of her thoughts. She looked to her right to find Tom staring at her. "I think the guy in front of you is about to turn around and punch us in the face. You haven't stopped bouncing your leg this whole time."

She looked down to find that she was kneeing the seat in front of her. She mumbled an apology to the man in front of them, who answered with an angry grunt.

"We're going to Miami. A week of sun and beach and hot, tanned bodies," Tom said. He reclined his seat for a few inches of extra space, but he squirmed and still appeared uncomfortable in his tall frame. "Why are you so stressed?"

Ari reclined her seat too. In her case, there was plenty of room. "You know why."

"I've met dozens of people through apps, it's not that big of a deal. If you hit it off in person, cool. If not, we enjoy the beach."

Ari wished she had his cavalier attitude. The situation wasn't the same, and their personalities couldn't be more different. She was going to obsess over every little detail, there was no way around that. "This is so not the same as when you meet your hookups."

"I know. But it's also not as dramatic as you're making it. Not every relationship has to have love-of-your-life potential. Even if you like someone, things can change. Sometimes you hit it off, sometimes you don't. It's not the end of the world, even if it feels like it to you now."

Ari appreciated Tom's efforts to try to calm her down. They weren't working, but she felt grateful nonetheless. "I'm going to try, but no promises."

The minute they landed, Ari texted Dani. They still had an hourlong ride to the hotel, but as the moment of meeting Dani face-to-face neared, the butterflies in her stomach went into a frenzy. Her phone chimed with a reply.

**I just finished training, and I'm heading back to the hotel too. We will get there around the same time.**

Perfect. Not only was she minutes away from meeting Dani, but now she was also at risk of running into her with no time to prepare herself. Ari hoped she could beat Dani there and at least make herself presentable. Nobody looked good after a flight.

During the ride to the hotel, she tried to force herself to enjoy the view out the window and not worry about whether they'd make it first. When they finally arrived, for a second Ari forgot about checking if Dani was around. Her jaw dropped, distracted by how stunning the place was. The lavish décor was intimidating, reminding her that she was from a different world, as if anyone would know she didn't belong only from looking at her. Tom, on the other hand, grabbed a welcome cocktail from the bellboy without hesitation.

He nudged her shoulder. "I'm so glad you're dating someone rich. This is amazing."

"We are not officially dating," Ari protested half-heartedly.

"Details."

Ari could only nod as the hotel concierge explained that they had a beachfront suite, fully paid for, with unrestricted access to any restaurant or bar on the property. As she was handed the key to their room, someone called her name.

Her heart started beating faster on cue. She already knew who it was, but she took a deep breath and forced herself to turn around and confirm it. A familiar face greeted her—a vision she'd already enjoyed several times before through the screen, but one that hit different this time, knowing she could reach out and touch her.

Dani stood six feet away, wearing the same kind of athletic clothes she always did for their calls. To have Dani so near overwhelmed Ari. But the fact that Dani focused solely on her, with that warm and inviting smile she'd fallen for, froze her in place.

To Ari's relief and panic, Dani started walking toward her with confident strides. In less than a second, the woman who had occupied her dreams for months now was standing in front of her. Before she could react, Dani reached down and greeted her with a kiss on the cheek.

"So happy you're here," Dani said, beaming. "How is everything going so far?"

Everything happened so fast that Ari wasn't sure it happened at all. The faint memory of Dani's lips on her cheek was the only proof left, and the urge to reach up to trace her fingers along the spot where Dani had touched her was overwhelming, but Ari fought against it.

She mentally shook herself and answered, "Great. It's going great. We got our keys." She dangled the plastic card in front of her face.

"Awesome. I need to shower and change, and I'm sure you want to rest a little too." She started walking away, but Ari remained rooted to the spot. After a few seconds, Dani turned around.

"Let's get you to your room," she said with a smile and a wink.

Ari managed to trail behind, trying to appear calm and composed on the outside while panicking on the inside.

Tom sidled up to Dani. "Girl, do you have a job opening on your team? 'Cause if this is what it's like to work with a tennis player, I'm in. Who needs to finish law school. I'll be your personal ball boy." He was undoubtedly trying to give Ari some time to recover. As always, she was grateful to him, and moments like this were why she had asked him to come with her.

Dani snickered. "Personal ball boy? I have a personal fitness trainer, a hitting partner, therapist, and physio, but I've never heard of a personal ball boy. Maybe you're onto something, though. Igor always makes me clean up the court after we train. He thinks it builds character or something, but I would totally pay you to do that."

Ari smiled at the way Dani was chatting and laughing with Tom without problem. She was as charming in person as she always was on their calls. Ari noticed, too, how Dani kept glancing at her every chance she could. Instead of unnerving her or increasing her anxiety, the way Dani looked at her helped calm her. There were still butterflies dancing in her stomach, but the warmth in Dani's eyes made them easier to ignore.

A few minutes later, they opened the door to their suite. Ari gasped at the sheer size of the enormous living room and two bedrooms, each one with its own ocean-view balcony. The suite dwarfed Ari's apartment, and it was bigger than some of the places she'd lived growing up.

After the tour, Ari and Dani returned to the living room while Tom ran around opening doors and trying each piece of furniture.

"I'm going to change into my swimsuit. See you soon!" he shouted, closing the door to one bedroom and leaving them alone. Ari had a hunch he'd done it on purpose and was eavesdropping.

Now that they were alone with nothing between them to serve as a distraction, the tension in the room started rising. Even with the air conditioning blasting, drops of sweat slid down Ari's back. She moved to sit on the sofa, more because she was trying to find something to do than because of a genuine need to rest. Dani sat next to her, close enough that her warm breath tingled on Ari's skin. Speckles of light reflected in her brown eyes.

Dani rested her hand on the couch, right beside Ari's. The sudden closeness made Ari eager to close the gap separating their hands. The idea of being able to touch Dani was stronger than her shyness. She moved her hand slowly, until the tips of her fingers brushed Dani's.

Dani looked down and finished bringing their hands together. "I'm so happy you are here."

"I'm happy to be here," Ari answered. "This room is amazing, by the way."

"I'm glad you like it. I made reservations at this wonderful Cuban restaurant for tonight, if you are up for it. I've got to warn you, though. Arantxa insisted on coming—she demanded to meet you. I hope you don't mind."

Ari nodded. “Sounds great.” Anything with Dani sounded great.

“Good. I will let you get settled and will text you later.” Dani stood and walked several steps, only to turn around and sit again. This time, she sat facing Ari, with one leg crossed under her. “There’s one thing I want to do before I go,” she said in that low, husky voice that drove Ari to the edge.

Ari swallowed, trying to clear the lump that had formed in her throat. If Dani’s flirty tone turned her into a mess over the phone, she wasn’t prepared for the effect it would have on her in person. Her own eyes betrayed her by moving down to study Dani’s lips—the same lips Dani was licking slowly. Ari forced herself to snap out of it and meet her gaze.

“Yeah?” Ari braced herself, sensing a change in the mood.

Dani moved closer and stared into her eyes, and Ari knew that she wouldn’t be able to say no to anything asked of her. “I’m okay with staying friends if that’s what you want . . . but I would love to kiss you right now.”

Ari felt the air catch in her lungs when she tried to answer. She wanted to kiss Dani—of course she did. But the undivided attention from Dani’s eyes, the closeness of her lips, and the warm tickle of her breath made it hard for Ari to focus or utter a word. Unable to voice her agreement, she opted for leaning forward and pressing her lips against Dani’s. Only two seconds passed before she moved away, startled by her own movements.

What she’d intended as a kiss turned out to be nothing more than a chaste peck. Heat rushed to her cheeks, but she hoped the act was enough to help her convey what she wanted. Thankfully, Dani was much smoother than Ari could ever hope to be. In other circumstances and with anybody else, Ari would have assumed that the huge grin on Dani's face was mocking, but she knew it wasn't.

Dani moved closer, and it took all of Ari's will to not melt into a puddle of feelings right there and then. "That's not what I had in mind," Dani whispered.

As she moved closer, her warm breath danced on Ari's lips like a ghost of the kiss to come. The anticipation was killing Ari, but she stayed quiet, immobile, waiting. The only movement she made was shutting her eyes the moment Dani put her hand on the back of her neck.

Even with her eyes shut, Ari could sense and follow every one of Dani's movements. The way she leaned forward and caused the couch to shift, the heat as her lips came closer, the way she paused right before closing the distance, probably because she enjoyed the tease.

After an agonizing wait, Ari finally felt Dani's soft lips on hers, and together they moved in sync like a melody she'd never danced to before but somehow knew all the steps of. There was no rush to escalate the kiss. Dani gently pulled Ari's lower lip between hers and caressed her with a hint of tongue, but she didn't push beyond that. She didn't need to. Without doing anything else, Ari's knees were weak, and a rush of heat warmed her core. She savored the kiss, which left her craving more. She forced herself to open her eyes.

Dani watched her intently. "That was better." She cupped Ari's face with her hand, finger drifting from her cheek to pass over her lips like a second kiss. "I'll see you tonight."

"Yes," Ari said in a voice that sounded coarse to her own ears. She cleared her throat before speaking again. "See you tonight."

Dani planted another quick kiss—this time only a peck—on Ari's lips before standing up and walking to the door.

◈

After kissing the woman who had been on her mind for months, Dani was walking on air. She left Ari's suite with a smile firmly in place, looking over her shoulder and fighting the urge to run back and kiss Ari again.

She'd imagined the way their lips would meet for the first time more often than she cared to admit, but the kiss surpassed all her expectations. From the way their lips melded together as if they were designed for each other, to the tingles that spread all over her body with just one touch. Her favorite part was the way Ari became a mess around her.

She hoped the kiss helped Ari feel more at ease and that it silenced the doubts and insecurities she knew Ari felt. Ever since Ari had confirmed her trip to Miami, the anticipation had been killing Dani—she hadn't been that nervous since she served for her first Grand Slam win. The minute she saw Ari in person, all fears faded away, leaving only one certainty behind: she wanted Ari, and wanted her to know it.

She decided then that she had to kiss Ari as soon as possible because the more they waited, the harder it would be to break the awkwardness. Her plan had been simple: avoid all the tiptoeing, the speculation, and the reading between the lines. Ask a direct question and get a direct answer.

If Ari didn't want to kiss her, or wasn't ready, they would spend the week as friends. But if Ari kissed her back, they could shake the tentativeness away, avoid walking on eggshells, and enjoy their time together with their intentions clear.

Dani always had a game plan, and her week with Ari was no different. The first step had been to figure out if the attraction they felt during their virtual meetings would translate into chemistry in real life. So far, mission accomplished. The second step of the plan was to go on a date, and that part was already in motion.

# Chapter Eleven

Ari didn't know where they were going, and she didn't care. Dani's hand in her own was all she needed. She was happy to let Dani lead the entire way through the spacious hallways of the hotel as they headed to the lobby.

She'd lost any hope of fighting her attraction to Dani the minute their lips had touched. Hell, the minute she'd seen Dani and the strength of her presence had drawn her in like a magnet. But after the kiss, her mind was fixated on when those lips would press against her own again.

First, she needed to get through dinner with their friends. As much as she craved Dani's lips, meeting the people in her life made Ari's heart flutter almost as much as the thought of another kiss did.

When they arrived in the lobby, Arantxa waved to them through the window. She was waiting for them in the hotel's driveway next to an unassuming black car, and she hopped in the driver's seat.

"That's why I let Arantxa come. I hate driving," Dani whispered in her ear. They were standing so close that the air that passed through her lips tickled Ari's neck and sent a shiver down her body. She would have sworn that Dani did it on purpose to tease her if it wasn't for the fact that as soon as she finished talking, Dani walked toward the car with Ari's hand still in her grasp as if nothing had happened.

When they reached the car, Dani surprised her again by asking Tom to take the front seat. Ari expected her to ride next to Arantxa, but it was clear Dani had other plans. They sat unnecessarily close to each other in the spacious back seat, and Arantxa raised her eyebrows at them through the rearview mirror.

Ari wasn't going to complain about this arrangement. She wanted the contact and was glad Dani was eager to offer it. Ari looked down at their intertwined fingers and marveled at how perfect they were for each other. Her smaller hand fit inside Dani's with ease, the same way she imagined her body would fit pressed against Dani's.

Ari forgot about the two other people in the car until Arantxa spoke. "It's nice to put a face to Dani's mystery woman."

"Arantxa," Dani replied in a warning tone before Ari could react.

"What? What did I say?"

Ari laughed. Arantxa's bluntness didn't make her uncomfortable, it amused her. In a way it made Dani more real. She was just a regular person with meddling friends who worried about her just as Ari's did.

"Thank you," she said. "Nice to meet you too."

"See"—Arantxa glanced back briefly and shot a smirk at Dani—"unlike you, she has manners." She turned on the car's radio.

Ari stared through the window and watched the Miami scenery fly by. She basked in the view of the highway elevated over the turquoise water, the white buildings in the distance, the wind hitting her face. Before she knew it, they were parking on a colorful street, the sound of music guiding their steps, almost inviting them to dance.

"You can't come to Miami and not eat Cuban food," Dani said, leading her into a small restaurant. "This is one of my favorite places here. I visit it every year."

The aroma of garlic, onion, and some unknown spices made Ari's mouth water. Dani spoke with the host and servers with familiarity as they were escorted to a table in the back, where an outdoor patio was hiding. Ari wasn't a fan of eating outside in the heat, but as the night fell, a fresh breeze made the setting perfect.

As soon as they sat, Arantxa ordered a round of mojitos. Ari hesitated, afraid of appearing rude, but before the server left, she blurted a change in the order. "Just water for me, please." Arantxa glanced at her but didn't speak, and Ari answered the silent question anyway. "I don't drink alcohol."

"Let's add that to the list of things that make you a perfect match for Dani," Arantxa said. "I always have to force her to have a drink with me, even to celebrate. I swear she thinks it will make her forget how to play tennis."

"You know I'm a lightweight and get sick with one drink," Dani quipped.

When their drinks came, Tom rushed to grab his own and take a long sip. "Mmm, this is the best mojito I've ever had. I guess we are the perfect match for our best friends." He raised his glass toward Arantxa for a toast. "Are you also the romantic one of the pair like I am?"

"I wouldn't say I'm a romantic, but I enjoy having some good company. Working with this one"—she tilted her head toward Dani—"doesn't leave much time for anything else, but I believe in love, even if it only lasts a night."

"I can see that you're my kind of girl. Well, cheers to love."

Tom and Arantxa clinked their drinks together between laughs. Ari raised her glass of water and joined them. She was about to put hers down when Dani clinked it with her own. Their eyes met, and no matter how much Ari tried, she couldn't decipher the expression in Dani's eyes. She only knew she couldn't look away.

"To finding love," Dani said without breaking eye contact.

◈

Maybe it was obvious to Tom and Arantxa how little the other two needed them around, or maybe they truly had things to do. Ari wasn't sure what was true or not. All she knew was that Arantxa claimed she had work commitments, while Tom assured them that he had a date waiting for him. In other circumstances, she would have ended him for dropping her for a random guy, but she knew he was only leaving because he could tell she was comfortable with Dani. And to be fair, she couldn't wait for them to be alone together.

Ari and Dani left the restaurant and spotted a pair of dancers gathering a crowd across the street. Dani pulled her toward the group so they could watch up close. The performers never lost the beat of the music, and the streetlights reflected on the black-and-silver sequin dress of the female dancer's every movement.

"Want to give it a try?" Dani's breath tickled the back of Ari's neck, and she held her hand out as an invitation.

Ari rushed to say no. She wasn't a terrible dancer, but it wasn't something she felt confident enough to do in public, much less after admiring the two in front of them who moved with a speed and practiced ease that seemed impossible to match. Some spectators around them paired up to dance, while others simply watched. Dani stood behind her, hands on Ari's waist and head resting on top of her shoulder, swaying from side to side with the music.

For a minute Ari contemplated turning around and taking Dani up on her offer. The possibility of having Dani pressed against her, moving to the rhythm of the music, was incredibly tempting. But the surrounding crowd intimidated her, even if nobody was paying attention to them.

Ari let out a small sigh when the dancers ended their show, not because of them but because she'd gotten used to the feeling of Dani's body so close to hers. As they resumed their walk, Dani didn't hesitate to grab her hand again. The feeling was becoming familiar despite it being less than a day since they'd touched each other for the first time.

"You're a dancer?" Ari asked, fascinated by this new piece of information.

"I'm an awful dancer."

Ari burst out laughing. She assumed Dani was good at everything—the idea of her being bad at anything never crossed her mind.

"Don't laugh. I think there's something wrong with tennis players' sense of rhythm. Like our bodies have adapted after years of training to only a certain set of movements. I haven't met one tennis player who's a good dancer."

"You had me fooled back there."

"Oh, I love dancing, I'm just not good at it. But I don't let that stop me most of the time."

"I've gotten the impression that applies to a lot of things in your life."

"It does. When I want something, I stop at nothing to get it," Dani said, turning to look at Ari as they walked. "I still want to dance with you, though. I won't let you get away next time."

Ari already knew she was incapable of denying Dani anything she wanted, but she didn't say so outright. The tiny amount of self-control left in her allowed for a much more subdued answer. "As long as it's not in public, I'm happy to dance with you."

"Deal."

When Dani asked Ari what they should do next, she answered that she wanted to do stereotypical tourist stuff. That's how they ended up at Wynwood Walls. Ari loved the buzz of the neighborhood. They walked around, took a hundred selfies with colorful murals as backgrounds, and sat down to admire the works of art. No rush to get anywhere, just happy to enjoy each other's company.

"This is not our first date."

Ari's eyes widened, surprised by Dani's exclamation. After their kiss earlier that day, it seemed clear they both were interested in something romantic. Ari hadn't thought of this outing as a date, but the sudden need to clarify was strange. "Okay . . ."

Dani raised her hands in defense. "No, sorry. That came out so wrong, like I don't want to date you, when I mean the opposite."

Ari let Dani arrange her thoughts and explain, but she couldn't control the smile tugging at the corners of her mouth at seeing Dani be the one to stumble with her words for once. "Go on."

"I had a lot of fun today, but I don't want you to think this is our first date. I want to take you out properly, and officially, the two of us alone."

Ari grinned. "I didn't come all the way to Miami to not go on a date with you, so my answer is yes, if that's what you are asking."

"I mean, I wasn't exactly *asking* . . . I kind of already have everything set up," Dani said with a smirk.

Ari rolled her eyes and mirrored it back. "Oh, is that so? My bad to think I had an option."

"You always have an option. Does Wednesday work for you?"

Ari knew that Dani had only been joking, but hearing that she always had an option—that she was the one who could make a choice—hit her hard. She always accommodated other people's needs, and she didn't know how nice it would feel to have someone think of her instead.

"I'm on vacation, so yeah, any day works for me."

◈

When they arrived at the hotel, Ari felt like a teenager coming back from prom, waiting for her date to make a move as they stood awkwardly in front of the door. The difference was that back then, she dreaded the moment and rushed inside as soon as she could. On this night with Dani, though, she waited in anticipation.

"Do you want to go to my room for a while?" Dani asked.

Ari's eyes widened at the implications, but before she could answer, Dani spoke again. "To talk and watch a movie, I swear. I just don't want the night to end yet."

Dani's clarification caused a hint of disappointment in Ari, which she knew was ironic. She wasn't planning on sleeping with Dani. Casual sex, even with someone she liked as much as she did Dani, was something she'd never enjoyed. The few times she'd slept with someone, it had been after she was already invested in the other person. Not in love every time, but close.

A lot of those things—the connection, the attraction—already existed with Dani. Ari was comfortable with her, and she saw herself trusting Dani enough to let herself go soon, but not yet. Ari didn't want to say good night yet either, though. She wanted to make the most of the limited time they had together. "I also don't want it to end."

Dani's room was as big as Ari's, with a king bed, a living room, a kitchenette, and a balcony overlooking the bay. Ari couldn't help noticing how organized it was. The only things she saw at first glance that showed evidence of someone staying here were two tennis bags standing against the sofa; other than that, there was nothing out of place.

"Where's all your stuff?" Ari asked.

Dani raised an eyebrow at her. "In the closet. Where else?"

"You put everything in the closet for just two weeks?"

"Yeah, I like the structure of it. When you travel from place to place all the time, it's hard to feel at home anywhere. Not having to take everything out of a suitcase is nice."

Ari thought about her own suitcase lying in the middle of the room, clothes already scattered all over the place after only one day. "I get it."

Dani smiled at her, that knowing smile that Ari was getting used to. "You mind if I change clothes? I can lend you something too, or if you want, you can go to your room and change."

"I will take something from you."

When Dani opened the closet to look for some pajamas, Ari couldn't stop herself from sneaking a glance. Despite their conversation, she was still surprised there were stacks of neatly folded clothes, not one out of place.

Dani handed her a simple blue T-shirt and matching shorts. "These are the smallest clothes I have. I hope they fit you."

Ari waited until Dani disappeared behind the opaque glass doors that separated the main bedroom from the bathroom to turn around to change. The borrowed shorts were loose in her hip area, and the shirt was wider than she needed in the shoulders, but they were comfortable and she was glad to be out of the yellow sundress she'd worn to dinner.

Ari was in the middle of debating if she should sit on the bed when Dani returned from the bathroom. Her outfit was almost identical, but it fit perfectly. The shirt clung to her body, accentuating every one of her muscles, and her strong legs filled the same shorts Ari was swimming in. Ari knew she was staring, but she couldn't stop her eyes from roaming up and down Dani's body.

"You look adorable in my clothes," Dani said, walking around the bed to sit.

Ari fidgeted with the bottom of her shirt, feeling shy because of the attention despite the fact that Dani was looking at her with pure warmth in her eyes.

"Do you mind if we watch an action movie or something mindlessly fun?" Dani asked.

Ari didn't care about the movie. Her nerves had returned with full force once she and Dani settled in the bed. "Yeah, whatever you want is good."

An ocean of pillows separated them. Ari wanted to move the pillows away and close the space between them, but she didn't dare. Instead, she watched Dani fumble with the pillows, sit up, put them behind her back, then take them out again. The entire time, Ari remained rooted to the spot, not moving one inch.

Dani let out a chuckle. "This is ridiculous. You look uncomfortable as hell, and I am too. Do you mind if we get closer together? There's no need to sit as far away as possible, unless you prefer that."

Ari smiled. "I'm okay with getting closer."

"Come here, then."

Dani scooted to the center of the bed and offered her hand to Ari, who took it and moved to sit next to her. Half of Ari's body ended up in the pillows, and half pressed against Dani's side. Dani didn't hesitate to raise her arm so Ari could nestle against her chest.

Dani looked down into Ari's eyes. "Perfect."

Ari expected a kiss to follow, but it didn't happen. Instead, Dani turned toward the TV and hit Play on the movie.

It wasn't long before sleep overtook her. She had a faint memory of fighting heavy eyelids, and the next thing she knew, her foggy brain was battling between waking up and remaining in a peaceful slumber. She wasn't sure if the hand caressing her cheek was part of her dreams or part of reality, until she opened her eyes to find Dani's face welcoming her back to consciousness.

"Hey," Ari said, trying to stop a yawn. "Sorry, I guess I was more tired than I thought."

"Don't worry. I was trying to wake you up softly. I hope I didn't freak you out."

"Not at all. My mom used to yank the covers off to wake me up, so this is a pleasant change." She finally let the yawn escape and snuggled closer on instinct, only to panic as soon as the warmth and softness of Dani's body registered in her brain. Despite the embarrassment, she fought the urge to move away because she felt comfortable and safe in Dani's arms.

"I will use that method next time," Dani said with a small laugh. "I've been trying to wake you up for like twenty minutes."

"Please don't. It makes me so mad." Ari turned to look up at her. "What time is it?"

"It's late. You are welcome to stay the night, but I didn't want to assume."

The way Dani kept thinking about what she wanted warmed her heart. As tempting as it sounded to spend the night, with the way she was falling for Dani, it was safer to give herself some space.

“I should go to my room,” Ari said.

Despite her words, neither of them moved.

“I want to kiss you right now,” Dani said, gently cupping Ari’s face with her hand. She shifted as she did, and it had the side effect of bringing their bodies closer, ending with Dani half lying on top of her. Not that Ari minded.

In the short time they’d shared together in person, Ari had discovered that Dani was not one to hide her feelings or agonize over a decision—she simply did it. She wished she could be the same, instead of always overthinking everything. She was glad for Dani’s forwardness because it helped her embrace her own desires without the fear of being rejected. In that moment, she felt overwhelmed by how much she wanted Dani to close the space between them. And eager to let Dani know.

It was one thing to know what she wanted to do, and another to put it into motion. She tried to speak, but her voice didn’t come out. She closed her eyes to calm herself down. The darkness heightened the feeling of Dani’s hand caressing her face and the way their lips were already so close.

When Ari opened her eyes, the words she wanted to say finally came out in a breathy whisper. “What’s stopping you?”

Dani grinned but didn’t move. She seemed set on dragging out the moment, her lips lingering inches away, building anticipation in a way Ari could no longer handle. She surprised herself by moving forward to close the gap between them.

Ari knew they were treading on dangerous waters when the kiss deepened. Dani's hand moved down to settle on Ari's waist and grasped her harder every time their tongues met, causing soft moans to escape from her lips at the contact. Ari could feel the heat radiating from their bodies, and even though her brain screamed at her to slow down, her body didn't want to listen. Her hand went to the back of Dani's neck, pulling her down and closer.

After what felt like hours, they separated slowly, letting their foreheads rest against each other, their ragged breaths punctuating the silence of the night. They never broke eye contact, but there was a question in Ari's mind, one she didn't voice: *Should we stop?*

The question faded away when Dani pressed her lips down against hers again, this time softer, without the same desperation of the previous kiss. Ari was trying, unsuccessfully, to remember why she thought they needed to stop as Dani kissed the corners of her mouth, first the left, then the right. Her lips hovered over Ari's neck and jaw for a second, before she placed a kiss there too. Ari didn't feel capable of stopping, not when she wanted Dani more with each touch. She moved her hands to the small of Dani's back and pushed them under her shirt, where they rested against soft skin.

Dani chose that moment to move back up from Ari's neck, retracing the same path she had forged minutes before, until their lips met again. *One last kiss*, Ari told herself. *One last kiss, and I will leave.*

Her resolve wavered more with each one, but she needed to trust her instincts. Before she could find the words to express her thoughts, Dani stopped.

"I would love to keep kissing you. Are you okay with that?"

Ari swallowed, distracted by the way Dani's chest moved up and down as she caught her breath. She looked down at Dani's lips, plump and red, tempting her by their mere existence.

Ari winced. "I would love to keep kissing you, but . . . I think it's better if I go now."

Dani nodded with a soft smile. "I understand."

Part of Ari regretted the choice, but she knew she wasn't ready yet. When Dani didn't move from her position, Ari cleared her throat and stared at the hand Dani had resting next to her—the one she'd been using to hold herself up, which now held Ari in place.

Dani fumbled as she realized her mistake. "Right, sorry," she said, moving away.

Ari took her time to walk to her room with Dani, who insisted on accompanying her. Once they made it to the door, Dani booped the tip of Ari's nose with her finger.

"Good night, beautiful."

Ari smiled at the pet name and raised herself up on the tips of her toes to plant a quick kiss on Dani's lips. "Good night."

◆

Dani watched Ari enter her room with a mix of wistfulness and nostalgia. She refused to miss even one opportunity to bask in the beauty of Ari's sun-kissed brown skin or the cuteness of her small frame swimming in the oversized clothes she'd lent her.

The good-night peck tingled on her lips, filling her heart with joy. As Dani walked back to her room, she wondered exactly when and how she'd started falling for Ari. When their random Tumblr conversations had turned into more. As much as she tried to remember, she couldn't find one exact moment when it had happened. But what she knew with certainty was that for months, Ari had been the first person she wanted to share her thoughts with every day, and being with her in person only reinforced that feeling.

The way Ari turned around to look at her one last time before going inside her room, and the small blush still coloring her cheeks as she ducked her head were all the confirmation Dani needed to know that she wasn't the only one getting in deep.

She crawled into bed with a grin on her face, hugging a pillow as she tried to fall asleep with only one thing on her mind: she was going to take Ari out on the best date of her life.

# Chapter Twelve

For the rest of the week, Ari developed a routine with Dani. She would spend her mornings and early afternoons with Tom, either exploring the city or relaxing at the hotel, while Dani focused on her training and media obligations. In the evening, they had dinner together and spent the rest of the night watching movies, playing board games, or simply talking in either of their suites. A dose of normalcy in the middle of extraordinary circumstances.

In the days Dani had a match, Ari and Tom sat in the first row every time. They became experts at navigating the behind-the-scenes of the tournament and made friends with the staff and volunteers, and even Igor started acknowledging them with a curt nod as a greeting when they joined the player box next to him.

Today, the plan would be different. She and Dani were finally going on the promised official first date, and even though she'd been spending as much time as possible with Dani, Ari's stomach was in knots from the anticipation. So much that the soft beep of her phone made her jump from her seat.

**I hope you are ready to go. I'll pick you up in fifteen minutes.**

She didn't know where Dani was taking her. The only information she had to go on was that Dani had asked her to dress light and beach ready. A soft knock interrupted her pacing. She took a deep breath and opened the door to find Dani looking as beautiful as always in shorts, a polo shirt, and sunglasses.

A silver convertible waited for them outside the hotel. Ari glanced at Dani with a questioning look.

"I hate driving, but if I have to do it, I may as well do it in style. Besides, I'm trying to impress a girl," Dani said with a wink.

Ari tried to hide the grin taking over her face. "Where are we going?"

"It's a surprise."

Ari's grin disappeared as she bit her lip to stop herself from speaking. Her restraint didn't last long. "I kind of hate surprises."

Dani raised her eyebrows. "You do?"

"Well, I don't hate the surprise itself. I hate knowing there's a surprise coming and not knowing what it is. The anticipation is unbearable." Ari clenched her teeth, worried she had ruined the date before it even started.

Dani simply shook her head with a laugh. "We are taking a boat to a beautiful beach for an afternoon of snorkeling, and we'll finish the day with a kiss as we watch the sunset. Do you like the idea?" She looked intently into Ari's eyes.

Ari blushed at the mention of a kiss but didn't dispute the plans. She didn't doubt Dani would do just as she said. It wasn't even arrogant, when it was a fact that Ari was dying to kiss Dani again too.

"I love the idea. Thank you for telling me."

"My mission today is to make you happy. No point in hiding the date if that's only going to stress you out."

As Dani drove, Ari relaxed thanks to the bright sun shining down on them and the sea breeze blowing in their faces while they crossed Miami. In less than half an hour, Dani pulled over into a parking lot next to the harbor. They strolled among the boats until they reached a yacht that was at least thirty feet long. Dani walked on board, pausing to extend her hand toward Ari to help her onto it too. For a second Ari stood motionless, realizing that if she got on the boat, there would be no going back.

"You're not terrified of boats, are you?" Dani said, panic written all over her face.

Ari gulped but fought to shake her nerves. "I've never been on one before, but I think I'll be fine." She took the extended hand and stepped onto the yacht.

"You good?"

"Yeah, I'm good. It's less scary than I thought it would be."

"Are you sure you want to go ahead with what I have planned? We can go grab lunch somewhere if you'd rather not do this."

Ari's stomach did a somersault. The way Dani was always worried about her well-being and comfort made her more open to try new things, because she knew that Dani would always listen to her if she changed her mind.

"I'm good, I promise. It caught me by surprise, but I'm excited to see what you've been working on all week."

Dani's broad smile was all the confirmation Ari needed to know that she'd made the right choice. "Okay, let's get settled, then."

Ari followed Dani to the cabin, where she realized there was nobody else with them. “Umm . . . Dani, are you going to drive the boat?”

“Wow, you look super thrilled about that.”

Ari’s eyes widened. “Are you?”

Dani stayed silent for what seemed like an eternity before breaking into laughter. “I know how to drive a boat. As a matter of fact, I have my own in Mallorca. But I hired a professional to handle that part while we enjoy the ride.”

“Oh, okay.”

Dani snickered. “Someone is relieved.”

“I’m sure you can do it, but I don’t need that stress in my life right now.”

“Fair. But when you visit me in Mallorca, I will be the captain.”

The motor rumbled to life, and the boat started to move. To Ari’s surprise, the sailing was smooth, with no hard movements or sudden jumps. She was grateful it wasn’t as rough as she expected.

Dani stood and offered her hand again. “Do you want to go to the bow? I love watching the ride from there.”

“The what?”

“The front of the boat. We can lay down some towels and sunbathe or just enjoy the view.”

Ari realized there was no point in accepting to take a boat ride if she then was going to hide in the cabin. Besides, she already felt more confident and relaxed. She took Dani’s hand and walked with her to the front of the boat, where there was enough space for them to lie comfortably, as well as a rail for safety if they wanted to stand and take in their surroundings.

When they approached the rail, Dani stood next to her, left hand holding on to the bar on the other side of Ari's waist. Ari appreciated the extra layer of security that small gesture provided.

With the blue sky and clear water surrounding them, and Dani's steady presence next to her, it was impossible for Ari not to relax. She let her body loosen and melt into Dani's side, who didn't hesitate to hold her.

"Are we going somewhere in particular, or is that a surprise too?"

"We are going to this spot close to the Bahamas. I've been a few times, and the water is amazing. It's like being in paradise."

"I'm assuming you love the ocean."

"It's hard not to when you live on an island, but mountains were my first love."

"Really?"

Dani nodded, leading Ari away from the rail to sit on the deck.

"The city I'm from, Medellín, is a valley surrounded by beautiful green mountains. I was young when we left, but I still remember waking up and looking out my window to stare at them. Even to this day, when I go back and see them from the plane as we get closer, my heart feels so full. "

"You could have tricked me into thinking you are all about the water."

"I learned to love the beach growing up. As a kid, I spent my life training, playing tennis for hours every day. But when we went to the beach, it was the one place where I could forget about tennis. As much as I love the sport, it can be hard to focus so much on only one thing."

"That makes sense. I guess it's kind of like meditation for you to be in the ocean."

"Yes, that's a good way to describe it. It's the one place, besides a tennis court, where my mind goes blank. No worries, no overthinking."

"That sounds nice," Ari replied, looking toward the horizon.

She felt Dani's eyes on her, observing, analyzing, but for once she ignored it. She kept her gaze focused on the vast ocean in front of her, realizing that right there and then was the first time in a long time that her head was clear of all the thoughts usually swirling around.

"You must have a place like that too," Dani said.

"A place where my mind goes blank? I don't know, I don't think I ever stop overthinking," Ari replied, still watching the waves around them. "The library," she added after a minute of silence. "Ever since I was a kid, I would hide there. As soon as the bell rang, I would run to the library instead of getting lunch and would spend the whole hour reading. Escaping to a different world through the words on a page is the only time I stop worrying." She lowered her voice as she spoke, almost embarrassed at how silly she sounded.

Dani didn't comment. Instead, she simply wrapped her arms tighter and kissed her cheek. "What has you so worried?"

"The usual," Ari said with a shrug. "Being a complete failure and disappointment to my parents." She let out a self-deprecating chuckle. "Let's go back to you. I'm ruining our date."

"No, you're not. Come on, I want to know everything about you."

The way Dani was looking at her, the warmth in her voice and her eyes, made it impossible for Ari to contain her thoughts and emotions.

"I decided to go to law school because I wanted to change the world, and at the time being a lawyer really seemed like the way to do it. The one way to influence the laws that affect everyone." Ari paused and leaned into Dani's embrace even more. "My parents were so excited. Two of my older brothers are doctors and the other one is an engineer. Wanting to be a lawyer made them proud."

"I can imagine."

"Going into debt sucked, but my parents always thought that education was the only way to have a better life. And at the time I didn't mind, either, because I would get a good job after school, pay off my debts, take care of my parents, and change the world. You know."

"Sounds like a great plan, yeah."

"Except when you realize that the jobs where you make enough to pay your six-digit debt are at law firms that work for big corporations, where I'd be doing exactly the opposite of what I dreamed of when I chose this path. But not taking a job with a big law firm means drowning in debt forever and not being able to help my parents. They've worked so hard and sacrificed so much for me to have a good life here."

The thoughts weren't new and had been plaguing her for months, but the way her insecurities were all coming out was the unusual part. She hadn't even shared with Tom how troubled she was about her choices, beyond a comment here or there. It seemed unfair to complain, when deep down she knew the choice she would end up making. If Ari wanted to be honest with herself, she would admit that her guilt didn't come from having to choose between those two paths, but from knowing she would be betraying her initial dream.

"I don't think there's really a wrong choice here," Dani said. "You should do whatever makes you feel better. From what you've told me, your parents only want what's best for you, so they would understand. If you end up going down the corporate path, there's no shame in doing what you need to do to take care of yourself. You can always do good in other ways."

"I guess."

Ari appreciated Dani's words and her attempt at making her feel better, even if she wasn't convinced she was right. But she wasn't going to fix her dilemma in one afternoon when she'd been agonizing over it for months. Right now, what she wanted was to forget all of her worries, and she knew Dani could make that happen.

"Enough depressing talk," Ari said, turning around to look into Dani's eyes. "Today is about enjoying ourselves, so let's forget about that topic for now."

As if reading her mind, Dani leaned down and gave her a long, sweet kiss that made her forget about everything for an instant. They sat in a comfortable silence, looking at one another with soft smiles on their faces. The moment felt right. The fact that they could enjoy each other's company without feeling an obligation to break the silence, without it being awkward, was one of Ari's favorite things about Dani. She filled any space with her personality and bright smile. She could be loud and imposing, but she also knew when to be more subdued.

It was Ari who spoke first. "I hope your master surprise plan includes food because I'm starving. I skipped breakfast."

Dani brightened at Ari's words. "I'm glad you brought that up because I planned a feast for us. Let me show you."

She walked back to the cabin and returned with a large cooler and a bag, carrying them with no effort. Ari watched in amusement as Dani set up a picnic on the boat.

"We have water and sodas. I'm not sure which one is your favorite. And if you want to get fancy, I also brought some ginger beer and nonalcoholic cider."

"I will take a Coke and water for now. We'll see about the cider later. Depends on how the day goes," Ari answered with a smirk.

"Well, I'm just getting started, so I'm pretty confident you'll have some cider with dinner."

Ari didn't doubt those words. The care Dani had put into their date had already impressed and charmed her, but she was also looking forward to finding out what else was in store.

"For food, I got some different options just in case. What about a trio of ceviche to start: white fish, shrimp, and octopus. I also packed some smoked salmon, cheeses, and charcuterie. Oh, and some Colombian and Argentinian empanadas. Don't tell anybody, but as much as I love Colombian empanadas, Argentinian ones are my favorite."

"What's the difference?"

"Well, Colombian ones use corn dough and are deep-fried. Argentinian ones are baked and made with normal wheat flour. They are great no matter which one you choose."

"Let's start with the Colombian empanadas. I think it's my duty to try them."

Dani pulled out a ginger beer for herself and a platter of empanadas. Ari took a different kind in each hand and pretended to be torn about which one to try first. She thought it was an unfair competition because deep-frying improved everything, and this was no exception. She was a fan of the crispy exterior and the soft, flavorful filling.

"I have to say I love the Colombian one," Ari said.

"Of course you do." Dani winked, making her blush.

Ari didn't know why she even tried to out-flirt Dani, who always got the better of her.

◆

When the boat stopped, they were surrounded by turquoise water, prettier than anything Ari had ever seen. Nearby, a white sand beach completed the idyllic view. She stared ahead, mesmerized by the scenery, until Dani stood up from their shared spot on the deck and stretched her arms and back. The way Dani's muscles moved hypnotized Ari, making her forget about the landscape.

She followed every movement with her eyes—the way Dani's hand ran up and down her leg as she applied sunscreen, how she bent over and reached down to her ankles, then went up again over her long legs. Ari's eyes traveled along with

Dani's hands as she moved to her shoulders. She was so transfixed that she didn't register the fact that Dani was speaking to her until Dani waved her hands in front of her face to get her attention.

Ari blinked and cleared her thoughts. "I'm sorry, what?"

Dani smiled. "Can you help me with my back?"

"Of course," Ari mumbled, taking the bottle of sunscreen.

She moved Dani's long hair out of the way and squeezed the bottle. At least she tried to, but nothing came out. Ari laughed and shook the bottle a couple of times before squeezing again. A giant splash of sunscreen came out, landing on Dani's naked back.

"Shit!" they exclaimed at the same time.

"Sorry!" Ari said, grimacing.

"It's okay, it was just cold."

Ari focused on spreading the sunscreen over Dani's skin with her fingers, grateful for the thin layer of separation the cream provided, because the sensation of Dani's skin under her fingertips was sending shivers down her spine. Ari couldn't see Dani's face, but she imagined the smirk on it. Dani enjoyed torturing her and had already proven to be a tease; Ari was sure that this time was no exception.

"Do you need help with your back?" Dani asked when Ari finished putting the sunscreen on her.

"No, I'm good," Ari rushed to answer, not trusting herself to resist if Dani touched her.

When Dani handed her a life jacket, fins, a mask, and a snorkel, Ari's anxiety returned. She wasn't a bad swimmer, but doing it in the middle of the ocean was on a different level. They used the stairs on the side of the yacht to descend into the water, something Ari was grateful for—the thought of jumping from the boat filled her with fear. Dani went in first, swimming gracefully but waiting close by.

The water was clear enough for them to see the white sand and coral under them, even though their feet didn't touch the bottom. Dani floated without effort; her hands stretched in front of her in a way that allowed Ari to use them as a crutch while she gained confidence.

"How are you feeling?" Dani asked.

"I'm a little scared, but I'm good."

"I'm right here. And Marcos, our boat captain, is also ready to step in if we need help."

Ari looked up to find Marcos waving at them, trying to reassure her. She nodded and started swimming.

"Snorkeling is easy," Dani explained, "but it can be scary the first time you do it, so we will go slow. Just put your head underwater and try to breathe."

Ari did as instructed. She broke the surface of the water with her head, looking through the mask and trying to breathe. It felt different, and Ari worried the air wouldn't come through or that her mask would fail and fill with water. She was about to take her head out in a fit of panic when she saw, out of the corner of her eye, that Dani had submerged her face next to hers. Remembering Dani was there looking out for her allowed her to push through the fear for a few more seconds. Enough to calm down.

Dani pulled her head out of the water, so Ari did the same.

"How did that feel?" Dani asked.

"Scary, but after a while it wasn't as bad."

"That's a normal reaction. Breathing through the snorkel feels different. You think you can do it? Or do you want to just swim or lie down to bask in the sun? We can do that too."

"I want to try it. I feel like I already did the hard part."

"You have. Take my hand. I will be next to you the whole time."

True to her word, Dani guided Ari every step of the way while they swam around and marveled at the beauty beneath them. Once Ari got over her initial apprehension, she fell in love with the sensation of being underwater, looking into another world. The area was full of colorful fishes that swam around her as if she were a mermaid. One of them was the strangest, most vibrant fish she could imagine, a mixture of pink and turquoise, almost fluorescent.

Ari started to feel the heat on her shoulders despite the sunscreen, but she was too excited about all the beautiful things she was seeing to care. She lost track of time as they swam around, the most fun she'd had in a long time.

They emerged from the water and climbed back onto the boat, where they were met by mouthwatering aromas. Marcos had set up a grill and was already cooking lobster and fish for them.

Ari wrapped herself in a towel and walked to the grill. "God, this smells amazing."

Dani arched a brow. "Hungry again? I might go broke at this rate."

"Hey, swimming makes people hungry," Ari answered, bumping Dani in the shoulder.

As the day drew on, it became harder and harder for them to not gravitate toward each other. Alone, miles away from anyone who knew them, they had no reason to stop themselves—so they didn't. They leaned against the rail, Dani's arms surrounding Ari while they watched the sun set on the horizon, stealing kisses every few minutes.

Dani took over serving the grilled lobster and fish, and she presented Ari with the cider bottle. She didn't have to say anything—Ari understood what she meant. Dani was daring her to argue that this perfect and romantic date didn't deserve a toast.

Ari answered without words too, reaching for the champagne glasses Dani had in her hands and setting them on the table to be filled. Dani's wide smile while they clinked the glasses together was Ari's reward.

◈

Saying goodbye to Ari was the hardest thing Dani had done in a while. After spending a perfect day together, it was the last thing she wanted to do, but she had to. She had an early match the next day and she couldn't lose, or else she'd have to face Igor's wrath.

He was already unhappy with her recent "distractions," as he called them. He didn't outright say he disapproved, but some of his comments made it obvious. He always wanted her to put tennis above everything. She usually obliged, but this time she couldn't. She had the rest of the year, the rest of her life to play tennis, but she only had a few days with Ari.

After seeing Ari's radiant smile that day during their date, the only thing Dani wanted was to make her that happy again. She couldn't do much to help Ari with the issues bothering her about school and her career, and to be honest, she wasn't sure she fully understood them. But she could help her forget them, at least for a while.

Dani opened her phone and started scrolling through the many pictures they'd taken. Ari looked beautiful in all of them, laughing and relaxing. For the first time, Dani didn't see a hint of sorrow in her eyes, and that was exactly how she wanted to keep things. One picture in particular caught her eye. She had asked Marcos to take it so they had at least one that wasn't a selfie, and she couldn't have asked for a better outcome: Dani stood with her arm around Ari's shoulders as Ari held on to her waist, and they looked into each other's eyes with ocean water still glistening on their sun-kissed skin and the glow of the sunset behind them.

As Dani admired the photo, she saw herself staring at Ari with a softness she didn't recognize at first, but she quickly realized that it was the only way she looked at Ari. She hoped the love in her eyes was as clear to Ari as it was to her. They were only starting to fully know each other, but in a few short days, Dani was sure of what she wanted—to keep Ari in her life as much as possible.

After staring at the picture for longer than she would ever admit, Dani shared it with Ari over text.

**At the risk of ruining my cool image, I have to say that I already miss you. But at least I have this picture of us to keep me company.**

**You're the one who ditched me ;)**

**Ouch. Ditched? There's nothing I want more than to walk to your room right now, but I need to be responsible or something.**

**I think I remember something about having to go to sleep early, yet here you are.**

Dani laughed.

**Well, it's your fault. I can't sleep because I'm thinking of you, and I needed to let you know. But I'm going to bed now so that our sacrifice is not for nothing.**

**Good night . . . If it makes you feel better, I can't stop thinking about you either.**

**It does. Sweet dreams, beautiful . . . And yes, by that I mean I hope you dream of me ;)**

**Good night, Dani.**

Dani slipped into bed, thoughts of Ari still lingering in her mind. Right before she put her phone down for the night and fell asleep, she opened Instagram and posted the picture she'd been staring at.

*The best day, with the best company.*

# Chapter Thirteen

**From: dani@danielamartinez.com**

**To: ari3nunezar@virginia.edu**

I realized just now, right after I left you at the airport and said goodbye, that I never asked you on a second date. We need to fix that.

The downside of doing such a great job planning our first date is that now I have it harder. But I won't let anyone outdo me, not even myself :P So I'm coming out with the big guns. What do you think about spending two weeks in Paris with me this summer? I'll be playing part of the time, but we'll have time to explore and vacation too.

And before you say anything, I'll pay for everything. I'm sorry, but this time I won't even allow a discussion. Take it as your early or belated birthday gift or something. I don't want you worrying about the money.

What do you say?

**From: ari3nunezar@virginia.edu**

**To: dani@danielamartinez.com**

Normally I would be making a list of reasons why I can't accept you just flying me off to Paris . . . but to be honest, I can't wait to see you again, so yes. I would love to meet you there.

I finish school in May and don't have to start my summer associate job until late June, so if the dates match, let's do it.

**From: dani@danielamartinez.com**

**To: ari3nunezar@virginia.edu**

Perfect. I can't wait to see you again and show you Paris.

You know your start date already? Does that mean you made a choice? Whatever it was, I'm proud of you.

**From: ari3nunezar@virginia.edu**

**To: dani@danielamartinez.com**

Yeah, I accepted one of the offers I had. I took the job at the firm one of my professors recommended me to. It's a big firm, and there's a possibility they'll take me as an associate after I graduate, so it was the smartest choice careerwise. I hope it's not as bad as I dread it will be.

I did offer to volunteer part time with the refugee NGO too. I wish I could take the job with them, but since I can't, I want to at least feel like I'm doing some good, even if in a small way.

Are you still proud of me?

**From: dani@danielamartinez.com**

**To: ari3nunezar@virginia.edu**

I'm even prouder because I know how hard it was for you to choose the "safe" option instead of the one you really want. I play sports for a living, so I don't think I'm in a place to judge anyone for choosing a better-paying job and stability. I'm lucky I get to do what I love, but I know that's not always an option.

I can hear the self-criticism in your words, and really you have nothing to be ashamed of. There's nothing wrong with looking out for yourself and what's best for you. I'm sure you will find a way to also do good and help people, because I can tell you want it so much. You're already inspiring me

—I've always worked with charitable foundations and have my own in Colombia, but I feel like I could be doing so much more. See, you're already creating change.

◈

Going back home to her routine wasn't easy for Ari. She didn't think it was possible to get used to someone's presence so fast, but she missed waking up early to have breakfast with Dani, missed their strolls on the beach and the late movie nights, even if she always fell asleep.

A week before, her only worry had been getting to Dani's matches on time. Now she was walking to her apartment after her civil procedure class with ten different assignments she needed to do, once again regretting the amounts of debt she was getting in for the privilege of hearing an old guy talk. It had been less than a week, and Ari was already counting the days left until the end of the semester and her next trip with Dani.

As soon as she got to her apartment, she called her mom. She'd neglected doing so during her stay in Miami and needed to make it up to her before she got on her case. As usual, the phone rang three times before her mom answered with a "Hi, baby," followed by a frenzy of blurry images while she moved the phone to an appropriate position—one that allowed her to keep working on whatever she was doing while they talked. Ari, used to the routine, waited for her to get settled.

A minute later Ari had a view of the entire kitchen, and her mom was back to chopping vegetables after putting the phone on a stand on the counter. Next to her, a pot sat on the stove, steam rising from it in a way that made Ari inhale deeply on reflex. Even though her mom was on the other side of the country, Ari swore she could smell the mix of garlic, onion, and peppers floating in the air back home.

"Finally, you call me. I was starting to think you'd forgotten about your poor mom."

Ari fought the urge to roll her eyes. She loved her mom, but her antics were too much sometimes. "I called you like a week ago. It hasn't been that long."

"For five minutes. It doesn't count."

"Well, I'm home now. We can talk while we both make dinner."

"What are you cooking? Not ramen, I hope. No man is going to want a wife who only cooks ramen."

Ari looked down at the pack of ramen in her hands and pushed it aside, grabbing something else instead. "I also make an amazing mac and cheese," she said with an air of triumph, bringing the box up to the camera.

Her mom's mouth twisted and she shook her head. "So, how was your trip?"

Ari noticed a weird inflection in her mother's voice. The question was innocent, but it was a tone she recognized. It always meant her mom was up to something. "It was good. Tom and I had a lot of fun."

"Speaking of Tom, Alizee told me she saw you both on TV or something."

Ari paused in her efforts to make dinner, surprised to hear that anyone in her family circle was interested in tennis enough to catch them on

TV. "Oh, yeah, I guess some matches we attended were broadcasted to the public."

"I've never paid attention to tennis, but Alizee's youngest nephew got a scholarship to play in college, so she knows a little about it. She said you were like special guests."

Though Ari hadn't been expecting the conversation to lead in this direction, she decided to go with it. She didn't see any reason to lie, and it wasn't like her mom would suddenly realize she was gay because she was friends with a popular tennis player. "Yeah, a friend invited us to the tournament."

"So, it's true?"

Her blood ran cold at the question, but she quickly dismissed her reaction—her mom had to be talking about something else. She opted for playing dumb until she knew for sure what her mom was getting at.

"What's true?" Ari asked nonchalantly.

Her mom stopped her chopping and looked at the phone. "That Tom is dating that tennis player."

Ari couldn't help letting out a big, relieved chuckle. "No, they are not dating. We're all friends." She considered reminding her mom that Tom was gay, the one fact about him she conveniently forgot all the time.

"Good. I was worried you'd let him get away."

Ari suppressed a groan. "Mom, I've told you plenty of times that Tom and I are just friends. And he's gay."

"Well, you don't like any of the family friends I've tried to introduce to you, and you spend all your time with Tom. What am I supposed to think?"

"I want to focus on my studies right now."

It was the excuse she'd used since high school. Back then, her mom was more than happy to brag about how Ari had no interest in boys and how proud she was of her daughter's determination to get an education. Even though she was still proud, she brought up the possibility of dating and marriage more and more. Ari wasn't even sure if telling her mom about her sexual orientation would stop the pestering about how single she was, but she wasn't ready to tackle that conversation yet.

"I know, I know. My beautiful future lawyer. I'm so proud of you, but I worry. You need someone to take care of you."

"I can take care of myself, Mom."

"That's not what I meant. I know you are an independent woman, but there's nothing wrong with having someone you can lean on."

An image of Dani flashed in her mind. In the short time they'd spent together, Dani had always gone out of her way to take care of Ari, to make sure everything was perfect.

"I actually met someone," Ari said before she could stop herself.

"You did?" Her mom dropped the knife for the first time since their conversation started. "Tell me everything. What's his name? What does he do?"

Part of Ari regretted her outburst, when of course her mom assumed she meant a man. Definitely not ready for that conversation yet. "It's pretty new, though. I will tell you when things get serious."

Her mom gave her a disapproving look, the same one that would make her tremble with fear as a kid. After so many years, it still sent a wave of panic through her body, and the way her mom was brandishing the knife as she spoke only amplified the effect.

"You can't drop a bomb like that on me and then leave me hanging," her mom said, accentuating every word with a movement of the hand that held the knife. "I will let you off the hook this time, but I want details soon. I'm really happy, though. You've always been too lonely."

Ari ignored the last part. She was used to those judgmental comments, even if her mom didn't mean them that way. Part of her regretted her choice of saying anything. Patience wasn't her mom's strong suit, and Ari would have to deal with her trying to find out more information every time they talked. But another part of her was looking forward to telling her mom more about her own life and her relationship with Dani once she was ready.

"I promise you'll be the first to know," Ari said, and as she did, she realized she meant it. She wanted to share with her mom the one thing that was making her happier than ever. It wasn't a question of if, but when.

◈

Mallorca was Dani's favorite place in the world. Spending a week at home after months on the road was enough to energize her for the upcoming clay season, her favorite surface. So far, her three Grand Slam wins had been on hard courts, at the US and Australian Opens. But she'd grown up playing on red clay, like all Spanish players did, and dreaming of winning Roland-Garros. In a month, she would have another chance to turn that dream into a reality, and as the winner of the last two Grand Slams, all eyes would be on her.

Another advantage of being in Mallorca was that she could train at the academy she'd grown up playing at, which felt familiar in a way nowhere else in the world did. She always played her best tennis there, and it was the perfect place to fine-tune her game and increase her confidence right before one of the most important tournaments of the year. And she'd have a perfect view of the ocean the whole time.

Not that Igor let her enjoy that view while she did these training drills. She ran from one side of the court to pick up her racket off the ground and then to the other side to hit the ball coming her way.

Igor's thunderous voice reached her ears. "Another five sprints and then we'll focus on your forehand. It's been breaking down under pressure in recent matches."

Dani didn't answer. She kept running from side to side to hit the ball, fully concentrating on the task at hand.

The sun was setting when Igor finished the training session for the day. "It's good to see you so focused again," he commented while they picked up their gear.

*Let it go*, she told herself. But she was getting tired of his nagging, and if he had something to say, she would rather he came out with it outright. "What do you mean 'again'? I'm as focused as always."

She walked away holding a bottle of Gatorade in her hand, leaving her tennis bags behind so Igor was forced to carry them. It was a petty, childish power move, but that small win made her feel less annoyed. Igor picked up the bags without a second thought and caught up to her as she left the court.

"That's a matter of opinion," he said. "From where I'm standing, you haven't been up to your usual standard. Miami was kind of a disaster."

Dani picked up the pace, eager to get to the parking lot and escape the conversation before she lost her temper. "I made the semifinals. I wouldn't call that a disaster."

"In tennis there's only win or lose. You lost to someone you've never lost against before, someone who was in their first ever semifinal. You were the favorite." Igor placed the bags in the backseat of Dani's car. "It doesn't matter anymore. Now Roland-Garros is all that matters, and I'm happy to see you have no . . . distractions around to keep us from that goal. I feel like double training sessions every day this week would do you some good."

Dani decided to ignore his emphasis on the word "distractions." She knew exactly what he was trying to insinuate, but she didn't want to start a fight about it. Once they were in Paris, he would have to deal with the fact that Ari was there no matter if he liked it or not. She wasn't changing her plans.

"Double sessions it is," she said, starting the car and leaving without a goodbye.

She drove faster than she should have, eager to get home and take a shower to wash away the sweat of training and the annoyance over her conversation with Igor. As she was parking, her phone rang. A smile broke out on her face, but it went away when she saw it was Arantxa.

"I hope this is a friendly call 'cause I'm not in the mood for sponsorship nonsense or media appearances."

"Well, hello to you too, Dani. Yes, I'm good, enjoying my time at home in Madrid. Thank you for asking."

Dani rolled her eyes but silently conceded that Arantxa shouldn't have to deal with the consequences of her frustration with Igor. "Hi, Arantxa, how are you?"

"Better than you, it seems. I thought you were all sunshine and rainbows now that you are the embodiment of a rom-com."

"You really don't want to try me today, Arantxa. Igor was already on my case about how distractions are affecting my tennis, and I don't need you to get on that train too."

"I honestly was only calling to chat, but I don't feel like being your punching bag if you are in a bad mood."

"I'm sorry, I won't take it out on you," Dani replied. "How's Madrid treating you?"

"It's good to be home, but all my plants died. I don't know why I keep trying when they die every time. And Rosana got a girlfriend while I was away and called off our casual hookup situation." Arantxa's voice didn't show a hint of sadness, but Dani still felt a pang of sympathy.

"Sorry to hear that."

"It's fine, plenty of fish in the sea. I've already got a date for this weekend."

"I meant the plants," Dani said in a deadpan voice that made Arantxa let out a loud chuckle. "I appreciate having you around so much, but don't you get tired of all the travel, never being home, losing your relationships because you're gone?"

"No, not really. I took this job and travel with you as much as I do because I want to. I love visiting a different country every other week, the excitement of having a demanding job that has me on-call all the time. I don't like being still, and I don't want people holding me back. If they can keep up with my lifestyle then they're welcome in my life. If not, it is what it is and it's better for us to part ways. I love my life just the way it is."

Dani nodded, and it took her a few seconds to realize Arantxa couldn't see her. "That makes sense."

"You seem all in your feels today. What did Igor tell you?"

"Just his usual lecture about *being a hundred percent focused on tennis all the time*," Dani said, imitating his deep voice. "I actually need your help setting up everything for Ari to stay with us in Paris, and that made me think about the future. I really like her, and right now she is excited to travel and explore the world with me when she can . . . but what you said made me realize that eventually the novelty will wear off, and she may not want my lifestyle or be able to fit into it. I like her a lot, and I wouldn't want my career to come between us, but you know tennis will always come first."

"Long-distance relationships are a thing, and it's obvious that girl is head over heels for you. It's written all over her face. I'm sure you can find a way to make it work."

"Yeah, you are right. It's probably just Igor's words getting in my head," Dani said as she arrived at her house. "I'll talk to you later. I really need to take a shower."

"Wait," Arantxa interrupted. "Now that you mention Ari, there's one thing I want to talk to you about."

Dani groaned. "I knew you weren't calling only to chat."

"I was, I swear! But this is a good moment to bring it up since we're talking about it. Have you checked your Instagram comments lately?"

"You know I try to not look at them."

"Right, that's good. Well, the newest addition to your entourage in Miami didn't go unnoticed by the media or the fans, and then the picture you posted on Instagram brought even more attention."

"Your point?"

Arantxa cleared her throat. "I know there have been rumors about your sexuality forever and you've never cared. Our stance has always been to never confirm the rumors but never deny them either. But you've also never been in a relationship before, so I want to check with you if there should be any change."

Dani sighed. This was the part she hated the most about her career—having people she barely knew intruding in her life. "What are they saying?"

"Fans are just speculating about who the mystery woman in your picture is, wondering if you'll officially come out, stuff like that. Some of the press, ironically, think you are dating Tom, and . . ."

"And what?" Dani snapped.

"And that your love life is affecting your tennis."

"Ugh . . . Roger Federer travels with his wife and four kids but nobody ever says that's distracting him from tennis. I have one date, and suddenly losing in the semifinals is newsworthy?"

"Don't shoot the messenger."

Dani took a deep breath. "Ignore them. Ari and I are only starting, and the last thing I need is to bring a public coming out into the picture. Make sure to divert attention from her, but as far as the rumors about me go, they can keep talking."

She hung up the phone before Arantxa could respond, but she knew her manager would handle things. She slammed the car door and jumped into the shower as soon as she stepped in the house in an attempt to bring her blood pressure down.

◈

**Are you free for a call?**

Instead of answering Dani's text, Ari immediately hit the button to start a video call, a rush of excitement racing through her. The first image she saw was of wet hair clinging to Dani's head and shoulders, causing Ari to momentarily lose herself in a vision of her stepping out of the shower with water dripping down her toned body. It had become difficult for Ari to stop her mind from wandering whenever she thought about Dani. Since their meeting in Miami, she'd ended several nights in her bed with tangled sheets and Dani's name dancing on her lips. If she were braver, she would insinuate something to Dani, but every time she tried to get herself to do it, she chickened out. This time was no exception.

"Hey, what have you been up to today?" Dani asked.

"Studying. I'm almost done with my finals. What about you? I'm sure it was more interesting than my day."

"Not really. Igor is killing me. I just got out of the shower after training all afternoon."

At the word "shower," Ari lost focus again, going back to the mental images of Dani standing naked under a cascade of water. She pictured every drop sliding down Dani's body, hugging every curve in a way Ari could only dream of one day doing. She was grateful they didn't move beyond making out in Miami, even if it had been almost impossible to stop some nights. But now a part of her regretted it—the part that was getting turned on just by looking at Dani through a phone screen.

Ari became painfully aware of the fact that she had spaced out and, in her rush to get back into the conversation, blurted out the first thing that came to her mind. "I need a shower too."

"We can shower together. I have an amazing bathroom, enough space for two," Dani said with a wink, never missing the chance to steer their conversation into risqué territory.

Ari swallowed. She knew Dani would drop the topic without even commenting on it if she asked her to, but this time Ari didn't want to stop. She was terrified, though not of Dani or of having sex

—well, virtual sex. She was worried about sucking at it. It had been a long time since she'd had sex with anybody, but she forced her fear down and trusted that Dani would be there to catch her.

With as much confidence as she could muster, even if she wasn't feeling it, she dropped her voice to sound sexier and answered Dani's challenge with one of her own. "Will it be hot?" She paused for a second and let the implication linger. "I don't like cold water."

Dani, unlike her, didn't pause before answering back. "I can make it as hot as you want it to be."

Ari bit her lip. "I'm sure you can."

Dani stared into her eyes without wavering. "Do you want me to tell you all the things I would do to you in the shower?"

Ari had thought she was going to melt under Dani's gaze before, but it was nothing compared to what those words did to her. Dani was giving her another chance to back out, to stop, but it only made Ari want her even more.

Ari wanted to not only say yes but make it clear how much she craved Dani, no matter how nervous she felt. "Yes, please tell me. I haven't been able to stop thinking about all the things I want you to do to me since we said goodbye in Miami."

"Um . . . you will have to tell me about those someday."

"I will," Ari breathed out. "But it's your turn now. I believe we were about to go into the shower."

Dani smiled. "Yes, we were."

Ari's heart raced inside her chest from the way Dani was looking at her, with eyes full of hunger and passion.

"I imagine that we're coming back from a nice day at the beach here in Mallorca. There are few clothes for us to take off because we spent all day in our swimsuits—which is a shame, because I would love to take off every piece of clothing you are wearing. Today you will have to do it for me, though. Can you do that, Ari? Take off your clothes for me?"

Ari didn't even have the impulse to panic. Dani's sultry tone was like a spell she couldn't break. She looked down at herself and lamented the fact that she wasn't wearing something sexier; she was in her usual home outfit of an oversized T-shirt and shorts.

When she touched the waistband of her shorts, her stomach tied into knots, but she kept going. She would've loved to take them off in a graceful and sensual way, but it didn't happen. Standing up would've been the best choice, but in her rush, that thought didn't occur to her. Instead, she opted for lifting her hips from the mattress to bring the shorts down to her thighs in what was supposed to be a quick and effortless motion. But Ari lost her balance and fell on the bed with her legs up. It wasn't the plan, but she forced her embarrassment down and went with it.

She finally pulled the shorts off in an awkward manner, throwing them into a corner of the room before sitting back up. Dani was regarding her with attention, following every movement with her eyes, unfazed by Ari's lack of coordination. Once she was back to her initial position, Ari lifted her shirt over her head in one swift motion and tossed it next to the discarded shorts.

When she looked at Dani again, she felt not exposed but desired. The raw passion in Dani's eyes left no doubt that if there wasn't an ocean between them, Dani would be on top of her in an instant.

"You look amazing. Better than all my dreams about you," Dani said, and Ari believed her.

She remained silent, lost in the way Dani was eyeing her, a shy smile the only response she gave.

"Once I have you naked in front of me, I don't think I will be able to stop myself from kissing you, tasting you. But I would try, because I want to savor every moment with you. I would let you step into the shower first, and I'd take a minute to admire the water running down your perfect back and legs before getting inside with you. The moment I do, I would press my body against yours." Dani's voice became sultrier. "Can you imagine how my breasts would feel against your back, with my hand resting on your hip and my lips kissing your neck?"

The way Dani looked into Ari's eyes while talking was enough to drive Ari to the edge. Her own breath came out loud and ragged, but she didn't care. She wanted Dani to know how much she affected her. In a spur of bravery, she decided to tease Dani the same way Dani had teased her so many times before. "I didn't take you as the soft and slow type."

Dani laughed. "Now I really need you to tell me what those fantasies of yours were about."

Ari bit her lip before answering. "Maybe next time. I want to know what else you have planned."

"Well, I'm full of surprises. I can do fast and hard, soft, rough, whatever you want. You only have to ask. But today . . . today I want to make you squirm with anticipation. The longer you wait, the more you want it, the better it is."

She couldn't argue with Dani's logic. She'd been on fire for minutes now, and the more Dani dragged the fantasy out, the hotter Ari got. "Is that so?"

"Yeah, and you know what I would love? I would love to hear you beg."

Ari let out a mix between a moan and a "fuck." The idea of Dani asking her to beg for more, teasing her until she was on the verge of coming and had to receive permission for release was almost more than she could handle. So far, she had been clutching her sheets, trying to keep her arousal under control, but it was becoming too much. Her body was moving, rocking against the bed for some friction, too turned on to care about appearances.

"You look so sexy right now. Would you touch yourself for me?"

Ari didn't know what it was about Dani's voice that made everything better, but hearing Dani tell her to touch herself made her lose the little control she had left. She assumed Dani expected her to reach down and put her hand down her panties, but that wasn't what Ari wanted.

Instead, she reached for one of her pillows, positioned it between her legs, and started riding it. The friction of the pillow against her thin underwear was enough to send a rush of pleasure through her body. She knew it would be enough to send her over the edge eventually, but it gave her time to enjoy the process. With Dani's voice whispering in her ear, she was in no rush.

She'd almost lost herself in the sensation when a soft moan from Dani brought her back. Feeling bold, she spoke between ragged breaths. "Are you going to touch yourself too?"

"Do you want me to? I will if it makes you feel more comfortable, but today it's about you. I don't want to miss a single one of your movements or expressions. I want them ingrained in my brain so I can remember them every day until I see you again."

A part of Ari wanted to hear Dani come undone for her too, but she was also eager to give Dani exactly what she wanted. Besides, she was already too lost in her own pleasure, in the longing and want that had been building inside her. She would put on a show for Dani this time, and there would be time for that favor to be returned later.

It was hard to focus on talking, but Ari made an effort because she wanted Dani to hear what she was doing to her. "You . . . You can watch this time, but I need you to tell me more."

Ari saw Dani smile before her eyes closed to focus on the sensations rippling through her.

"I have you pressed against the cold shower glass with your hands raised above your head and restrained by my left hand, while my right hand travels down your body."

Ari's panting and Dani's voice were the only sounds reverberating around the room. The pace of her thrusts against the pillow increased with every word.

"I bite your shoulder and suck your neck while my hand presses down against your center. I start with just one finger, and it's enough to make you squirm and say my name."

Mirroring the scene described by Dani, Ari let out a moan.

"You are so wet as my finger slides in and out of you, and I turn you around to have better access. I add another finger and start slow, dragging out every second. My fingers go in and out of you, but I pick up the pace when you ask me for more between your moans and screams."

The way Ari's body reacted to Dani's words felt like a trance, a hypnotic act. As soon as she mentioned going faster, Ari couldn't stop herself from increasing the rhythm of her rubbing.

"You grab my back and shoulders with your hands. It hurts, but I don't care. I know it's because it feels so good for you, so it only makes me want to fuck you harder."

The image Dani was describing translated with vivid detail to Ari's mind. Lost in her arousal, she had long ago stopped caring about how she looked, with her eyes closed, her mouth parted, and the moans increasing in volume and frequency. She knew Dani was still talking, but it became harder to focus on her voice. Soon, she was screaming Dani's name.

Ari wasn't sure how long it took for her senses to return to her. When she focused again on the world around her and opened her eyes, she found Dani looking back at her with a smile.

"That was so hot," Dani said.

Ari let out a soft chuckle. "Yes, it was."

To her surprise, the virtual encounter didn't satiate her desire for Dani. Quite the opposite, making it grow stronger.

◈

First tennis and now soccer. Apparently getting into one sport had opened the floodgates of athletic interest for Ari—or at least had made her usual excuses to get out of Super Bowl watch parties and school games useless, even if she still didn't care about sports.

"Aren't you happy I forced you to leave your apartment and come to the game with us?" Tom asked.

"Not really. Watching a soccer match is not my idea of fun."

"It won't kill you to show some school spirit. Besides, we are having a picnic afterward to celebrate the end of classes, and you can't miss it."

"It was really the picnic that made me come. I'm always down for food," Ari said. "Do we even have a chance to win?"

"It's only a friendly exhibition game, so it doesn't matter. But their top scorer, Camila Sanchez, is a beast of a player, so our chance of winning is about . . . none. That won't stop me from partying later. If we win, then to celebrate. If we lose, then to commiserate."

Ari laughed despite herself. The beautiful, sunny day marked the start of her summer break, and even if she never admitted it to Tom, it was fun to be out with her classmates doing something different. She didn't care if they won or lost, but having the people around her brimming with excitement was contagious, and she found herself on the edge of her seat more than once.

When the first goal was scored, she jumped up and cheered, only for Tom to yank her down immediately. “That wasn’t our team,” he whispered.

She had no time to feel embarrassed because the beep of her phone pulled her attention away from the game and anything else happening around her.

**I’m taking a shower right now and can’t stop thinking about you.**

Ari bit her lip and glanced around before starting to type an answer. Her response was more risqué than usual, but she’d become more comfortable sharing texts like that with Dani ever since they saw each other in person—and even more after their latest FaceTime. It was impossible to not feel confident and wanted when Dani reminded her every day how much she liked Ari.

**It’s not fair to tell me that when we can’t do anything about it.**

**Who says we can’t?**

Ari could almost see Dani’s mischievous grin in her mind as she read the text, and a smile was mirrored on her own face.

**I’m out with some friends (against my will, I must say, and now I regret it even more). I don’t**

**think they would be down for a show right in the middle of campus.**

Ari felt Tom looking over her shoulder, mostly because he didn't care to be subtle about it.

"Those Flirting 101 online classes are paying off. Look at you, one step away from sexting," he said.

Ari rolled her eyes at him. "I'm sure you're sad your assistance is no longer necessary."

"Not really, I'm happy to see the student surpassing the teacher. Not that you have surpassed me, but I'm glad that you are no longer a disaster." He looked away for a second to focus on the soccer match because this time it was actually their team almost scoring. "It's a relief to know you will be able to handle yourself. Since you'll be traveling alone to Paris to see Dani while I enjoy my bachelor life in New York, I won't be around to rescue you."

"I talked to Dani on my own for like six months before you even knew she existed in my life, so you don't get to take all the credit just because you helped me with one message."

"Yes I can and yes I will," he said with an exaggerated motion of his head. "I've already worked that tidbit of information into my future best man speech."

Ari snickered at him as another beep alerted her to a new message.

**Have fun with your friends today. You can have all of me when we see each other next week ;)**

# Chapter Fourteen

*Ari should land in Paris soon.* That was the only thing on Dani's mind all morning. For the first time in her career, during the week before a Grand Slam, she wasn't worried about training or what rivals she would be facing. The one thing occupying her thoughts was how to enjoy Paris with Ari.

With Arantxa's help, Dani had arranged her schedule to have as much free time as possible, but there were things she couldn't get away from. The fact that she was training instead of waiting at the airport for Ari was one example of it.

Instead of focusing on hydrating herself, she used the brief break to check her phone. No news from Ari, but a quick online search confirmed that her flight had landed half an hour before.

She was about to put away the phone when Igor's stern voice reached her ears. "You should withdraw from the tournament and go where you want to be. No point staying in it with that attitude."

Dani gritted her teeth, not appreciating his tone or implications. He was strict, that wasn't new, but she wasn't going to allow him to meddle in her personal life. "Looking at my phone for a minute is not going to prevent me from winning the tournament."

"I'm not talking about looking at your phone, and you know it," he said, walking closer to her.

"When we started working together, we made a promise. You give me your all, and I give you my all." His eyes softened. "I've been keeping my part of the deal, but lately it seems like tennis is the last thing on your mind. Training is useless if you don't have the motivation."

Dani looked away for a second. "Just because I'm not breathing tennis every second of the day doesn't mean I'm not motivated. I am. I still want this more than anything, but I can't sacrifice my personal life forever. I'm not a machine."

"I'm not saying don't have a personal life. I'm saying that when you are on the court, I need all of you focused, not daydreaming away."

Dani clenched her jaw to stop the biting remark she had on the tip of her tongue from coming out. Despite her anger, part of her knew he was right. There would be time for her to enjoy Ari's company, but while she was playing tennis, all her energy needed to go to it.

"That's fair. I'll give you my full attention now."

"No," he said while packing up his gear. "Go rest or do whatever it is you want to be doing right now, but tomorrow we start fresh. There are only two days left before the tournament starts, and I need a hundred percent commitment from you."

"You got yourself a deal. Tomorrow is tennis only, I promise."

She picked up her gear and rushed to the locker room to shower and change. She was grateful for the extra time with Ari, but she would fulfill her promise to him. As exciting as having Ari in her life was, as much happiness as it brought her, she couldn't let its novelty consume her. She needed to find a balance, for both of their sakes.

◈

Dani returned to the hotel right on time to greet Ari as she arrived. She engulfed her in a hug that wasn't enough to show how much she'd missed her but would have to do in a public setting. In the middle of the lobby with dozens of players and their teams walking around them, she had to restrain herself. When they were in private, Dani could kiss her for as long as she wanted.

Ari returned the hug with equal fervor, nestling into her chest in a way that made Dani wish she didn't have to let her go. When she stepped away, ready to tell Ari all about her plans for their first day in Paris, she noticed the heavy bags under Ari's eyes and the way she could barely keep them open.

She leaned closer again to kiss her head and whisper into her hair. "You should have let me pay for that first-class ticket."

"I'll be fine after a shower and a nap. There's no need to waste money," Ari answered with a yawn.

"At least I get to tuck you in." Dani took her hand.

As they walked to their rooms, the thought of what would happen once they were alone occupied Dani's mind. They'd been by themselves in a hotel room before, but things had changed since then. Their relationship had evolved, and they'd broken a barrier with their virtual sex.

It didn't mean they had to jump into doing something as soon as they were alone, but the question of how their relationship would progress now that they were sharing the same physical space hung in the air. The soft blush adorning Ari's cheeks and the way she gripped Dani's hand harder as they got closer to the room told her that she wasn't the only one with those thoughts in her head.

When they got to the room, Ari busied herself putting her luggage away while Dani watched her. The way Ari fidgeted around, moving all over the room and finding things to do to avoid her gaze at any cost, reminded Dani of their first meeting. She let out a low chuckle at the realization, and after one last sip of water she walked with purpose toward Ari.

She put her hands on Ari's waist and turned her around, pressing their bodies together. "Can I get a hello kiss?"

As soon as Ari nodded, Dani wasted no time bringing their lips together.

"I'm so happy to have you here." She rested her forehead against Ari's. "You look tired. I'll leave you alone so you can clean up and rest." She gave her one last peck on the lips before walking to the door.

"Can you stay?" Ari said as Dani reached for the handle. "I've never slept better than when I'm with you."

"I'll stay, then."

Dani retraced her steps and kissed Ari again. When they broke apart, Ari glanced down and pressed her lips together as if she wanted to say something else but didn't dare. Dani remained silent, occupying her time by softly tracing the contours of Ari's face as she waited. Ari grabbed her hand and looked up into her eyes. Dani smiled but said nothing, hoping that was encouragement enough.

"I wouldn't mind if you joined me in the shower," Ari said. "Not for sex," she added in a rush. "I don't have the energy for that right now. But I want to make the most of our time together."

Dani knew how hard it was for her to be direct, and the last thing she wanted was to embarrass her after a moment of vulnerability. "Sounds like a great plan. I'll follow your lead."

Ari walked toward the shower, and Dani followed one step behind. She watched every movement silently, enjoying the way Ari discarded her clothes shyly and how she jumped away when a spray of cold water hit her face. Dani stood by while Ari tried to find the perfect water temperature—burning hot if the steam surrounding them was anything to go by—and admired the view of how Ari's body looked under the water, the steady stream embracing her from head to toe.

It wasn't until questioning eyes glanced her way that Dani moved to take her own clothes off. "I was enjoying the view, but I'm joining you now." She deliberately explained everything she was about to do to give Ari the chance to stop.

Dani stepped into the shower. For the first time, they saw each other fully exposed with no barriers, virtual or physical, between them. After months of miles being in the way, the distance separating them had become next to nothing, but it still felt too big for Dani. She moved closer, as close as she dared without merging their bodies together.

To her surprise, Ari didn't seem embarrassed as usual. She was ravaging Dani's body with her eyes, looking her up and down without shame. Dani savored the moment too, tracing with her fingers the path marked by the drops of water sliding down Ari's curves. She wanted to run her tongue over each of them, but she didn't think she could stop if she did. Instead, she planted a short, chaste kiss on Ari's exposed shoulder before stepping forward to join her under the cascade of water.

Their lips eventually found each other. Their kisses, some more passionate than others, accompanied their shower, but they always stepped back when it felt like things could get out of hand. Soft fingers ran over exposed skin, bodies pressed close together while they washed off, but they never let it go beyond that.

After the shower, they helped each other dry off and, without a word, got into bed together. Even in their state of nakedness, it didn't faze Dani when Ari nestled herself between her arms.

Dani planted a kiss on Ari's temple as her eyes fought to remain open. "Go to sleep, beautiful. I will be here when you wake up."

The steady rise and fall of Ari's chest lulled Dani to sleep too, her eyelids becoming heavy and harder to keep open. With her last vestiges of consciousness, she gave Ari another kiss before letting her own eyes close.

◆

Dani woke up to her arm tingling after supporting Ari's weight for hours. She opened and closed her hand, trying to help the blood flow to her fingers again. Carefully, she tried to drag her arm out, but with every movement she made, Ari sought her comfort by snuggling closer and making it impossible for her to move. Not that Dani had any desire to escape. She was happy to stay here for as long as possible, even as the tingling in her arm became more painful.

She took advantage of the time alone to bask in Ari's presence. She stared at her chest, admiring how it rose with each breath, how the blanket covering their bodies rested over Ari's hip bone, how the bright white of the cover made Ari's brown skin look even more beautiful. There were so many details Dani wanted to lose herself in—the plump lips slightly parted while Ari slept, the brown curly hair falling over her eyes, framing her face.

She stared until Ari showed signs of consciousness. Dani smiled at the way she stirred and turned around before cuddling close again. When Ari's eyes finally opened, Dani was incapable of waiting one more second to kiss her. It was a slow, languid kiss that left her craving more.

"What time is it?" Ari said in a low, raspy tone as she stretched the sleep away. Dani found every movement of hers sensual and tempting.

"I have no clue, and I don't care. I'm happy never leaving this bed again."

It was Ari's turn to lean over and claim her lips. "I wouldn't mind staying in bed, but I think I remember you promising something about dinner?"

The adorable way Ari was looking at her was not enough to stop Dani from teasing. "Oh, I see.

Food is more important than me."

Ari gave her another soft peck. "It's more important when I've had nothing to eat but airplane food for like a day now."

With great effort, Dani rolled away to check the time on her phone. In the back of her mind, she was aware of how comfortable they were with each other, even while naked. It had taken months, even years, for Dani to build that level of comfort with other people in the past, but with Ari it was already there.

"It's only five," she said. "I made a reservation for dinner at eight, but we can go out and have a snack so you don't starve."

"Yes, please."

Despite their words, they didn't leave the bed. They got lost in each other's eyes until, without realizing, they both closed the distance separating their lips. The movements were instinctive, unplanned.

Dani took the lead, grabbing Ari's lips between her own and biting them before going in for a deeper kiss. She let her tongue explore Ari's mouth without restraint, alternating between pushing it deeper and slowing down to savor the moment. The sucking and biting sharpened her senses.

The raspy breaths coming out of Ari's lips and the way she gripped Dani's shoulders, trying to bring their bodies closer together, told her that Ari was as ready as she was to make their calls and texts a reality.

She rolled over to hover on top of Ari, her hands planted next to her head, knees digging into the mattress next to Ari's thighs. When their eyes met, Dani froze, lost in the pools of passion looking back at her. With only inches between their lips, it was impossible to not feel the warm, panting breaths coming from Ari that mixed with her own.

She lowered herself, claiming Ari's lips again only for a few seconds before moving to Ari's jaw, cheekbones, and ears. The loud moan that Ari let out when Dani's tongue licked her ear made Dani pay extra attention to that part of her body.

"I wasn't expecting my ears to be that sensitive," Ari said between gasps.

"Do you want me to stop?" Dani asked. An enthusiastic head movement let her know she was welcome to continue her ministrations.

"Don't you dare," Ari replied.

Dani was happy to take her time making Ari squirm under her every time she touched her ear with her tongue, before moving to her neck. There, she let her teeth press into the soft skin, not biting but running down the length of Ari's neck with her tongue. The reaction from Ari was not as intense as when Dani focused on her ear, but still loud enough to let her know it was welcome too.

Dani continued to travel down, letting herself rest more of her weight on top. She ran her tongue from Ari's shoulder blades to her chest, taking her time to tease each nipple with the tip of her tongue. Ari's moans and movements turned more frenetic, but Dani didn't let that stop her from her mission.

"I want to taste every inch of your body," she whispered.

"Please," Ari hummed.

Dani kept going, leaving a trail of small kisses down Ari's stomach and sides before moving farther down. But even then, she didn't go straight to her center. She moved around it and planted kisses on exposed thighs, some long and slow followed by deeper and harder ones, getting close, closer, but never there. As she inched nearer, she allowed herself to breathe in the intoxicating smell of arousal and sweat, before looking up at Ari's pleading eyes.

There was only one thing Dani desired more than finally tasting Ari, and that was to hear her ask for it. "Tell me what you want."

"I want you," Ari begged. "Please, Dani."

She had barely finished talking when Dani let her tongue stroke along the length of Ari's center, the moan Ari let out the only reward she needed. She held Ari's hips down in an attempt to control her desperate movements because Dani didn't want to lose the perfect spot she'd found with her tongue.

Dani held Ari's body in place as her moans intensified, and continued to hold her even after she'd screamed her name and went limp under her. Dani didn't want to stop because Ari's taste was already an addiction, but a soft hand on top of her head reminded her that she needed to move away, at least for a while. The lazy smile on Ari's face and the glint in her eyes spurred Dani to retrace her steps, covering Ari's body with kisses on her way up to find her lips.

They remained like that for a long minute, foreheads pressed together and breaths mixing, until Dani couldn't help herself any longer and planted small kisses all over Ari's face.

"That was amazing," Ari whispered. "But I'm even hungrier now."

Dani laughed and gave her one last deep kiss before getting out of the bed. "Let's get you some food. I don't think I want to find out how you get when you're hangry."

◈

Ari would never get tired of the way Dani defied her expectations every single time. She'd done it so often that Ari had started to believe that Dani could never let her down. She would have never dared to suggest going out to eat instead of returning the favor after sex if it wasn't for Dani always showing that she would never be judgmental or dismissive.

It wasn't like Ari wasn't dying to give Dani as much pleasure as she had given her . . . but she was also really hungry. Maybe a small part of her was also panicking at the prospect, and some extra time to prepare herself wouldn't hurt. Ironically, Dani's reaction and willingness to stop as soon as she asked only served to encourage Ari even more to take that next step in their relationship.

The first thing Ari noticed once they stepped outside the hotel was the Arc de Triomphe visible in the distance. It didn't appear to be farther than a few blocks away, and as soon as Ari saw it, her inner tourist took over. She dragged Dani in that direction, forgetting about her hunger.

When they got close enough to it, Dani took her phone out and insisted they take a selfie with it as a background. They took one with both of them smiling and then, feeling bold, Ari stood on her tiptoes to kiss Dani's cheek as she took another picture. The wide smile that took over Dani's face warmed Ari's heart and made her want to show Dani how much she meant to her more often.

"It's weird. I visit Paris and other cities every single year for at least a week at a time, but I rarely explore them," Dani said while putting her phone back in her pocket. "I'm always focused on tennis, but it's nice to enjoy it like a tourist for a change." She reached for Ari's hand.

Ari gasped and placed her hand to her chest. "Are you telling me you don't have a cliché picture at the Eiffel Tower?"

"I don't," Dani answered with a grin. "I always stay in the same hotel. Every year I see the Arc from my window but rarely walk to it, and I've only been to the Eiffel Tower once. Never been to the Louvre either. We should do that too."

Ari bumped her shoulder softly. "You can count on it. I didn't travel this far just to sleep with you." At Dani's raised eyebrow, Ari's newfound confidence faltered, and she rushed to elaborate. "Maybe that was a factor . . . but it's not the only thing I plan on doing."

Dani laughed, moving to steal a peck from Ari. "Of course. We have at least two weeks here, so there's plenty of time for us to explore . . . and do other stuff too." She winked.

Ari ignored the way heat rushed to her face. "At least two weeks? Someone is confident."

"Being confident is part of being successful. I'm the best player in the world, and clay is my favorite surface. There's no reason for me to not make it to the final."

"It's adorable how you talk to me as if I understand tennis when I haven't been able to grasp the scoring system after all this time. But I trust you and look forward to those two weeks of exploring and watching you win."

"So do I. My two favorite things, winning and you."

# Chapter Fifteen

Standing at the edge of Court Philippe Chatrier, ready to step on the red clay for her first-round match at Roland-Garros, Dani glanced at her player box and looked for only one face among the crowd. She and Ari had spent every possible minute together the days before, and whenever Dani wasn't training, they were exploring the city hand in hand. As happy as it made her to have Ari with her, she had a goal she couldn't forget: to win Roland-Garros.

As she walked to the net to greet her rival, Dani met Ari's eyes across the court. She gave her a small smile before turning all her attention to the upcoming match. The bandage on her right thigh served as a painful reminder that she wasn't in top shape. The injury was the result of a bad movement in training the day before, but she wasn't worried about it affecting her play. She had won entire tournaments before with one functioning leg—one small tear on her thigh was nothing.

She started the first game with an ace, to make a statement, but everything was downhill from there. After a few games, the increasing pain in her leg started hindering her movement.

At 2–2, her rival hit a crosscourt backhand that made her stretch to prevent a winner on her part. Immediately after she returned the ball, a flash of pain shot through Dani's leg. She managed to ignore it as she raced to the other end of the court, trying to save the point again after her opponent's powerful forehand. That time she failed to make it, and the same was true in the next point, where she barely moved to catch a powerful return. Then, a drop-shot volley after a long rally made her lose her serve.

The injury was limiting her speed and ability to react to even easy balls, and the score reflected her struggles. Soon she was down 2–5 and on the edge of falling behind a set. Dani stood behind the baseline, waiting for her opponent to close out the first set with her serve. The ball landed on her backhand side, and she tried to put all her weight on her left leg to reach it, but she was too slow. An ace, and the set went to her opponent.

She fought the urge to slam her racket against the clay, stopping herself when her arm was mid-movement. Instead, she walked to her seat and asked the chair umpire to call the trainer. She hated doing that, especially after losing the first set. Some people would accuse her of faking the injury to cover her ass in case she lost, but she also knew there would be no way for her to win this match if she didn't get some help from the trainer. He wouldn't cure her, but if he lessened the pain at least a little, she would be able to play closer to her usual standard.

While the trainer massaged her leg and rubbed anesthetic cream on it, Dani sneaked a glance to her player box. Igor had taken off the cap that always covered his head and was now rubbing his hand up and down his bright, uncovered scalp. Arantxa was harder to read, face half covered by the sunglasses she insisted on wearing, but the constant tap of her fingers against the rail in front of her gave her away.

Their worry was getting to Dani, so she shifted her gaze to Ari, where it was a different story. A bright smile lit up her face, no sign of worry evident. Dani wasn't sure if it was only because Ari's knowledge of tennis prevented her from realizing how dire the situation was or if she simply had that much faith in her.

Being one set down with an injured leg and, worst of all, a rival who was playing some of her best tennis didn't bode well for her—even Dani was forced to recognize that fact. But Ari's smile almost made her believe everything would be okay. She would find a way to win. Despite the pain still throbbing in her leg, she smiled back at Ari, who beamed in response.

The trainer finished wrapping Dani's leg in medical tape. She stood up and jumped in place a few times to test it, and though it still hurt, she could at least move. She glanced at Ari once more, which filled her with energy right before she ran to her side of the net.

The downside of getting treatment was that it gave her opponent additional ammunition against her. Now that everyone knew her mobility was hindered, the drop shots and short-angled shots became her opponent's main weapon. Despite her best effort, Dani lost most of those points.

Another short ball landed on her side of the court, and when she pushed down on her leg to run, pain shot through her leg and made her lose valuable seconds. Once again, she reached the net as the ball bounced for a second time.

"Game: Stephens. Stephens leads 6–2, 4–0," the umpire said.

Dani walked slowly back to the end of the court with her jaw clenched. *If I'm going down, I'll go down swinging.* A ball boy threw a ball in her direction. She caught it with her left hand and bounced it on the court four times. The injury wasn't affecting her serve as much as the rest of her game, so she went for a big serve, as fast and hard as she could hit it to the corner of the service box. Her opponent was unable to return it, so Dani used the same tactic again and again, not caring if it was the first or second serve.

"Game: Martínez. Stephens leads 6–2, 4–1."

The next game, Dani implemented the same strategy. She couldn't run, and the best way to not have to run was to win—or lose—the point as fast as possible. The number of points she won had to outweigh the ones she lost. As her rival prepared to serve, Dani stepped slightly inside the court, anticipating the side where the ball was going to land. She moved to return it with her best shot, her forehand. She hit the ball hard and fast to the center of the court, right at the feet of Stephens, who had no time to react and control the ball. The next serve went to her backhand, and she sent it to the corner with a parallel return.

"Game: Martínez. Stephens leads 6–2, 4–2."

Dani let a small smirk break free when Stephens mouthed exasperated words toward her box. She was getting in her opponent's head, making her doubt herself and think that Dani could close the match against her despite her significant lead. That was exactly what Dani wanted. A sliver of doubt could spiral into unforced errors that would help her turn the match around. As she bounced the ball four times before serving, she caught her rival moving two steps back, prepared for another one of her fast serves. Dani decided to mix it up, alternating her first serves between power and placement. More than once, she caught the other player out of position.

"Game: Martínez. Stephens leads 6–2, 4–3."

*Come on, one more break*, she told herself while hitting her injured leg softly with her fist. She knew from experience that if she managed to break and level the match, her opponent would beat herself up over losing the advantage, and there was a big chance she would become tense at the possibility of all her effort landing her back at square one. When the first serve bounced far past the service line, Dani decided to change her strategy. Instead of going all out, she would put the ball back in play and test if her rival would give her some free points with mistakes from her nerves. Indeed, she did.

"Game: Martínez. Stephens leads 6–2, 4–4."

Dani fist-pumped while Stephens threw her racket against the wall. Dani knew she still wasn't out of trouble, and the pain in her thigh was coming back stronger than before, but she still had a chance and wasn't going away without a fight.

The next two games would be crucial. If she won them and took the set, she would metaphorically destroy her inexperienced rival. Dani wasn't counting on it, but it was highly likely that her opponent wouldn't be able to recover. That's what she was hoping for deep down, even if she knew that focusing on the next point, not getting ahead of herself, was the best strategy.

She intended to start the game with another thundering serve, but as she jumped to hit the ball, a pull in her thigh stopped her momentum, making the ball fly from her racket slower than planned. Stephens returned it with a crosscourt backhand that bounced out of Dani's reach.

Dani cursed silently. Her next serve was a wide slice shot she hoped would get Stephens in a bad position in the return, but what she got was a lightning-fast forehand she was unable to control. It seemed like Stephens was taking a page out of Dani's strategy book and fighting fire with fire. Her nerves seemed to be settled and the silly mistakes had stopped, making things harder for Dani. After a long, hard-fought game, Dani lost her serve.

"Game: Stephens. Stephens leads 6–2, 5–4."

The first point of the game was a drop shot that tested Dani's speed and determination to turn the match around. She ran from behind the baseline to almost one inch away from the net with everything she had. She made it right before the ball bounced for a second time and used a subtle touch of her racket to pass it to the other side of the net and win the point.

As she walked back to the baseline, a sudden, intense jolt made her stop walking. She'd played long enough to recognize a muscle tear, and she knew without a doubt that, two points away from losing, she had aggravated her injury. She gripped her racket harder and did her best to not limp as she walked.

In the next point, Dani saw clearly how the serve was aimed at her backhand, but when she tried to move to that side, her leg failed again and she could only watch as the ball sailed past her. The same happened again in the following and final point.

Daniela Martínez, number one player in the world and recent champion of the Australian Open, had lost in the first round.

The umpire's voice rang out clear as day as Dani walked to the net. "Game, set, match: Stephens."

This was not the first time she'd had a disappointing result. Losing was a fundamental part of tennis, and it was impossible to play almost every single day of the year and not lose. But it had been a while since she had such a terrible loss at a Grand Slam. The unexpectedness of it made it hit even harder. While preparing to leave the court, Dani looked at her box again. Igor wore a scowl, Arantxa's expression was unreadable, and Ari still smiled at her. This time, though, there was no joy in Ari's eyes. Only worry.

◈

After losing in the first round of one of the most important tennis tournaments in the world, the only thing Dani wanted was to get out of the tournament grounds. She canceled her mandatory press conference, not caring that she would have to pay a fine for missing it, and left for the hotel immediately.

In her room, the physical trainer assessed the extent of her injury while Igor sat across from them, watching the procedure but avoiding Dani's eyes. Arantxa paced behind him, typing nonstop on her phone. Ari sat on the other side of the room, as far from them as possible. She looked Dani's way often with a mix of concern and love on her face, but no matter how much Dani tried, she couldn't muster a smile in that moment, not even for Ari. Even when Ari let the corners of her mouth rise in a slight smile, Dani quickly looked away.

Igor said nothing to her, which was worse than having him yell. Dani knew he was disappointed. He couldn't blame her for being hurt, but she'd won matches while injured before. She could have done more; she *should* have done more.

Their conversation from a few days before kept circling in her mind as loud and clear as if he were speaking right then. The cold gel and the metal running up and down her leg were the only distractions from her self-recrimination.

"We'll need an MRI to confirm but I suspect there's a muscle tear on your thigh, but it's nothing some rest won't solve," the trainer told them.

Dani opened her mouth to speak, but Igor beat her to it. "How long?"

"Two weeks at least, maybe three. If she rests and lets it heal, it shouldn't take more than three weeks. Should be fine by Wimbledon if that's what you're asking."

Wimbledon, the most important, most prestigious tennis tournament in the world. It hadn't crossed her mind until then, but of course that was what her coach would be worried about.

"We'll focus on rehab the next two weeks," Igor told her, "with some work in the gym for upper body conditioning. We will reassess in two weeks.

If it's fully healed, we will have a week to train on grass."

Usually, Dani hated when Igor told her what they would do, but the plan made sense and she felt guilty enough about the Roland-Garros disaster to agree without a fight.

"Sounds good," she replied. "Let's head back to Mallorca for the recovery and then travel to London one week before the tournament."

Just as his words left no room for discussion, neither did hers.

◈

Dani looked out the small plane window to see the stunning blue water and beaches of Mallorca beneath them. Knowing she was close to her home, to the place where she could forget about the outside world, lifted a weight off her shoulders.

She had been trying to pretend she was fine. Pretend that losing early at Roland-Garros didn't hit her as hard as it did. It was a lie, of course. She was pissed at herself. Dani suspected that everyone around realized how upset she was, and it was only out of politeness, fear, or pity that they didn't mention it. Except Arantxa, of course, who was happy to call her out on her foul mood.

"Lighten up, would you? There's a beautiful island waiting for you, and a stunning woman right here waiting for you to get over yourself too," Arantxa said as if on cue.

Dani didn't bother replying. She knew her manager wasn't looking for a conversation and only wanted to snap her out of the funk she was in. This was her own way of caring. Dani appreciated it; it was exactly what she needed. Anyone trying to walk on eggshells around her would end up infuriating her even more.

She followed Arantxa's advice and looked at Ari sitting in front of her, doing her best to pretend everything was normal. As if the fact that Dani had made them all get on a private flight to Mallorca the day she lost was at all normal. Dani appreciated Ari's understanding, and she committed to making sure they had an amazing time here.

"I'm sorry about ruining Paris, but you are going to love it here," Dani said. "I will show you every corner."

"I'm here to be with you. Paris or Mallorca, it doesn't matter," Ari answered with a sincere smile.

Dani couldn't help but return it, probably for the first time since her loss. She reached for Ari's hand, and the repetitive motion of rubbing her thumb up and down Ari's exposed palm calmed her.

"Now that I know you won't chew me out if I speak, there's something I need to talk to you about," Arantxa interjected, ruining Dani's mood again.

She gave Arantxa what she thought was her most intimidating look, but her manager ignored it.

"Rumors are getting harder to contain. There are several articles today about how a trusted source told journalists that your loss had more to do with a distracting love life than an injury."

Dani scoffed and let go of Ari's hand. "Are you kidding me?"

Arantxa nodded in response.

"Did they give any more details?"

"No. They don't have much—yet. But I had to intervene to buy some pictures of you two out and about in Paris before they made it to the media." She pointed at them both, as if they wouldn't know who she was referring to otherwise. "It's my job to anticipate these things, and I can see where this is going. Once we get to London, it will only get worse. You know how awful the English tabloids are."

Dani frowned. She was not ashamed of being a lesbian. Many people already knew about it, and she'd never attempted to hide it. However, coming out to the world had never been in her plans, and she also had to think about how it would affect Ari.

"This is bullshit. There are male players changing their model girlfriends every other month and I don't see anyone writing articles about how it distracts them." Dani vented, even though she knew exactly why that was. "What do you suggest I do?"

"For now? Nothing." Arantxa paused as if preparing herself to say something she knew Dani wouldn't like. "But eventually we'll need to choose a side. I can go all out to hide and deny it if that's what you want, or we can share it on our terms. It's your decision, but I want to warn you that I won't be able to contain the rumors forever if we are in this I-won't-hide-but-don't-want-people-to-know limbo."

Dani looked at Ari, then back at Arantxa. "Noted."

For the time being, Dani planned on enjoying herself. She didn't want to think about tennis or what the media was saying about her. She would worry about when and how to come out to the world later. For the next two weeks, she only wanted to focus on Ari and recovering from her injury.

# Chapter Sixteen

Ari woke up to Dani walking into the room with a tray stacked with food. Her stomach growled as soon as the smell of fresh baked goods filled her nostrils. She stuffed a piece of sweet bread into her mouth the minute Dani rested the tray on the bed.

When Dani opened the thick blinds covering the windows, Ari squeezed her eyes shut at the sudden brightness of the room. "Waking up this early should be a crime," she said with a groan, but she quickly forgot about her hatred of early mornings when her eyes focused on the view.

Visible through the wall-to-wall windows, an infinity pool overlooking the beach greeted her while Mallorca's blue sky completed the picture. She could hardly believe her life now, that she got to share part of her summer with a beautiful and amazing woman in one of the prettiest places she'd ever been.

"It's eleven in the morning. I already went to the gym with Igor, did physiotherapy, showered, and made you breakfast," Dani answered while leaning down to give Ari a peck.

Ari smiled into the kiss but then pouted when Dani's words fully registered in her half-asleep brain. "I can't believe you showered without me."

"I promise to wait for you next time," Dani said, kissing her again. "I'm sorry for ruining Paris."

Ari rushed to swallow a piece of food. “Don’t be silly. I had a great time in Paris while we were there, and I really don’t care where we are as long as I get to spend time with you.” She took another bite and looked down at the spiral-shaped pastry she was eating. “What are these, by the way? They are so good.”

“Ensaïmadas. They are a traditional dish from Mallorca,” Dani replied, leaning down to steal a bite from Ari. “I love them, and I maybe wanted to soften the blow of how awful yesterday was with some baked goods.”

“It wasn’t awful, but consider yourself forgiven.” Ari hadn’t finished the pastry in her hand yet, but she reached for another one anyway. “So good,” she said, mouth full.

Dani watched her with a small smile, and Ari quickly tried to control her eating in case that was the cause of the amusement on Dani’s face. But even as she put the food back on the tray, Dani’s expression didn’t change.

“I hate losing, but this time it stings a little less since it gives me more time with you. I already told Igor I’ll only be available for training or therapy in the mornings, so the rest of the time I’m all yours.”

Ari choked on the tea she had just taken a sip of. For once, Dani didn’t put an ounce of innuendo in her words, but they still sent Ari’s mind into overdrive. She was thankful when Dani ignored her mishap and kept talking.

“It’s still early. What do you say we enjoy a day out?”

Ari tried to think of a single reason why they shouldn’t go out and explore the city together but there was none, except for her own selfish desire to keep Dani all to herself.

As if reading her mind, Dani leaned down and whispered in her ear. "The pool, the house, the bedroom . . . All of it will be here when we get back."

Ari's skin broke out in goosebumps, but she forced herself to swallow before speaking, to try to hide the tremble she was sure would betray the thoughts swirling in her mind if she didn't control it. "I guess I should get to know the island since I'm here."

The two of them were soon packed into Dani's car, the wind blowing through the open windows. Ari closed her eyes, getting lost in the feeling of the breeze caressing her face, the smell of salt water, and the way Dani softly rubbed her thumb over her hand.

◈

Dani set a course for one of the best views in Mallorca, Cap de Formentor. Though it was on the other side of the island, an hour and a half away from her house in Porto Cristo, she knew the view would make the trip worth it.

The drive was easy and fast on the almost deserted highways, giving Dani time to glance at Ari every now and then as she drove. She was able to admire the soft smile adorning Ari's lips and the placid expression on her face. Ari looked so content, so at ease looking out the window and humming softly with the radio that Dani couldn't help but smile too. She basked in the realization that she'd never felt as happy as she did while sharing her city, her world, and her life with Ari.

When they arrived at her favorite lookout point, Dani parked and offered her hand to Ari as soon as they stepped out of the car. “Come on, it’s only a short walk to the best view of the island,” Dani said, pulling Ari eagerly toward the stone path that bordered the cliff.

They walked hand in hand up the stone steps at a leisurely pace because there was nowhere else they needed or wanted to be. They stopped every few steps to take pictures and drink in the scenery that became more breathtaking the higher they climbed. When they reached the small mirador that offered a 365-degree view, Ari’s mouth opened in awe. Dani had seen the deep-blue water nesting between the mountains at least a hundred times, which never lost its appeal, but it was impossible for her to look at it with the same joy and wonder reflected in Ari’s eyes at discovering something for the first time.

“I . . . Wow . . . You were right, this is amazing.”

“Now I don’t know if I should feel jealous that you think *that* view beats *this* view,” Dani said, gesturing toward her own figure. She expected Ari to blush, but she was pleasantly surprised when Ari’s eyes raked over her body.

“It’s a tough competition.”

Dani grinned. She loved how Ari was growing more confident around her, even if she could still see hints of shyness in the way Ari looked away as soon as she spoke.

“There’s so much more I want to show you. Let’s go,” Dani answered, excitement filling her voice.

She drove up the mountain to take Ari to the white lighthouse at the top, one of Mallorca’s most popular tourist spots. Despite the crowd, Dani knew how to maneuver around the people to find the best place to look out at the bay. They stood on the balcony and gazed at the beautiful view in front of them, nothing but water as far as the eye could see.

Ari leaned into Dani. "Huh, you really brought me to the edge of the world," she said jokingly.

Dani glanced down, savoring how beautiful Ari looked with the sunshine dancing on her face. "I'll take you wherever you want to go, as long as it makes you happy."

Three small but scary words fluttered on the tip of Dani's tongue as they embraced, with the Mediterranean sea as a backdrop. To stop them from coming out, she took Ari's lips between her own.

◈

After eating lunch in a small restaurant overlooking the beach, Dani drove them back home for a relaxing afternoon at the pool. Dani felt as if she were in paradise as she lay on a towel with her eyes closed, the afternoon sun hitting her face and Ari resting next to her. Her injury and Igor's nagging had become faraway memories incapable of disturbing her peace. She would have to deal with them at some point, but she was going to enjoy herself as much as possible first.

A burst of energy shot through her body when the chords of one of her favorite bachata songs started playing. She turned around, holding herself up with one arm to look at Ari, who seemed almost too serene to disturb. She poked her softly in the ribs to get her attention.

"Are you up for a dance?" Dani asked.

"I don't think I can get up. I'm so happy here." Ari half opened one eye to look back at Dani. "I also have no clue how to dance to that."

Dani nodded. This was the most relaxed she had been in months, maybe years. Closing her eyes and going back to bask under the sun sounded great, except now she couldn't shake the idea of dancing with Ari from her mind.

"I'll lead you," she said, standing up. "And I seem to remember you owe me a dance."

She offered her hand to Ari, who didn't appear as excited at the idea of dancing instead of sunbathing, but she grabbed Dani's hand anyway. The moment their fingers touched, Dani pulled Ari forward with all her strength until she flew into her arms. Ari gasped at the movement, and Dani wanted to assume it was because their closeness affected Ari as much as it did her.

"Okay, follow me," Dani instructed. "One, two, three, four. One, two, three, four." They moved in sync, as if they were always meant to move together. As Ari got more confident, Dani stopped counting. "I told you it was easy."

They stared into each other's eyes in silence, without losing the beat even once. Dani pressed her forehead against Ari's and tightened her grip around her waist. She wasn't sure if Ari still needed her to lead, but she kept her hand there anyway, helping to sway Ari's hips side to side with a subtle nudge here and there.

It was hard to not notice the heat rising with the closeness of their bodies, the feel of skin touching skin, the intermingling of legs, and the mixing of breaths. Fire radiated from every inch of Dani's skin and pooled in the lower part of her body, but she ignored it because she wanted to focus on the moment.

She wanted to marvel at their closeness and breathe in Ari's essence. She was in no rush to move beyond dancing, no matter how obvious it was in Ari's eyes that that's what she wanted too. She was happy letting their want for each other build up until the heat rose from their cores to engulf them. She knew that the more they waited, the bigger the anticipation, the more powerful the release. So, she kept dancing. Slowly, closer.

Dani was not sure how many songs they danced to, but as the sun started to set on the horizon, Ari melted into her arms. Dani's hand traveled north from Ari's waist to caress eager lips, before finally allowing their mouths to merge into one.

◈

All of Ari's thoughts left her mind the instant Dani's lips touched hers. She'd never cared about dancing, but maybe she'd been missing out, because she'd never felt as turned on as she did in that moment. The closeness and the unspoken promise from Dani's movements were enough to affect Ari in ways nobody had before.

"Why are you smiling?" Dani asked as she pulled away from Ari after the kiss.

Ari didn't bother to answer—she was possessed by an urgent need to have Dani closer. She pulled Dani's head down and kissed her with as much passion as she could. “I’m smiling because I just realized I finally have you all to myself.”

Dani smirked. “And why do you want me all to yourself?”

Ari felt like this was an intentional challenge. Usually, Dani was the one who took charge and Ari was happy to let her. Instead of being annoyed at the way Dani pretended she didn’t understand what Ari was trying to do, she took it as her chance to show Dani how much she wanted her.

She moved her lips to Dani’s neck, slowly sucking and licking her soft skin. “I think you know.”

Dani leaned down to meet Ari’s lips, and as they kissed, they started walking toward the bedroom. She didn’t bother to open her eyes; she trusted Dani to lead them, and she didn’t want to stop kissing her. Not then. Not ever.

When they finally broke apart, Ari had no time to process the absence of Dani’s lips because suddenly she was being raised from the floor. She let out a surprised yelp and wrapped her legs around Dani’s waist on instinct. They were as close as humanly possible, bodies pressed together and intertwined. She looked down at Dani and immediately lost herself in her eyes.

Dani smiled, turned around, and started walking them both to the bed. Each step was accentuated by a kiss, as if Dani knew that every instant their lips were apart felt like an eternity to Ari. Or maybe Dani didn’t want to spend a second without kissing her either.

As they fell on the bed, Ari had to fight the urge to surrender to the moment. As much as she loved having Dani on top of her, tonight was going to be different. She wanted to take the lead, she wanted to let go of her inhibitions. And the one thing she wanted more than anything was to know she was the cause of Dani's pleasure. She wanted to make Dani come undone the same way she had so many times before.

It was hard to focus on her goal with Dani's tongue ravaging her neck, but she forced herself to. Softly but with determination, she pushed Dani off her and onto her back, then climbed on top to reverse their usual positions. Dani raised an eyebrow at her but didn't question beyond that. The curiosity in her eyes, the expectation, made Ari hesitate for an instant, insecure about the next step. But she tamped down the self-doubt, trusting that her instincts, her desire for Dani, would take over.

She focused on Dani's neck first, savoring its taste, the way every stroke of her tongue made Dani moan. She felt an overwhelming urge to bite her, to take as much of Dani as possible, and Ari tried to restrain herself until she realized there was nothing stopping her from doing what she wanted.

She started by softly grazing the base of Dani's neck with her teeth, making the other woman shiver with anticipation. Once she confirmed her nibbles and bites were welcome, Ari increased their intensity. She bit harder, harder, harder. And each time, Dani moaned louder and louder. Ari felt on top of the world, her confidence growing each time Dani whispered her name as a prayer.

Her short nails scraped along Dani's sides, her legs, her back—any part Ari could reach. As she moved with purpose on top of Dani, she realized that Dani's legs had parted in an invitation Ari was happy to accept.

But before she could fully indulge herself, she needed to remove every piece of clothing from their bodies. The fabric barriers had become an annoyance, an obstacle she couldn't stand. She peeled each one off slowly, taking her time with every garment. First, she slipped out of her own bikini with purposeful movements while Dani stared at her without blinking.

Ari stood by the edge of the bed fully naked, and for the first time in her life she didn't rush to cover herself, to hide under the sheets or turn off the light. She let Dani look, enjoying every second of the way Dani drank her in, caressing her with the softness of her gaze. She then moved up Dani's body, helping her discard her own clothes. She traced Dani's skin with her fingers as she pulled down wet bikini bottoms, smiling at the way she left a path of goosebumps behind.

If Dani's skin tasted like ambrosia, the sight of her naked body was paradise. Ari could have admired her curves for hours if it wasn't for the aroma of arousal calling her, taunting her, begging for her touch.

She leaned down and kissed Dani, letting her body rest softly on top of hers. The moment their skin touched again, the kiss became more forceful, almost like a battle to drink in as much of the other person as they could. Ari didn't mean to tease, as eager to touch Dani as Dani seemed to want to be touched; she was simply distracted by how good it felt to kiss her.

That's why the words that came out of Dani's mouth caught her by surprise. "Please, beautiful. I need you."

The plea not only reminded Ari about her initial plan but also made her tremble with excitement, being desired the biggest turn-on of them all.

"Soon, baby. There's just so much of you I want to experience. I need time. Is that okay?"

Dani let out a cross between a moan and a groan. "I want you to do whatever you want to me," she said, giving Ari a peck.

Ari bit her lip and took a deep breath to calm the rush of nerves that went through her body at Dani's words. The woman who had taken over her thoughts and impulses for months now was fully at her mercy, open and willing to do anything Ari chose to. . . and she was frozen in place, overwhelmed by the reality of the situation. A hand caressing her cheek pulled Ari out of her thoughts.

"Hey, it's just me," Dani said with a smile.

Ari returned the expression and leaned down to capture Dani's lips, calmness overtaking her. It was just Dani. The same person who had showed her time after time that she never judged her, that Ari could trust her. As they kissed, Ari's confidence grew, as did the urgency to explore more of the delicacy that was Dani's body.

Slowly, Ari broke apart from the kiss, only giving herself a few short seconds to stare into Dani's eyes before moving her lips to the smooth skin of Dani's chest. As she gave tentative kisses up and down Dani's collarbone, her hands moved steadily south, tracing over ribs and landing on sculpted abs. The soft tremble of Dani's body under her ministrations emboldened her enough to grab her waist harder and move her mouth closer to the things she'd been craving from the start—those beautiful brown nipples she was eager to take between her lips, caress with her tongue, and softly graze with her teeth.

The subtle murmurs of pleasure coming from Dani encouraged Ari and filled her with enough confidence to keep moving down. She traced her breastbone with her tongue until she found her stomach and covered it with kisses. She loved the way the firm muscles moved up and down with the sharp intakes of breath Dani took anytime she touched her.

"Turn around," Ari said.

Dani arched an eyebrow but didn't say a word, simply rolling onto her stomach. Ari lost herself for an instant looking at Dani's sculpted back before planting kisses all over. She ran her tongue from the small of Dani's back up to her neck and marveled at the shivers and whimpers Dani let out.

"You have no idea how much I love knowing I'm the one making you feel this way," Ari whispered in her ear after another kiss to her neck.

Dani laughed softly. "Well, I'm really happy to let you go on."

Ari didn't need to be told twice. She went for Dani's neck again and, feeling bold, grabbed her hands and held them above her head with her own.

"Leave them there," Ari commanded.

"I'm really enjoying this bossy side of you so don't worry, I won't move them."

Of course Dani would make a joke during sex, but Ari didn't mind. If anything, it made her braver. She gave Dani's hands a firm squeeze before releasing them and bringing her own down to push Dani's hips up. While she kissed and sucked on her neck, she ran her hands up and down Dani's body, bringing them closer and closer to her center. Dani's breath increased speed with each movement Ari made.

The urge to feel Dani around her fingers became impossible to delay any longer, every touch increasing her desire, her need, to give Dani as much pleasure as possible. The deep moan that Dani let out when Ari finally slid inside her sent a rush of heat to Ari's own center.

Her position on top of Dani had their bodies fully pressed together, close enough that with each motion of her hand, their synced, rocking movements filled Ari's senses with gratification.

She accompanied each stroke of her fingers with a kiss to the exposed skin on Dani's back or neck. The moans and quivers coming from Dani in response filled her with purpose, making her want to lose herself in Dani's body and live forever in that perfect instant punctuated by Dani's moans. She tried to extend the moment as long as she could, but eventually their energies faded away and they drifted off to sleep in satisfaction.

◈

After a few days of waking up with a view of the beach and Dani between her arms, Ari stopped caring about what day it was or when she would have to leave. For two weeks she and Dani lived in a realm of their own, a cocoon of love where the outside world didn't matter. Except that morning, the luggage standing by the door served as a stark reminder of the fact that their time together had come to an end.

She wasn't even gone yet and nostalgia was already weighing heavy on her soul, a longing to stay suspended in that magical, perfect place with Dani forever. She wanted to forget about her own responsibilities back home, about the job she didn't want to do anyway, and beg Dani to let her stay. Instead, she grabbed her backpack and smiled when Dani asked if she was ready to leave.

"Yeah, all set."

"I'm gonna miss you," Dani said, then leaned down to kiss Ari. "It's a shame you can't come to London, but I can't wait to visit you in your dorm after the US Open. I've always been curious about the whole school experience."

Ari smiled. The kiss filled her heart with warmth, and the words reminded her that this was only a brief goodbye. As hard as it was to part ways, at least she had the certainty that it was only temporary. "I can't wait to show you around."

Dani moved in to kiss her again, but the sound of someone clearing their throat cut the moment short.

"Sorry to interrupt," said Igor.

Dani's coach was standing by the door, not looking sorry at all. It was hard to tell because he always wore the same rigid, stern expression, but during the few times they'd crossed paths, Ari felt like he didn't particularly like her.

"Are you ready?" he said to Dani.

She fumbled around the four suitcases and the backpack she had lying around. "Shit, I think I forgot my earphones. Be right back."

Ari watched in horror as Dani ran into the house without a word, leaving her alone with Igor. He focused on his phone right away and didn't even look her direction. She could have chosen to do the same and pretend like he wasn't there, but she couldn't stop wondering what she'd done for him to dislike her.

"Can I ask you something?" she said. After several seconds without an answer, she spoke a little louder. "There's something I want to ask you."

This time Igor glanced her way and raised his thick eyebrows in what she gathered would be the closest she would get to an actual invitation to talk.

"Do you have a problem with me?" she asked.

Ari regretted the words as soon as she said them. What did she care if Dani's coach liked her or not? Except she knew he was like part of Dani's family, and the idea of not being accepted by them hurt her. His impassive face made it impossible to decipher what he was thinking, which unnerved Ari. She was about to tell him to forget about it, when he spoke.

"My job is to help Dani win tennis tournaments, not to have an opinion on her personal relationships," he answered coldly. "But since you want to know. I'm sure you are a nice girl, but you are an obstacle when it comes to Dani's success. Lately, all she cares about is you, so sorry if I don't throw a parade every time you're around and getting in my way."

It was her own damn fault for asking, but Ari hadn't expected the disdain in Igor's words. She stopped the apology itching to come out of her lips because she knew there was no reason for her to be sorry, even if Igor had made her feel like there was. Dani's return saved her from the awkwardness of being incapable of finding a good comeback.

"Found them!" Dani said, dangling a pair of white earphones in the air. "Let's go."

Ari sat in the back of the car with Dani while Igor drove them to the airport. As Dani's house disappeared, Ari focused on Igor's stern eyes in the rearview mirror and then on the island they would be leaving behind. Dani cupped Ari's face and turned it around softly to look at her.

"Hey," Dani said. "Don't be sad. This is just a brief intermission. I'll go win Wimbledon, you go and slay at that summer job, and in a couple of weeks we'll see each other again."

Ari smiled despite the uneasiness Igor's words had caused. As long as Dani wanted her, that was all that mattered.

# Chapter Seventeen

**From: ari3nunezar@virginia.edu**
**To: dani@danielamartinez.com**

How do I look? I thought if I was going to have to dress up, I should at least get something out of it (besides, you know, appearing professional in front of the partners and associates I'm trying to impress at the firm), so I may or may not have spent my lunch break taking selfies in the bathroom.

**From: dani@danielamartinez.com**
**To: ari3nunezar@virginia.edu**

I didn't know I needed to see you in a power suit until this picture, but now I'm obsessed. As cute as you look in your sundresses or in shorts and T-shirts, there's something about seeing you in a suit. It's sexy . . . but what about a picture with only the blazer?

**From: ari3nunezar@virginia.edu**
**To: dani@danielamartinez.com**

Only the blazer . . . I could arrange that, but I think you should earn it. I'm not in the habit of sending sexy pictures just like that. If you win Wimbledon, I'll send them to you. What do you say?

**From: dani@danielamartinez.com**
**To: ari3nunezar@virginia.edu**

I think you mean *when* I win Wimbledon. You better use these upcoming two weeks to find your best angles, then (not that you have any bad ones).

◈

The view that greeted Ari outside her window couldn't be more different than the one she'd left recently. Instead of the beautiful blue ocean, a sea of gray buildings stood on the horizon. New York was nothing like Mallorca, but it would be her home for the next six weeks during her summer associate job.

She'd been here for a week already, sharing an apartment with Tom, who was clerking for a judge. After an exhausting first few days of trying to settle in at her firm, she was happy to spend her day off watching Dani play.

Tom knocked on her bedroom door at eight o'clock sharp and dragged her out of bed so they could follow Dani's opening Wimbledon match.

"I made strawberries and cream!" Tom said, shoving a bowl into her hands.

Strawberries and cream? Was her half-asleep brain missing something? Ari yawned and sat in front of the TV next to him. "What's the deal with this?"

"It's a thing at Wimbledon, trust me."

By the time Dani appeared on her screen, dressed in immaculate white clothes, Ari had already finished eating. Waves of nausea made her regret eating whipped cream so early in the morning, until the commentators started talking about Dani and she started feeling even worse.

The food wasn't causing Ari's upset stomach. Her anxiety over the match was.

She'd watched Dani wake up at six in the morning every day to do physical therapy on her leg, observed her training for hours once her leg was better, listened to her talk on and on about how excited she was about recovering in time for Wimbledon. How she was going to make everyone forget about Paris when she raised the trophy for the first time. Dani had sounded so confident that Ari never showed signs of doubt that she would do exactly as she said—except for the sudden pain in her stomach when the match started.

"*After her first-round loss at the French Open, Daniela Martínez must be eager to prove that she is still the player to beat. She is still the top-ranked player in the world, but that could change this week, as there are several rivals waiting for her to make a mistake so they can overtake her.*"

"Those commentators are always trying to stir up drama," Tom said with a half-chewed strawberry still in his mouth. "She is playing great, and this match is going to be a breeze."

As much as she wanted to believe Tom, Ari was unable to shake the uneasiness she felt. The nerves lessened with every point Dani won, with every powerful serve and trip to the net to define the point with masterful volleys, but it never went away. Not even when the umpire said, "Game and set: Martínez," or when Dani took a 5–1 lead in the second set and prepared to serve for the match.

Dani was graceful, powerful, and merciless. She seemed more focused than ever . . . until the first match point in her favor. Two balls into the net for a double fault provided her rival with new life.

*Smack!* Dani's powerful backhand that had given her several winning points the entire match landed long this time, giving her opponent a break.

*"If there's one thing Daniela Martínez is known for, it's being ruthless. I don't think I've ever seen her squander a lead like this. Leading* 6–2, 5–1 *with six match points, and now she is on the verge of losing the second set in a tie break.* Nobody *saw this coming. The question is if she will pull herself together for a third set or if the ghost of her loss at the French Open is still on her mind."*

Ari's hands ached from clenching them into fists as another one of Dani's serves met the net, causing her to lose the second set. Dani slammed her racket against the ground, splitting it in half.

*"That is quite the racket smash. Daniela Martínez is mad, and she has reason to be. A match she had in absolute control is now going to a third set. Her rival, ranked number one hundred and forty-three in the world, is now the one looking confident and ready to take the win."*

Ari winced with every long ball, biting her lip and expecting, against all odds, that Dani would somehow turn things around. But she didn't. Half an hour later, she and Tom stared at the screen in silence, not believing Dani had lost in the first round. Again.

Ari had been there for the aftermath of Paris, so she knew Dani would be devastated and angry. She wanted to express her support, of course, but if she were in Dani's shoes, she couldn't think of anything worse than having to talk to somebody, no matter who, right then. She opted for a text message instead.

**I'm here if you want to talk. I'm sorry.**

◈

The more time that went by without Dani answering her messages, the more worried Ari got. A delay wasn't unusual because of the time difference, but it had been two days. Dani had never gone this long without answering.

Ari tried to distract herself with her job, reading, and watching TV, but she could barely get anything done while glancing at the phone every other minute. Of course, the moment she went to the bathroom, the phone rang.

She barely avoided falling as she ran to her bed to answer before the person on the other line hung up. In her rush, she picked up without checking who it was, sure it had to be Dani.

"Hey! I'm so glad you called!" Ari said between heavy breaths.

"You're glad I called? You're the one with no time for your mom."

Ari winced. "Sorry, Mom, I thought you were someone else," she said, unable to hide her disappointment.

"You went off to have fun in Europe and forgot about your poor mother."

"I'm sorry. The time difference made calling hard, but I thought of you all the time. I bought you a bunch of cute things!"

As Ari expected, her mother's mood picked up at the mention of gifts. From there, the conversation went as usual. Her mom told her about the latest news from the family, with Ari chipping in occasionally.

She wasn't sure why or at what point she decided that this phone call was as good as any to tell her mom she was dating someone. A female someone. For years she'd thought about how to tell her parents she was a lesbian. She had practiced speeches, wrote letters she never delivered, fantasized about family dinners where she stood up and made a big announcement. It never felt right—not as right as it felt in this moment.

Her parents had always supported her, encouraged her to be and do anything she wanted. She hoped this wasn't the exception. She was confident it wouldn't be, but that didn't make the lump in her throat go away.

Maybe treating her coming out as something natural, a minor announcement, would make things easier. It was the one scenario she never thought about. But right then, as her mother babbled on the phone about this or that cousin, the urge to just do it grew stronger.

A big part of her newfound courage was the time she'd spent with Dani, when she felt so happy, so free. She couldn't imagine not sharing that with her parents. It wasn't only about Dani, of course. It would be foolish to make such a big decision because of someone else. But she couldn't deny she had fantasies swirling in her mind, of Dani meeting her parents and spending time together back home in California. Those thoughts were the last push she needed to go through with it.

Her mom kept talking, and Ari smiled at the fact that *she* would be the main topic of conversation in the next few family calls between her mom and her aunts. And from them it would pass to her cousins and uncles. The normalcy of that imaginary situation cemented her decision to share the one part of her she had always hidden from her mother.

"I have some news too, Mom."

"Oh! Really? Tell me."

"I'm kind of dating someone."

Her mother's squeal and excited reaction weren't unexpected, but Ari pushed herself to keep talking. She had to go through with it, show her mom the complete picture, or it would be a mess.

She took a deep breath. "Yeah. She is great. I can't wait for you to meet her soon."

Ari tried to sound natural, as if she was talking about the weather and not a life-altering truth her mom didn't know about. She almost managed it, except for the small quaver in her voice when the words "she" and "her" came out of her mouth.

For the first time in a call with her mom, there was nothing but silence for an unbearable ten seconds. Ari took a deep breath, suppressing the panic that was about to spill out of her, when her mother cleared her throat and spoke again with the same animated tone she always used. Or at least tried to. The strain in the effort was obvious.

"I would love to meet them. Her. Soon." Silence swallowed them again, this time not as long. "I'm sure your father would be happy to meet her too."

Ari understood the implicit question. Did she want her father to know? She did. And honestly, she preferred to let her mom handle it. "Yeah, I can't wait to introduce her to Dad too."

"I will let him know you may bring someone special to meet us soon."

They tried to go back to a normal conversation, with her mom asking a few more questions about the person she was dating and mixing it with some additional news from home. Their conversation didn't flow as it had before, but they both refused to hang up with awkwardness lingering between them.

Though the rest of the call was weird, a weight had been lifted, and Ari felt relieved. It was out there. Her parents would need time to process, and that was fine. She was sure they would be okay. Now she only needed one thing: for Dani to answer her back so she could tell her the news.

# Chapter Eighteen

Dani sat in the locker room what felt like hours. She should have showered, stretched, and taken an ice bath by then, but who cared when there were no more matches to play. When she'd lost again. She kept replaying the events in her mind. This time there was no injury to blame; she was fit and had been training full time for over a week. Her mind had failed, not her body.

She'd heard plenty of times that the key to being a successful tennis player was the ability to forget the losses, but this one would be hard to erase. Dani relived every single point, every shot she missed. That 5–1 on the scoreboard in the second set was tattooed in her brain. The only thing she was grateful for was the fact that as long as she stayed in the locker room, she didn't have to face the world. Not Igor, not the press waiting to hound her with questions. In the locker room she was safe.

Dani wasn't sure how long she stayed just like that, staring into space. Fellow players came in and out of the room, passing her by on the way to their own matches. Some looked at her with pity in their eyes, others with indifference.

Her mind fixated on one thing, the famous quote every player saw right before entering Wimbledon's Centre Court: "If you can meet with triumph and disaster and treat those two impostors just the same." Disaster—that was an accurate word to define the past two months of her tennis career. And no, she couldn't treat them just the same, no matter how much she wanted to.

She hung her tennis bag on her shoulder and walked toward the door, where she bumped into Olga Podoroska. Exactly what she needed, for her biggest rival to see her in her worst moment.

"Rough loss," Olga said.

Dani bit her tongue only because she wasn't interested in starting a confrontation in the middle of the locker room, but she wasn't fooled by Olga's innocent tone. The Russian had always disliked her, and after Dani's loss she was one step away from taking the number one position in the ranking.

"Yeah."

Olga smirked. "I was looking forward to beating you in the final, but I guess I'll have to settle for taking the title against someone else like I did at Roland-Garros."

"Funny, I would have sworn the last time we played I won. The last five times, actually." Dani put as much bite in her tone as she could muster. "Enjoy winning while I'm not around, because it's the only way you will get close to a trophy."

She walked away as soon as the words were out of her mouth. The expression on Olga's face, a mixture of shock and anger, almost made Dani forget about the loss as she closed the locker room door behind her. Almost.

Several hours later, Dani was on a flight back to Mallorca with Igor by her side. She looked at the empty seat where Ari had sat a month before and felt a pang in her heart. She'd seen the message

Ari sent her after the match but hadn't answered yet. The care and attention Ari showed her usually made her smile, but in that moment, she didn't want to talk to her. She didn't want to talk to anybody. The only thing she wanted was to find a way to get out of the funk she was in and win again, and she didn't know if she could do that and focus on Ari at the same time.

Dani knew it was unfair, and part of her felt like shit at the mere idea of cutting contact with Ari. But another part believed it was necessary. She didn't blame Ari for her losses—that would be ridiculous. She blamed her own lack of focus. Unfortunately, she didn't feel capable of focusing on tennis again, with the single-mindedness necessary to win, if Ari was in her life. Maybe with time she could balance the two, but right then it was impossible.

The only reason she was delaying telling Ari she needed some time for herself was because she was trying to talk herself out of her own decision. Dani knew that making a choice, a drastic change, in the heat of the moment was not ideal. She would give herself until the next morning. If she didn't change her mind by then, she would do it.

When they landed, she demanded they went to train without delay.

"It's okay if you want to take a day to process the loss. We don't have to train right away," Igor said.

Never before had Igor offered to cancel a session. Usually, it was her pushing for more time off and him telling her she wasn't training enough. Maybe in the past she would have been happy with the offer, but this time, she glared at him. “We are training.”

Without a word, he grabbed her bags full of tennis equipment and put them in the car’s trunk before getting in the passenger seat.

“I’m winning the US Open,” Dani said, joining him in the car. She shot him a look that almost defied him to disagree.

He nodded. “Let’s get to work, then.”

Once they made it to the court, she hit each ball fed to her as hard as she could for as long as her body let her. She kept going as the sun set and bright lights turned on to illuminate the court. When exhaustion became too much even for her anger to overcome, she stopped. It was eleven o’clock, and Dani ached all over. Her mind and muscles were exhausted, which was exactly what she wanted. That way, as soon as her body hit the bed, the world would fade away and she could finally stop thinking about her loss.

When she woke up the next day, her phone blinked with several unread messages. She ignored them all and opened the one Ari had sent the day before. She read the kind words again, and the image of sweet brown eyes came to her mind, making her resolve waver. Dani crafted a message of her own and hit Send before she could talk herself out of the idea.

**I need some time away to focus on my tennis. I’m sorry.**

She regretted the words almost as soon as she sent them, but she refused to backtrack. This was the only way to get her career in order. Just a few weeks and then she would have time to focus on Ari again. *Ari will understand.* With that thought, Dani turned her phone off and left for practice.

◈

When Dani finally answered her message, Ari wished she hadn't. She read the twelve words over and over to try to convince herself that they weren't real. It wasn't possible for Dani to change in only a couple of days, from loving and attentive to discarding Ari as if she were nothing because of one match.

The dismissiveness of not even calling her, treating her as an inconvenience to get rid of, gave her flashbacks of all the times Lara had acted that way. She typed and deleted several desperate messages before settling on something concise but direct.

**I respect your need for space, but can we talk? I think I deserve more than a text message.**

The hours until Dani answered back passed by excruciatingly slow.

**You're right. What time works for you?**

Ari hated to seem needy after Dani had dismissed her without a second thought, so she tried to sound nonchalant.

**Whenever is fine by me.**

Ari assumed they would set a date and time, that she would have some time to prepare, but the phone started ringing almost immediately. She should have known that Dani would want to get on with it as soon as possible. Probably try to shake Ari off so she could go back to focus on whatever it was she needed to focus on.

Ari took a deep breath before swiping right on her phone to answer the call. "Hey."

"Hey."

Silence appeared to be a common theme for her calls that day. Neither of them seemed to know how to start the conversation.

Ari took the lead. She had asked for the call, after all. "I saw your message, but I'm not sure if I understand what you mean. Is this it? Are we never talking again?"

"No! Of course not. I'm sorry. It was shitty of me to just drop a message with no explanation."

Ari bit her lip. She didn't want to sound petty, but she couldn't help herself. "Yeah, it was shitty."

"I'm sorry. I was only thinking about myself, and I knew if I didn't do it right then that I would never bring myself to do it at all. I regret the form, but I do need some time alone."

Ari tried to hold on to her anger, but she couldn't. The pain was stronger. When she spoke, her voice sounded small and defeated. "I don't get it. I've never tried to interfere with your tennis."

"It's not your fault," Dani said softly, but Ari couldn't bring herself to believe it. "Our time together was some of the best of my life. I was the one who didn't manage my time well and neglected my responsibilities. I'm the one who needs to find a balance, but right now I have only a couple of months to salvage my season and need to dedicate all of my energy to it."

"So you are not talking to me for two months? For whatever time you feel I'm getting in the way?" This time her anger made it to her voice, and Dani winced. Good. Ari wanted to see at least a sign of regret, shame, sadness. Anything that let her know Dani cared for her as much as Ari believed.

"We can text occasionally," Dani said. "I just won't be as available as I usually am or have time to plan dates and see each other in person. I'm dreading it too, but I think it's what's necessary for me to have a chance to win the US Open."

Ari tried to control the quaver in her voice. "I know how important tennis is to you, but I can't help but feel like you're throwing me away as if I'm nothing."

"I'm sorry."

The regret in Dani's tone did nothing to alleviate Ari's pain. If Dani wanted time and space, Ari would give it to her, but she wouldn't wait around. She'd done that in her past relationships, let the other person determine when and where she was worth their time, and she'd promised to never allow that again.

"I'm sorry too," Ari replied. "I lo—I really like you and want the best for you, but I don't know if in two months, or whenever you decide there is space for me, that I'll want to be there. I don't want to feel like I'm an object you bring into your life only when it's convenient."

"I understand." There was a subtle change in Dani's voice. Or at least Ari wanted to think there was a hint of sadness in her words. "I can't ask you to pause your life because of me, but I hope you know I do care for you, a lot. You have no idea how much. Maybe it's not the right moment for us, but I don't regret any of our time together."

"I don't regret it either." Despite the heartache, Ari let a small smile emerge at the memories of their time together. "Good luck, I guess."

"Thank you," Dani whispered.

After a long few seconds of silence, Ari hung up.

◈

Dani fought the urge to smash her phone against the wall. Instead, she gripped it in her hand as she replayed the conversation in her mind. Of course Ari was upset, and of course she wanted nothing to do with Dani. She'd been naive to think Ari would be okay with them not talking for months and would be waiting for her with welcoming arms. Dani resisted the temptation to call Ari, apologize, and backtrack.

Now that her decision of walking away from Ari had become real, she felt weak at the thought of losing her forever. But as much as her mind kept screaming at her to fix things, she didn't move a muscle. She'd made a decision, and now she had to own up to it and deal with the consequences. She needed to give herself a chance to reassert her tennis dominance with no distractions or doubts. The idea that her relationship was affecting her play would always be there, in the back of her mind. She needed to do this, as much as it hurt.

She realized how self-centered she'd been, how accustomed she was to everyone bending to do anything to guarantee her success, that the idea of Ari not understanding her decision hadn't crossed her mind. Her entourage was always focused on one thing and one thing only: Dani winning. Even her parents had left everything behind all those years ago so that she could become a professional tennis player. Other people sacrificing for her was so normal, she had expected Ari to accept her decision and wait for her.

Now it was clear that there was a real risk of losing the one person she wanted more than anything. But there was no going back, even if in two months the only thing she had to keep her company was a piece of metal. In the worst-case scenario, she would end up without a trophy and without the woman she'd fallen for.

More than ever, Dani needed to use her time for training. If her relationship with Ari was already ruined, the least she could do was win the damn thing. Holding up the trophy at the US Open wasn't a goal, it was a must. It was the only way to make the pain she was feeling worth it.

Dani left for the court. The plan was simple: she would train until every muscle in her body ached that day, and then she would train some more. When she played tennis, her mind emptied. She would have no thoughts, no sadness, no pain. No memories of Ari swirling in her head, no regret hanging heavy in her heart. Everything melted away. After training, her body would be so tired she would pass out until the next day. Rinse and repeat for as long as necessary.

If Igor had been the only one she had to deal with, that plan would have been perfect. Arantxa, however, was another story, and she'd picked that day to show up.

Dani ignored her arrival. If breaking Ari's heart hadn't been enough to stop her from training, Arantxa waiting on the sidelines wouldn't be either. To her surprise, Arantxa didn't interrupt them but instead stood on the sidelines while scrolling on her phone, as impeccable as ever in her sunglasses and high heels. She waited for over an hour without saying a word.

When Igor declared the training session over, Arantxa finally walked toward Dani. "I'm taking you to dinner. I'll wait for you in the car."

Dani frowned. What was all this about? Only her curiosity and her respect for Arantxa prevented her from bailing, but they didn't stop her from taking her sweet time showering and changing.

"What's up?" Dani said once she reached the car. "I have a hard time believing you were just lonely and missing me."

"You're right. I could be happy while relaxing at home or working on my new client, a Brazilian future football star that I'm sure won't give me as much trouble as you do. But no, right as I was about to finish work, I got an email that ruined my night."

"I feel some animosity coming from you. Why do I sense that you blame me for it?"

"Because I do. Mary Felton is getting fed up with my excuses, which are *your* excuses. She has a collection of paparazzi pictures and interviews with hotel employees in Paris and Miami. She could do the exposé of her career, but she is waiting for the interview we promised her."

"So what? Is she threatening to out me? Because she can do it, I don't care, and I won't give her the satisfaction of blackmailing me." Dani's voice was full of anger, leaving no room for discussion.

"No, she didn't say that," Arantxa replied in what Dani recognized as her appeasing tone. "Quite the opposite, in fact. She says she won't publish anything without your authorization, and she wants to give you a chance to do it on your terms. But we don't know if other journalists will follow the same code of honor."

"I thought you had taken care of that."

"I did. Nobody else has any material from Miami or Paris, but it's going to be hard work keeping things under wraps when you are spending so much time in public with Ari."

"Well, that won't be a problem anymore," Dani snapped. She then softened her voice. "We kind of broke up. I don't even know if that's what you'd call it, but we're not seeing each other at the moment."

Arantxa took her eyes off the road and looked at Dani for a split second. "What?"

"I need to focus on my tennis right now."

"Why are all tennis players so dumb?"

Dani's enraged look was enough to shut her up. The last thing Dani needed was someone else on her case—she was already drowning in her own sorrow.

"That makes things easier, I guess," Arantxa muttered.

They drove in silence until Dani broke it. "After the US Open," she said, hoping what she was about to say didn't turn into a decision she would later regret. "Tell her I will give her an exclusive, full-access, no-topic-off-limits interview. Make a contract promising it so she gets out of the way until then."

"Are you sure?"

"Yeah, the US Open is it. For better or worse."

# Chapter Nineteen

**From: ari3nunezar@virginia.edu**
**To: dani@danielamartinez.com**
**Status: Draft**

I know I won't send this, the same way I haven't sent the other ten letters I've written to you since the last time we talked. Sometimes I wonder if I should have taken your offer, if a message here and there would have been better than this unsurmountable distance, better than losing all of you in a single instant. But deep down I know that would only prolong the pain. That if we kept talking, I would feel the same sting of betrayal every time I got a text as I did the day you told me I was too much of a distraction.

It's better this way. At least that's what I tell myself. With the distance between us, I can at least hope to one day stop longing for you. I like to pretend our time together was a fantastic dream—it felt like one at the time—and I simply woke up to reality.

I came back to my routine of going to school, working at the library, and dreading my future life working at a firm. At some point Tom got a boyfriend, can you believe it? His name is Mark, and he lives in New York. I like him but now I have the added fun of being the third wheel on their dates and having them try to not so subtly set me up with some of his friends.

The worst part of losing you is not even that I miss your kisses, or the exhilarating feeling of not knowing what you might propose next, or the way you looked at me, or how you always made sure to ask what I wanted. The worst part is that I can no longer rush to send you a message any time something happens to me, no matter how silly or small. Yes, I miss the woman I met in Miami who made me feel on top of the world, but I miss my online friend—the one who was always there and always listened to me—even more.

I never knew I needed someone like you in my life until I had it, and now I must learn to live without you again. I'm sure I'll get there, but the process is harder than I expected.

I wonder if you think about me as I do about you. Probably not. I saw that you won the tournament in Connecticut, so congratulations. I guess you were right after all. You needed me out of your life and your head to start winning again.

◈

Dani's first match at the US Open felt like endless déjà vu, or a nightmare she couldn't wake up from. The similarities to her most recent Grand Slam matches were too many, too close for comfort. Again, she found herself down in the third set after leading in the first and second. So much training, so much sacrifice for nothing. Just a week before, she'd won a tournament, so it wasn't an issue with the quality of her game or her physical condition. Fear was consuming her, tightening her muscles before every shot and making them land where they shouldn't.

Was Ari watching and asking herself if *this* was what she had been tossed aside for? For Dani to lose again? Dani knew it was unlikely. The two months of radio silence were enough proof that Ari had forgotten about her, but she didn't need logic. She wanted to believe Ari was watching. She needed her to be watching. Pushing Ari out of her life was the hardest thing Dani had ever done, and she at least needed to show Ari with a win that it wasn't all for nothing.

The next game, every single shot landed inside the lines no matter how hard she hit it. Her serves bounced in the exact spot she wanted, and her backhand down the line won her one, two, three points.

During every point, only one thing hovered in Dani's mind: *This is for her*. If she lost, it'd be harder to convince Ari of the fact that she no longer cared about the stupid notion of distractions or interference with her tennis game. But if she won, she could go to Ari and show her that the victories didn't matter if they weren't together to celebrate. Dani wasn't sure if her logic would make sense to Ari, but it made sense to her.

The past two months had been miserable. There was no point in staying away from Ari when she was the only thing Dani could think about. She had known for weeks that she needed to try to win Ari back, but in her mind the only way to do it was to win. For the next hour, that idea fueled her enough to turn the match around.

Dani lay neck-deep in an ice bath when Igor entered the players' area. "Second round. Congratulations."

It was hard to tell if he was being sincere or sarcastic because his tone was as flat as ever. Looking at him, Dani was inclined to believe he meant it. It had been a rough couple of months for her, but also for him.

"Thank you," she said, then closed her eyes and returned to her thoughts.

Igor cleared his throat. "I'm sorry if I've been too hard on you."

Dani opened her eyes, unsure where his sudden softness was coming from. She'd never doubted that he cared for her, but he was never interested in showing it like this. "That's why I have you, to push me."

"I know. But you deserve to be happy. We all do." He sat on the edge of the bathtub. "I love tennis as much as anyone, but at the end of the day, all tennis careers end. There are other things that are forever."

Dani nodded, Ari's face flashing in her mind.

He cleared his throat again. "No morning session tomorrow. You should rest. We have a tournament to win after all."

Dani stayed in the ice, thinking over his words and about her own grand plans to win Ari back. She scoffed and shook her head at herself. It was time to stop waiting, hoping, preparing for an ideal moment that may never come. She had to just go for it. As soon as she stepped out of the ice bath, she did the one thing she had wanted to do for weeks, the one thing she should have done long before now.

**I'm sorry I was such a dumbass. I miss you.**

She wondered if it was too little, too late. But the only sure way to lose a match was to not try at all.

◈

An entire week had passed since she texted Ari and still no answer. In that time, Dani beat three players in straight sets, utterly dominating them, and was about to play her quarterfinal match—but the only thing on her mind was Ari.

The possibility of making the US Open final was so close, as was the reality that she wouldn't have Ari there to share her happiness. While her trainer finished wrapping her ankles, Dani grabbed her phone and texted Arantxa. There was one last thing she could do, one last-ditch effort to salvage what she'd damaged.

**I need you to buy two flights from Virginia to New York for Ari and Tom. I need the tickets printed, not digital. Let me know when you have them.**

If she could count on something, it was Arantxa's efficiency. Her manager would have those tickets ready by the time she finished her match. Then it would be Dani's turn to make things right.

Maybe it was a coincidence, or maybe it was Dani's eagerness to go back and put her plan in motion, but the quarterfinal was one of the most focused matches she'd ever played. Winning 6–0, 6–1 in less than an hour filled her with confidence.

After the match, she went to her room and used the free hotel notepad to write down everything she wanted to tell Ari, only stopping when an insistent knock forced her to drop the pen and see who it was. Arantxa stood at the door without talking as if enjoying the nervous energy radiating from Dani, savoring her suffering for some long, interminable seconds.

"Here is what you asked for," Arantxa said, handing her an envelope.

Dani opened it eagerly and found two tickets inside. She scanned them, then frowned. "These are for the day before the final."

"Well, I assume Ari will need some time to think. She can't just up and go without notice."

Dani had to admit that Arantxa's reasoning made sense. Adding even more time to her wait didn't make her happy, but Ari accepting her invitation wasn't even guaranteed. One day didn't matter, only that Ari agreed to come.

"I also thought that would give you some extra motivation to make the final," Arantxa added.

Dani couldn't even be mad at her. It was devious and a little cruel, but Arantxa was right—it helped motivate her even more. In four days, Dani would play in the US Open final, she was sure of it. The only question was whether Ari would be there to see her win.

By the end of the night, an envelope was on its way from New York to Virginia in priority overnight mail, with a letter and two flight tickets inside. Dani had played her best shot, and now the ball was in Ari's court.

◆

Ari had been staring at the piece of paper with Dani's messy handwriting for hours. She read the words scribed on it a dozen times and ran her thumb over the hotel's logo, which was printed on each page. The symbol made the letter feel more real, like a Polaroid snapped in the middle of the circus that was Dani's life during a Grand Slam. Imagining Dani scribbling away on the first piece of paper she found between rushing to training and press conferences affected Ari almost as much as the actual words did.

Dani's confession about not being able to stop thinking about her, about how much she regretted pushing her out of her life, sparked Ari's interest—but she was still wary. It wasn't until she noticed the hotel's logo that she fully believed the words, because it proved that even when Dani was so close to accomplishing what she'd been after all year, Ari was still on her mind. What Ari didn't know was whether that was enough to forgive the pain Dani had caused her.

Dani had once told her that meeting each other was fate. Ari had laughed then because she didn't believe in that kind of thing. But now she wondered if there was some truth to those words. Usually, she could go weeks without picking up her mail, and the only reason she checked it that morning was because she was waiting for a package from her mom. Any other week, the letter would have stayed unopened in her mailbox, containing only useless tickets and wasted words. Maybe it was fate, as Dani said, that they'd met online despite being from completely different worlds. And maybe it was fate that Ari was now holding in her hand a chance to fix their relationship.

The sound of the door opening snapped Ari out of her thoughts. She had texted Tom soon after finding the letter, so it didn't surprise her that he'd come by, only that it had taken him so long to arrive. The Starbucks cups in his hands were probably the reason for his delay.

"It seemed like a hot chocolate kind of moment," he said, sitting at the foot of her bed.

"Good call."

She exchanged the letter for one of the steaming cups in his hand. While he read each page, she blew on the hot chocolate.

"Hmm."

Ari waited for Tom to say more, but he didn't. "Hmm? That's all?"

He looked into her eyes and took a deep breath before speaking. "I gotta say, I appreciate the fact she sent a ticket for me too. Makes me feel important. But she won't win over my loyalty so easily."

Ari smiled at his attempt at levity.

"I know she hurt you," he continued, handing the letter back, "and you are the only one who can decide if you're willing to gamble with love and heartbreak again. The risk will always be there, with Dani or with anyone else. So, what does your heart tell you?"

Ari looked down and fidgeted with the pages in her hands before answering. "I knew I wanted to go the minute I saw this." She glanced up at Tom. "But I'm afraid. I don't know if I can handle always being second best, fearing being pushed aside the moment things get tough."

"That's reasonable. Maybe tell her all that? See if she can promise you to do better. There will always be the danger of being hurt when it comes to love, but if you two work together, I think you can fix it."

"You think?" Ari asked softly.

"Yeah. Take it from someone who has perfected the infatuation part of relationships but rarely makes it all the way through to real love. At the start, everything is easy and happy, but when things get tough, that's when you'll know if it's genuine." Tom raised his thumb and wiped away a solitary tear Ari didn't realize was sliding down her face. "It was easy when it was all about traveling and having fun, but now is the moment to take that next step. Only you can know if it's worth it. It will take work and you two may still mess up, but if both of you want it, I think you can build something amazing."

Ari pondered Tom's words. The time she'd spent with Dani had felt like a dream or a fairy tale where everything was perfect. But he was right. Sometimes things got hard or messy, and you could choose to stay and fight if you thought it was worth it. In a way, Ari had chosen to run away as soon as things became more complicated, and she wanted to give Dani—give *them*—another chance. She already knew there was no decision to make. She could never live with herself if she didn't try at least one last time.

"When did you become so deep?" she teased.

"I've always been a love expert; you just never pay attention to me."

Ari laughed and wrapped her arms around him. She rested her head on his shoulder as he held her.

"Should I pack, then?" he asked.

"Yeah, let's pack."

Despite her words, they didn't move.

Tom glanced at her. "She's playing right now, you know."

She knew. Even though she refused to watch Dani play because it hurt too much to see her, Ari always checked her scores and schedule. It was semifinals day, only one step away from what Dani wanted most.

She nodded, and that was all the cue Tom needed to turn on the TV. They caught the end of the third set, but Ari didn't pay attention to the score, too busy enjoying the sight of Dani for the first time in weeks. She only realized Dani had won when a scream and fist pump filled the screen.

A tradition in tennis that Ari had learned about through watching matches was that the winning player signed the lens of the camera. She didn't quite understand the reason for it, but this time her heart skipped a beat when they handed the marker to Dani, and instead of writing her own name, Dani used the same messy calligraphy from the letter to scribble the words "for you."

# Chapter Twenty

Dani's muscles ached after the long match she had the day before, but she savored the feeling. The pain was tangible evidence of her effort. If she lost a match, she left a tournament with nothing to show for it—no trophy, no celebration. But she always had pain.

As she stretched her muscles to relieve some soreness, her thoughts drifted to Ari. Had she read the letter? There was no way to know for sure. Based on the tracking, Dani knew it had been delivered, but she hadn't heard from Ari at all. No message, no call, nothing. Not even anything to tell Dani to leave her alone.

The flight Arantxa had booked for Ari was scheduled for that morning, so if she'd decided to give Dani another chance, she would already be on the flight. Dani was tempted to stay at the hotel so Ari could find her if she made it to New York. It was dumb, of course, as Ari could call or text at any time to find out where she was, but Dani couldn't deal with doing nothing. She also considered going to the airport to wait, but Igor would kill her if she skipped practice the day before a Grand Slam final.

She hopped out of bed, figuring that keeping busy would be her best plan of action so she didn't agonize over Ari all morning. Wondering if Ari was on that plane or not wouldn't do her any good. The possibility of Ari dismissing her letter floated in the back of her mind, and as much as she hoped that wasn't the case, if there were no signs of Ari by the end of the day, Dani would have to accept the implicit rejection.

If she'd made more mistakes than usual during training, Igor was nice enough to not mention it. Not directly, at least. "Are you nervous for tomorrow? You seem tense. I don't remember you being like this even before your first final."

"No, I'm good," she said with a shrug. "A little sore from yesterday, that's all."

"We'll do light training and set you up for a massage to loosen those muscles."

After training, she went back to her room. Despite how early it still was, she felt like climbing into bed. She put on the TV to have some background noise and spent the day looking at pictures of her time with Ari, glancing at the clock every few minutes. Each one that passed served as a stark reminder of the fact that Ari wasn't coming.

At eight o'clock, a loud knock on the door interrupted her wallowing. Dani jumped from the bed, too excited to even stop to check herself in the mirror or change out of the ratty pajamas she was wearing. When she found Arantxa on the other side of the door, the disappointment must have shown on her face.

"Well, hello to you too," Arantxa said. "It's nice to feel loved."

"Sorry, I was hoping it was someone else." Dani crawled back under the covers.

"I bet. Come on, let's go have some dinner."

"I'd rather stay here and order some room service," Dani said, defeated and suddenly unable to believe any longer that there was any hope of Ari showing up.

For the first time since she'd known her, Arantxa didn't press. She left quietly without further comment. As soon as Arantxa left, Dani buried her face in the blanket, willing sleep to numb her.

A loud rap on the door startled her awake. She didn't feel like talking to Arantxa again, but as the knocking continued, Dani reluctantly dragged herself from the bed.

She opened the door with a groan. "I told you, I want to be alo—"

Ari stood in front of her.

Was she dreaming? Maybe in her sadness, she'd conjured a fantasy of Ari to soothe her pain. But the soft smell of coconut shampoo confirmed that the person in front of her was real.

"Can I come in?" Ari said.

Dani shook her head to clear the thoughts swirling around a hundred miles a minute. "Yeah, of course." She stepped away from the door to let Ari in. She was dying to take Ari in her arms and plant a kiss on those plump pink lips, but she restrained herself. Instead, she said, "You came."

"I did."

They stood in silence until Dani couldn't endure it any longer and took two steps forward to close the distance between them. When her movement didn't meet resistance, she pushed the boundaries even more, raising a trembling hand to tuck a loose strand of hair behind Ari's ear and caressing her cheek on the way down.

"The flight was delayed because of bad weather."

"I'm glad you are here. I wasn't sure if you would come."

Ari looked down. "I wasn't sure either, but I am now."

Dani moved closer. She knew this didn't mean everything was perfect, but Ari was here, and it was a start.

"I know we need to talk," Dani said, "but can I kiss you first?"

Ari's nod was all it took for Dani to move forward, their lips colliding in a frenzy. The first passionate and forceful touch let the months of distance, longing, and desire out, and slowly their movements became softer. The need to enjoy every second overtook her, making her savor the way their lips moved together.

Dani pulled Ari closer until barely any space separated them. When they ended the kiss, Dani moved her lips to Ari's chin, neck, the corner of her ear, and anywhere she could reach.

Once they broke apart, Dani gazed into Ari's eyes, trying to convey with one look how much she meant to her. "Thank you for coming."

"It was a very convincing letter."

"I meant every word. I'm so sorry I was such a fool."

"As much as I love that you are admitting that, I need you to be more than sorry."

Dani frowned. "What do you mean?"

"I need to know you won't do something like this again. There's no point in apologizing if we don't change."

Dani moved away because the conversation deserved her full focus, and being that close only made her think about kissing Ari again. She sat on the bed and patted the spot beside her, and Ari sat down.

"I can't promise I won't mess up again," Dani said, taking Ari's hands between her own, "but I can promise to never run away like I did. I won't make decisions that affect both of us on my own."

"No leaving me for tennis?"

"Never again. I love tennis, but I love you more."

Ari's eyes widened. The words had spilled out of Dani's mouth by accident, but that didn't make them less true. She was sure of them, and there was no reason to wait to say them when she had learned the hard way that another day with Ari wasn't guaranteed. She may as well put it all out there, bare her heart.

"Yes, I love you," Dani said. "I've loved you for a long time now, since before we saw each other in person, even. I was holding myself back because of stupid reasons, but I don't want to keep it inside any longer. Even if you leave today, I want you to know I love you."

"You are so silly. Of course I love you too. I don't take a flight at a moment's notice for just anybody, you know."

Dani smiled and leaned down to give Ari a brief kiss. "Say it again. I like how it sounds."

"I love you, Daniela Martínez."

"Y yo te amo."

"Speaking in Spanish now? You're bringing out the big guns to try to seduce me."

"Is it working?" Dani said with a flirty grin.

"Maybe . . . We still need to work on things, but I want to try. I want to give us a chance."

"That's all I need."

Dani knew this was only the beginning, the cornerstone of the long road to build a lasting relationship, but their promise was all they needed for the time being.

Once the air was clear, the past forgiven, they allowed themselves to surrender again to the passion they had been holding back. Dani was running her tongue up the side of Ari's neck when Ari stopped her in her tracks with one thought.

"Don't you have a pretty important match tomorrow? Maybe we should try to sleep," she said with a laugh.

Dani smiled and kissed her quickly. "Yes, I have a match, but I don't care. We are not sleeping tonight."

"Oh, you don't care?"

"Not one bit," Dani answered, pushing Ari on her back and climbing on top of her.

◈

Dani felt like a creep for staring at Ari while she slept, but she had been deprived of Ari's presence for too long now and didn't want to waste a single instant. With that in mind, she made it her mission to wake Ari up so they could enjoy some time together before she had to leave for practice.

Wanting to be as romantic as possible, Dani ordered breakfast to the room and started leaving a trail of kisses all over Ari's shoulders to stir her awake. Ari soon grumbled something and rolled away, pulling a pillow over her face in the process. A string of muffled sounds came from under it.

"Sorry, babe. I can't tell what you are saying," Dani said with a laugh.

The groan that came next was loud and clear, even against the fabric barrier. Ari rolled around again, moving the pillow aside, eyes still half-closed as if it pained her to open them. "I said, I'm forgiving you this time but never wake me up again. I'm so sleepy."

Dani grinned and gave her a quick peck. "Noted. I got breakfast, though."

Ari bolted upright and took in the spread of fruit, tea, pancakes, eggs, muffins, juice, and toast on the room-service cart. "I may forgive you, I guess," she said with a shy smile.

Dani watched enraptured as Ari took a bite of a strawberry and then leaned forward to give Dani a kiss. The look of happiness and adoration in Ari's eyes when they broke apart was more important to Dani than the kiss itself. It reminded her of the mornings spent together in Mallorca with no worries, only love between them. The time before she messed things up.

"Stop staring," Ari said, covering her face with the sheet.

"Sorry. I was just thinking about how happy I am that you're here."

"You don't have to act as if I'm disappearing any minute," Ari said, moving closer. "I'm here to stay. I wouldn't have come back if I didn't mean it."

"I know," Dani answered sincerely. She started eating breakfast, suddenly realizing how hungry she was. "I'm going to take some time off after the US Open no matter what happens today. I would love to spend some time with you if you can spare it. I've missed you so much."

"Of course. I have school, though."

"I can visit you there. As long as there's a tennis court, I'm good. Or I can stay here in New York and travel back and forth on the weekends."

Ari smiled and kissed her. "Sounds good."

Dani hoped her effort to find ways to be together even if Ari couldn't travel to see her showed Ari how committed she was to making their relationship work. Ari's life and responsibilities were as important as her own, and Dani intended to prove that she was serious when she said she wanted to build a lasting relationship between them.

"I can also travel. It doesn't always have to be you, but sometimes it will be impossible for me to get away," Ari added.

"Don't worry, we'll make it work."

By the time they left the hotel room, Dani was running late for training. Between breakfast, kissing, showering, kissing, getting dressed, and kissing, it was a miracle they'd made it out of the room at all. Ironically, Ari was the one worried about Dani missing training, while Dani tried her best to convince her to stay in the shower a little longer.

"The least you can do is win this thing," Ari said, a stern look on her face. "Think of it as an extra reward. Once you finish the match, we'll have all the time in the world to ourselves."

"That's the best motivational speech I've heard in twenty years of playing."

Ari was right—the least Dani could do was win the damn thing.

# Chapter Twenty-One

Dani's usual pre-match routine included at least half an hour of solitude in the locker room. No conversations with her coach, no team hovering around her, only her own thoughts as company while she prepared to do what she did best. But fifteen minutes before she was due to play in the final of the US Open, she found herself in the locker room chatting with Ari, and she'd never felt more relaxed before a match. If she won—and she planned to—she was going to make it a new tradition.

While she finished putting on her shoes, Ari caught her up on the things she'd missed in the time they were apart. The conversation was so casual that it took Dani a moment to react when Ari switched from telling her about school and Tom's latest love adventure to something more important.

"I came out to my parents," Ari said out of the blue. "They took it well."

Dani's hands stopped moving, her shoelaces left untied as she looked up at Ari. "You did? That's amazing. How did it go?"

"It was a little awkward at first," Ari said shyly. "But they're doing their best to be supportive. I sometimes catch them trying to not mess up when they speak about my love life, but overall, it went well." She played with Dani's shoelaces as she talked. "They've started pestering me about meeting a nice girl, so I guess that means they accept it." She gave a small smile.

Dani returned it and reached down to take the shoelaces from Ari, caressing her hand softly in the process. "On the next call you can brag about having a US Open champion as your girlfriend."

"I will."

"You know, that reminds me of something," Dani said, standing up to stretch. "I've been thinking about this whole situation with being out in private and closeted in public, and I've decided that I want to be more open about my life." She started running in place. "If you are okay with it, I would like to tell everybody about our relationship. I want people to know I'm in love with an amazing woman."

Ari's grin was all the answer Dani needed.

"That sounds amazing. Now that my parents know, I've got no reason to hide."

Dani leaned down to kiss Ari when a loud voice interrupted them. "Five minutes until the start of the match. Players, please make your way to the court."

Dani sighed. "That's my cue." She grabbed her bag and moved toward the door. "See you soon."

Ari stood suddenly and ran to plant a soft kiss on her lips. "Break a leg?"

Dani let out a chuckle as she walked out of the locker room.

◈

Ari reached the reserved area in the stands of Arthur Ashe Stadium just in time to watch the players walk out to the sound of thousands of fans cheering them on.

The roar of the public as Dani stepped onto the court sent chills down Ari's spine, and her chest swelled with pride. She could only imagine how Dani felt peering up from the court at the blurred mass of people, but if it affected her then she didn't show it. She walked with the same confident stride Ari had seen so many times on TV.

Arantxa talked animatedly in Ari's direction. "This is Antonia Carvalho, my newest client."

The last thing Ari wanted was to look away from Dani. She could have stayed lost in the vision in front of her for hours, but she forced herself to turn around and be polite. "It's a pleasure to meet you."

"She just signed to play with a NWSL team and I'm sure she is going to become a superstar."

"I'm just a football player. Turning me into a superstar is more Arantxa's job." Antonia extended her hand toward Ari.

"Well, Arantxa is the best manager I know," Ari said. "She's the *only* manager I know, but that's beside the point," she added with a laugh.

While Tom, Arantxa, and Antonia talked around her, Ari had a hard time processing anything they said. She tried to smile and nod when appropriate, but she found herself unable to focus and sneaking glances at the court every other second.

"I thought some small talk would relax you, but I see I'm stressing you out more," Arantxa said out of nowhere. "Don't worry, I won't take it personally. Feel free to ignore us."

Ari's apology died on her lips. "Thank you. I don't know why I'm so nervous."

"We all are, but we have more experience dealing with it. Dani really wants this one."

Ari nodded. She knew how much Dani wanted to win. She knew better than anybody. After all, it was the reason Dani had decided to leave her, the reason they'd spent months apart. Maybe a piece of Ari was insecure about what would happen if Dani lost, despite the reassurances that she would never be blamed for Dani's tennis performance again. Or maybe it was simply because she wanted Dani to be happy, and winning was part of that happiness.

No matter the reason, Ari's worries lessened when Dani dictated play with deep, fast, and strong groundstrokes right from the get-go. She returned balls with lightning forehands, served aces, and defined points with down-the-line backhand winners or angled forehands that were impossible to reach. At least, that's what Tom told her Dani was doing and maybe after months she understood tennis a little more.

When Dani was forced to defend, she did it with as much ability as she attacked with. She ran from one side of the court to the other, returning unbelievably hard balls. When she chased down drop shots and lobs, she forced her rival to make mistakes time and time again. For the first half hour of the match, it seemed like Dani could do nothing wrong. The score line reflected it, and the first set went to her 6–2.

Ari let out a sigh of relief.

"She's got this," Tom whispered in her ear.

"Don't jinx it, Tom."

Dani's focus never wavered, but her opponent kept trying. The annoyance at every winner from

Dani was obvious on Olga Podoroska's face, but to her credit, she never gave up. Olga flew around the court and returned her fair share of impossible balls. More than once, Ari had to stifle premature cries of joy as Olga made a last-second save that Ari was sure would've been Dani's point.

That was exactly what happened during the first match point, when Dani was receiving the serve at 5–4 in the second set. At 30–40, Dani sent a crosscourt forehand to the corner that had everyone in the box, from Igor to Ari, jumping up in celebration. But one flick of Olga's wrist sent the ball back in a lob. Dani took her time to watch the ball fall to the perfect height before sending a swinging volley to the opposite side of the court, but her opponent anticipated it and was already running in that direction. Next thing they knew, Olga not only caught the ball but sent it back deep for a passing shot that left Dani standing in place.

The next match point arrived almost fifteen minutes later, with the score 10–9 in Dani's favor in the tiebreak. This time, it was her serve, and she did so with power and precision before rushing to the net. Ari watched in horror as what looked like an easy volley crashed against the net instead.

Ari could count the number of mistakes Dani had made in the whole match on one hand, but of course one of them came at the most important moment. To Dani's credit, she shook it off. When her rival won the next point and earned a set point, her face gave nothing away. She walked to the back of the court to get a towel, and on the way there, she glanced up to the player box. She gave them a little nod as if to say "don't stress, this isn't over." Igor nodded back and Ari tried to smile.

A second later, a forehand return winner set up another match point for Dani. With a powerful serve, followed by a long backhand return from Podoroska, Dani finally clinched the title.

Ari, Igor, Arantxa, Tom, and the rest of the team jumped and screamed in the player box. The umpire announced, "Game, set, match: Martínez," and Dani fell to her knees.

◈

It was only when she saw the ball bounce out that Dani allowed herself to feel the weight of the expectations she had placed on herself lift from her shoulders. As confident as she had tried to be the entire match, there was always a small, lingering doubt in the back of her mind. Winning the last point was the only thing able to silence it, at least for a few days.

When Dani looked toward her box, the urge to run to her people and hug them overcame her. She'd never done it before in any of her other Grand Slam wins, but it felt right. After shaking hands with Podoroska and the umpire, she walked to the edge of the court and started climbing the stairs. A security guard realized what she was trying to do and rushed to her side to help her reach the elevated seats, pushing through the sea of spectators eager to touch her and congratulate her.

Igor stood closest to her when she made it to the second-level seats reserved for her team. She didn't even have time to react because as soon as she was within reach, he engulfed her in his arms. Dani didn't understand what he was saying, but she didn't need to hear his words to know how excited and proud he was. The evidence was in the strength of his hug, the way he grabbed her face and looked at her with a barely contained smile, and the tears glistening in his eyes. He almost didn't let her go, but when she was able to move one step to the right, Arantxa swallowed her in another hug. Hers was faster and less intense, and she didn't pull her close against her body like Igor had done. Dani suspected it was because she didn't want to ruin her outfit with sweat.

Dani kept advancing between pats on her back, handshakes, and hugs until she reached the person she was looking for, the person who had motivated her to make the trip to the stands. Ari waited only a few steps away, but the distance stretched forever because everyone wanted to congratulate Dani. They locked eyes, the two of them connected no matter how many people stood between them.

When she finally reached Ari and they stood face-to-face, Dani had to muster every ounce of self-control she had to not claim her lips. Instead, she took her into her arms in a restrained hug that wasn't enough to quench her need.

"I want to kiss you right now," she whispered in Ari's ear.

"Then kiss me," Ari whispered back, and Dani did so without hesitation.

It was barely a brush of their lips that lasted only seconds. Dani wanted more, but the trophy ceremony awaited her, and if she kissed Ari again she wasn't sure if she would be able to stop. With one last lingering look, she walked back down to the court.

◈

Dani lifted the trophy above her head and presented it to the cheering crowd. If someone had asked her months ago, she would have said that nothing could beat that moment, those precious few seconds when it really dawns on you that you've won a Grand Slam. Now she knew better. As good as it felt to win, being in love felt better. Kissing Ari after a triumph was her new favorite thing to do, with hearing the crowd cheer for her now second on the list.

She'd never been good at the customary victory speech, but this time the words flowed from her mouth without her even trying. She started with the usual platitudes, thanking the sponsors, the tournament organizers, and her team. And then more words tumbled out. Words she didn't plan, ones she didn't know were in her head until she said them.

"I've been hearing about love my whole life, but not in the way most people do. Love–15, 6–love. It's curious how in tennis, love is the one thing you never want. It means you are losing. That knowledge is so ingrained in us that for a while I even convinced myself I didn't need the other kind of love. That it would only get in the way of winning. It's funny that in life, love is the one thing most people are looking for, and when I had it I ran away from it."

Dani wasn't sure where her candor was coming from, why she was confessing to a bunch of strangers all over the world some of her most intimate thoughts. But once she started talking, she couldn't stop. Maybe it was the months of pent-up feelings or the fact that once she won, the weight she had been carrying lifted from her shoulders. But she felt free, felt on top of the world.

She paused her speech for only a few seconds. A hush had fallen over the whole stadium as the crowd hung on to her every word. The same people who had been screaming their support—or disagreement—for two hours were now stunned into silence by Dani's sudden openness.

She could backtrack or change topics to speak about something more banal. About how much she loved New York, or how happy she was to win. But she didn't want to. Tennis fans had been involved in her life since she was a teenager. In a way, they were part of her family even if she didn't know them personally, so opening up to them made sense.

"Tennis is also a lonely sport; maybe the loneliest. You step onto the court with no coach, no teammates, no place to hide. I had a lot of matches this year where I wanted to hide, but I couldn't. All that loneliness teaches you to stand on your own, like I did today. But the key is to realize that even if you walk in alone, there are always people supporting you, like the amazing fans here in New York today." As if on cue, the spectators erupted in applause like Dani knew they would. The cheering gave her a break to gather her thoughts before continuing her speech.

"Like my coach and team, who stood by me during the good times and the hard times we had this year." She took a deep breath. "Like my beautiful girlfriend, Ari."

Murmurs broke out among the crowd, but Dani ignored them. She turned around to look at Ari, as if her words were only for her ears despite the thousands of people listening. "Since the day I grabbed a tennis racket for the first time, I've heard the word 'love' more than I can count, but it wasn't until I met you that I understood what love means outside of tennis. This win is for you, because you taught me that love is the biggest triumph of them all."

As thunderous applause surrounded her, Dani looked up at her box again to find Arantxa smirking at her and Igor as stoic as ever, but she could swear there was a hint of a tear sparkling in the corner of one of his eyes. And Ari. The most important person to her, the one who inspired her speech. She beamed at Dani through tears flowing down her face.

There would be a whirlwind of questions, sponsor calls, and social media outcry, but none of that mattered. As she smiled back at Ari, Dani realized her life was as close to perfect as it could be. Any challenge she might face would be worth it, because now she knew there was no need to tackle it alone.

She was happier and stronger with the people she loved around her, Ari being first on that list. Her successes and her triumphs meant even more now because Ari was part of her life. And now she wouldn't let her get away.

# Chapter Twenty-Two

Dani snickered when Arantxa stood and ordered everyone to shut up because she wanted to make a toast. She also fought the smile threatening to take over her face as her manager started the impromptu speech. It was true that Arantxa would take any excuse to raise a glass of cava and drink as much as she could, but Dani knew that her words were sincere and the drink just a nice bonus.

"I'll keep things short because I want to go back to eating, and I'm sure Miss US Open Champion over there would rather spend the night focusing on rubbing Ari's leg under the table instead of listening to me."

Usually, Dani would have made a show of putting her hands up just to prove Arantxa wrong, but she didn't want to spend even one minute apart from Ari. Instead, she gave Ari a quick, chaste kiss on the lips.

As expected, Arantxa rolled her eyes. "Now you are just showing off."

"I'm glad I got myself a boyfriend," Tom chimed in. "I don't think I would be able to handle third-wheeling with you two. You're too cute even for me." He leaned into Mark, who had joined them for dinner.

"You can't blame me for stealing a kiss while I can," Dani told Arantxa, "when we all know how hard it is to get you to stop talking once there's some wine in your system."

"Very funny. I don't think you should talk about speeches. I'm not the one who just declared her love in front of millions of people," Arantxa said with a teasing grin. "As I was saying before I was rudely interrupted, I want to make a toast. To a year that challenged us but also brought new, amazing things to our lives. I know we are supposed to be celebrating a win, but more than that I want to toast to finding what makes us happy and fighting for it. There will be many more tennis tournaments, many more wins, but what I'm looking forward to is being able to share those moments with this great family."

While Arantxa spoke, Dani looked around the table and basked in the glow of the faces, new and familiar, that surrounded her. Igor was sipping his favorite Japanese whisky and ignoring Arantxa in favor of joking with Dani's physical trainer. Tom had his glass raised but his eyes were fixed on Mark, the love and warmth in his gaze only matched by what was evident in the blue eyes peering back at him.

"And since everyone found love this year except for me, not that I'm bitter about it," Arantxa added, eliciting laughs from everyone, "let's toast to love."

Dani turned toward Ari without thinking, only to find Ari looking back at her. Dani smiled softly and leaned down to kiss Ari as a chorus of "to love" and "salud" sounded around her.

◈

Ari stirred the instant mac and cheese one last time and turned off the stove. A few feet away, Dani sat on her bed in her pajamas—a surreal sight Ari could hardly believe but one that warmed her heart all the same.

When Dani had mentioned the idea of visiting her at school, Ari hadn't expected her to make the trip. But a month after the US Open, they had started planning the details, and last night, Tom had driven her to pick up Dani from the airport. They'd cuddled to sleep on her too-small bed and woken up together after noon to rumbling stomachs.

"My specialty," Ari said, offering a plate to Dani. She was about to sit on the bed when a loud moan almost made her fall over.

"Mmm, this is so good."

"Stop messing with me, it's instant mac and cheese."

"I'm not, I swear. Maybe it's because I never have this kind of food, but it tastes like heaven." Dani ate another spoonful of the gooey yellow noodles.

Ari shook her head. "That's good news, then, since that's the most substantial meal in my pantry right now."

"Oh, we'll go shopping for other stuff. As much as I love it, I can't live off this for a week, and I promised Igor that my training and habits wouldn't suffer while I visited you."

Ari nodded as she took a bite of her own food. The thought of having Dani with her for a week doing domestic stuff like grocery shopping or walking around campus made her smile. It was everything Dani had promised when Ari accepted her invitation to New York and more.

Not only were they spending the week together, but they already had plans for when and how they would see each other again over the next few months. Coordinating time together while dating a tennis superstar who traveled all around the globe wasn't easy, but they were ready and eager to make it work.

The incessant ringing and beeping from Dani's phone interrupted their comfortable silence. Dani swiped up with one hand while she kept eating with the other. "It's a message from Arantxa. The interview I gave Mary Felton is out," she said, passing Ari her phone.

Ari read every word, a grin spreading over her face as she did. As she handed the phone back to Dani, she gave her a deep kiss full of love to go with it.

# Epilogue

*Daniela Martínez Opens Her Heart*

*An Exclusive Interview with the Tennis Icon*

*By Mary Felton*

*The first time I sat across from famed tennis player Daniela Martínez in a Melbourne restaurant ten months ago, I realized with one look that there was more to her than meets the eye. It was also obvious that talking to me was the last thing she wanted to do.*

*Since that night, a lot changed for the top-ranked player in the world. She went from the high of winning a Grand Slam to two consecutive losses in the early stages of some of the most important tournaments in the world, facing the scrutiny of tennis pundits who wondered if she would become another failed, fleeting champion.*

*If there's one thing that fuels Daniela Martínez, it's proving people wrong. It wasn't a surprise, then, when she turned her season around to win the last big tournament of the year. What nobody expected was for her to break her cold exterior, her unapproachable image, to share her love with the world.*

*I was as surprised as everyone else by her confession. Maybe even more than anyone, because I clearly remembered her guarded expression when I inquired about her love life during our interview in Australia.*

*"I don't have time or desire to focus on anything else," she'd told me then. The ice in her eyes and the hardness in her voice showed she meant it.*

*I remind her of those words as soon as I settle in the living room of her home in Mallorca. Ten months before, she would have snapped at me at that question, but with the happiness radiating from her every pore, I take a chance and am rewarded with a laugh.*

"I *sounded like a jerk, to be honest," she tells me with a teasing smile.*

*We all have been witnesses to Daniela's transformation. We've watched her heartfelt, viral speech more than once and we've seen her slowly open up on her social media to share glimpses of her private life, but we've also seen her fight tooth and nail for a win, leaving no doubt about her desire for success and her commitment to the sport. As I see her smile at a text message, I wonder if it is safe to assume her priorities have changed.*

"No. I *wouldn't say that," she tells me.* "It's *been a process of realizing I can prioritize two or more things at the same time and understanding that it doesn't have to be all or nothing. I love tennis and I've dedicated my entire life to it, but as a good friend once told me, all tennis careers end sooner or later. The only thing left is the legacy we've built and the people we've kept close. I still want to win as much as I ever have, but I don't want to wake up in fifteen years to an empty house full of trophies. Thankfully, I have someone amazing by my side who understands my life and in fifteen years I hope to wake up next to her."*

Sign-up to my mailing list at johanagavez.com/subscribe and gain access to deleted scenes from Match to Love, including Dani's apology letter.

# About Author

Johana is a proud Colombian that loves losing herself in stories and fantasy worlds. She loves watching cooking shows, even though she can barely cook, traveling to see her fiancée and spending relaxing afternoons reading in her hammock. At risk of becoming a stereotype, she loves to listen to Shakira, Maluma and J Balvin, but will always choose tea over coffee.

Her writing will always center Sapphic stories with romance at its core. She loves fluffy novels where love always wins. She reads and would love to write any genre, but romance and mystery hold a special place in her heart.

You can stay in touch with her via e-mail (johana@johanagavez.com) or on your favorite social media, be it Twitter, where she loves to share everything and anything related to lesbian romance, Instagram where she tries and usually fails to post beautiful pictures or Facebook.

She also has her own fancy website www.johanagavez.com to publish the occasional blog post with updates about her work and free stories.

Made in the USA
Columbia, SC
15 September 2021